Also by Gary Sernovitz

The Green and the Black
The Contrarians
Great American Plain

THE COUNTING HOUSE

The Counting House: A Novel

ISBN: 978-1-60801-253-4

Cover design by Kevin Stone.

First edition.
Printed in the United States of America on acid-free paper.

Library of Congress Cataloging-in-Publication Data

Names: Sernovitz, Gary, author.

Title: The counting house : a novel / By Gary Sernovitz.

Description: First edition. | New Orleans, Louisiana : University of New Orleans Press, 2022.

Identifiers: LCCN 2023011330 (print) | LCCN 2023011331 (ebook) | ISBN 9781608012534 (paperback) | ISBN 9781608012558 (ebook)

Subjects: BISAC: FICTION / Satire | FICTION / Political | LCGFT: Political fiction. | Novels.

Classification: LCC PS3619.E76 C68 2022 (print) | LCC PS3619.E76 (ebook) | DDC 813/.6--dc23/eng/20230308

LC record available at https://lccn.loc.gov/2023011330

LC ebook record available at https://lccn.loc.gov/2023011331

UNIVERSITY OF NEW ORLEANS PRESS
2000 Lakeshore Drive
New Orleans, Louisiana 70148
unopress.org

THE COUNTING HOUSE

a novel

GARY SERNOVITZ

To Dora,
for the daily reminders to love words and jokes,
and the urgency of stories

Managing Director of Private Markets Office July 13 (unscheduled)

"Can you interview her, please?" Emily asked, still standing.

"Interview her for what? The intern of the year award? Do we have an intern of the year award?"

Emily didn't smile. Normally, he could make Emily smile.

"I would say we need more permanent horsepower on the team."

"Then we should get a permanent horse."

Emily was the managing director of private markets. He was the chief investment officer.

"Why are you resisting?"

"Did I ever tell you what John Bogle once told me?"

"You have more than once told me what John Bogle once told you." Emily smiled this time. As she always did, she immediately covered her gums, biting her upper lip.

The CIO looked closely at her, hopefully without being noticed. After five years, he had never figured out if that gum shame was self-consciousness or a strategy not to leaven an office with too many smiles.

"Ah," the CIO said, "today apparently marks the day when I officially run out of material. Maybe that's—" He didn't finish. He didn't want to talk about their—his—performance today. He didn't want to know what Emily was hinting at with what more horses could do.

"Why *don't* you want to interview her?"

"Because what kind of recent graduate is still hanging around campus, looking for jobs, in June? The endowment is not the University Department of Post-Graduation Fallback Plans."

"There's an explanation for—"

"There's always an explanation for everything," the CIO said, maybe talking about the intern.

Emily dressed more Business Person than he did, or was necessary on campus. She smoothed her navy skirt. The CIO checked his own khakis for any stains that were obviously recent.

"I would say that we need more people," she insisted again.

"Is that true? Does Michael Hermann have more people? I think he trades from a cave in Bhutan, with a single goat by his side. And not even a particularly smart goat that provides excessive goatpower."

"Then I would say that you should reach out to learn the investment secrets of Michael Hermann."

The CIO felt a genuine laugh bubble up, warming from his lower belly. He was glad to see Emily laugh, too. She covered her gums.

He was going to joke again, about goats. But then suddenly the laughs smelled stale. Couldn't the art and science of investing on this campus go a week without the thought—the concept—of Michael Hermann?

Who had nothing to do with anything on this campus.

Emily said, "Please just interview her."

"As always, Emily, I will do as I am told. But just not today."

Intern interview
Office
July 14

"Does that apply to late capitalism, too?" the intern asked.

The CIO liked her, even if he had no idea why any of them thought that this was the best use of their open sky. "Is that what we're living in? Late capitalism?" he repeated, chuckling, a benign uncle. "Like, socialism, communism, capitalism, and mercantilism were told it was time for dinner, and capitalism showed up at 7:15 and missed the soup?" Her eyes had begun to dew. They were walnut brown, larger than her face needed them to be. He stared at her skin, trying to measure what made youth. "It was a joke. I assumed that you had already learned that there is an 80 percent chance that what comes out of my mouth is a joke."

"I'm sorry."

"You don't have to apologize. That is not your personality trait. That is my personality trait. Maybe you face the facts head-on, without the need for irony. For which you should consider yourself lucky."

She stared at him, the fact head-on, without a need for anything. The CIO should save this mask (if that's what it was anymore) for the hedge fund and private equity guys pitching them. He tried again, head still on. "Tell me again why you want to remain here to embark upon a career in endowment management?"

"I was really engaged by the projects I worked on during my internship. Figuring out whether a manager's track record was good or not was like, um... endlessly fascinating."

"Can I ask another question?" He tried not to mimic her uptalk. Maybe he had succeeded. "Did you apply for jobs elsewhere?"

"Sorry?"

They both knew it had been two weeks since graduation. "Did you go to New York to let twenty-five-year-olds from Morgan Stanley ask you why manhole covers are round or to guesstimate the number of laundromats in Pittsburgh?"

She smiled, almost easily. "I'm not really interested in moving to New York."

"Well, at least you were spared that experience. Maybe they are trick questions. Maybe there are no longer laundromats in Pittsburgh. And five hundred of your classmates are probably already in that channel of the meritocracy. Was there any interest in trying the other Golden Pole, seeing what life is like at a startup? One—I don't know—using artificial intelligence to optimize burrata?"

"I'm not—"

"That was a San Francisco joke. Apparently not the best one. I thought it was pretty... Anyway, the purpose of the internship program is partly educational but also instrumental. To help people get jobs. Out there. Off campus. Not that this isn't also out there, I guess."

He rolled his fingers into fists and heard his knuckles crack. He had to release the not quite completed grip.

"I'm sorry."

"Again, please don't apologize. You didn't do anything wrong. Maybe it's my fault. A couple of years after I took over as CIO, Jim Pascarella, one of our trustees, kept asking me if we could improve our performance by moving to New York. I tried not to take it personally. These khakis may not be the most intimidating pants, but our numbers were pretty good even without being more snazzily panted. The fact is that we are one of the last—maybe the last, other than Stanford—large endowments to be located on campus. Christ, Dartmouth has moved out of state. Before you were born, a few endowments came up with the idea that, to succeed, you had to hire real Wall Street types, and those dudes belonged in the high floors of skyscrapers, where the weakened gravitational pull required suspenders."

Nothing. Part of him wanted to let her stay if she really wanted to stay. Her sleeveless, eye color-matching dress was not quite casual but also not formal, like Emily's outfits. He continued, "Those type of guys are super unpopular now at endowments—maybe everywhere. I'm grateful for that. You really don't want to see a guy in khakis with suspenders unless he is threshing wheat. But even nowadays, if you want classic LP types—that's limited partner—the conventional wisdom is that it's hard to hire a team if they have to live among the gothic towers and particle physicists. I accept the social reality at some of our bigger brother—sister?—endowments, in which the 'managing director of real assets' is paid three times the best particle physicist. It's awkward to make eye contact when that fact becomes known. But I thought, screw it: if you work here, you have to make eye contact with particle physicists—if particle physicists are capable of making eye contact—because this is not some theoretical pool of capital we are managing. This is not particle physics."

The CIO smiled, for himself. "I want everyone to come in here every day and *see* what we are tasked with: last year, providing 264 million dollars to everything that goes on outside there." He hitchhiked his thumb to the quiet summer quad behind him. "That's 264 million, with the understanding that it better be 300 and then 400 million within five to ten years. I know that's an incredible amount of money—we're not running Microsoft here—but the university's operating expenses are three times that. And we cannot—I repeat, cannot—fail to provide that money. I'll get off my high horse before I start talking about the advancement of 'human thought and human character.'"

For a year after the *Times* article came out, he could give himself goosebumps with his words' easy nobility. But even last year it wouldn't have grabbed him so hard, how—why—*he'd* turned out on the funding side, rather than the receiving side, of human thought and human character.

And *human*? Versus monkey thought and beaver character?

"So anyway," he went on, "scholarships are expensive, art history is expensive, particle physicists are expensive. Their particles are really expensive, you have no idea."

No reaction from her. He could feel his own attempted smile coming out crooked.

"Again, a joke. I have no idea how expensive particles are. You'd imagine that they are not terribly expensive. They are, after all, particles." He pointed to the air. "I think that one is, like, only six bucks. The point I am trying to make, with the non-joking 20 percent part of my communicating ability, is that, unlike our endowment peers in New York or Boston or wherever, I don't want our office to be merely decorated with coffee table books—*Our College: Its Whiter Days*—gathering mold in the waiting room." He wondered if Emily, who was Black, would find that funny, unlike the intern, who was very much not. "I figure the trade-offs of awkward encounters are worth it to have us *in* this university, with the essential purpose of that call on 264 million dollars felt daily."

She was staring at him. Was *she* asking for paved routes to meaning, happiness, identity? He swallowed hard and looked down at his pants.

He had taken only this route. He had been taken only on this route.

He rubbed his hand hard over his eyes, clearing them, before dragging it over his closely trimmed beard.

"But I should be asking you questions. Wall Street's greatest product, as you may have already learned, is lectures on the way the world really works. Fifty percent of our job is listening semi-patiently to GPs—general partners, the asset managers—lecture us on how they have conquered fear, greed, and uncertainty in the more accurate prediction of the future. Not totally believing them is another 25 percent. The hardest 25 percent is figuring out what exactly to not believe. But anyway, back to you, why exactly are you avoiding the bright lights of big cities to work here of all places?"

She pounced: "There are the intellectual aspects to the work, which I find really appealing. And I think a career in finance is *important*. I learned both in classwork and in my internship how finance, as power, drives so much of the world. But I also need to be passionate about what I do. That's probably why I never wanted to do investment banking at Morgan Stanley, in addition to not really caring about the laundromat situation in Pittsburgh."

She smiled, not quite aware of the unnaturalness of her humor. He felt sad for WASPs for not being Jewish. But he also sensed values coming from somewhere planted. She went to a good school. She was a good person.

She continued: "And so I really admire you wanting the endowment to be on campus to be meaningful. That's really important to me, too: doing well by doing good."

"There it is," he said of the phrase, more dismissively than intended. He needed to revive a jocular tone, his 80 percent. He tried to be very clear. "Let me be very clear." That didn't exactly—"The conflict of values is unavoidable. Everywhere. We are not in some Neverland here. Although you meet a lot of Lost Boys." He rubbed his face again. There was anger he needed to pet calm, like a permanent horse.

For once, in one aspect of his life on Earth, he wanted to disprove the lies and hypocrisies that everyone told themselves were purpose.

To be, singularly, the disproof.

So why couldn't he just explain to this child his disgust at the totalizing nonsense of doing well by doing good? (Could he point to the Lost Boys, who wanted only to do well?) Why couldn't he start anew, on truthful grounds, for all of them, for his own children: a demonstration of the routes a career took you into yourself?

He didn't know where to begin. So he began the interview again. "What was your major again?"

"Economics and history."

"All you kids have double majors nowadays. In my day, we had only single majors. At this rate of change"—the CIO scratched the math out on some paper in front of him, the calming of arithmetic—"by 2080, students will all be octuple majors: economics, history, burrata AI, spaceship repair, apocalypse resilience, robot sociology... and phones. Just 'Phones,' sort of like 'English' now."

She looked composed. Or she just looked like what beauty gave you when you were twenty-two.

"Why did you choose those majors?"

"Coming out of high school, I thought I wanted to be an econ major. But after taking U.S. social history freshman year, it became clear that a narrow economics focus wouldn't allow me to understand structure. And in economics, especially macro, it all seemed so, um, bloodless unless you applied it to the real world."

The CIO smiled, relieved. Would Hannah grow up to be this thoughtful? Jane told him it was offensive to compare every female college student to a ten-year-old. But *would* Hannah want to do well by doing good?

"That's an interesting answer," he said, leaning back. "I was a history major, too." When he first landed on campus, he embarrassed himself by sharing that fact with too many faculty. "But even with a half double major, studying human motivation and coming to the best possible conclusions from ambivalent evidence is a good preparation for this work. Which is judgment. Correct judgment. Because that's our job. We have sixty or so GPs across asset classes. Each GP manages 1 to 4 percent of the endowment. They are all pretty smart in some way or they wouldn't—or, at least, shouldn't—have gotten in the door. They are also all, with too few exceptions, the rich white guys that everyone is exhausted by in our quest for Diversity, Equity, and Inclusion. We try to not back the ones that are *already* too vilifiable. For what is *our* job? It's not to judge the GPs as people. It is not to signal our own intelligence." That wasn't as accurate as he wanted it to be. "Our job is to judge the GPs' sometimes brilliance—sometimes actual genius—and know when is the right time to replace one of them because their blind-spotted brilliance isn't translating into our task of providing 264 million dollars to this educational institution.

"And we *can* replace them. There is an endless supply of asset management firms desperate to get some of this endowment to manage. Some of them are hustlers, some of them are creeps, all of them, deep in their hearts, believe it's their divine right to become billionaires. We are, I hope, mainly dealing with the least creepish cream of the crop. So I doubt these firms will disappoint us by stealing from us. However, I don't doubt as much as I want to that many of them—maybe most of them—will one day nonetheless disappoint us by being humanly fallible, limited, and leaving too much to luck. But, for now, we have an existing roster of managers. We add a few per year, drop a few per year, and spend a lot of time deciding how we adjust the ingredients—of how much capital each manager, each asset class should get. More salt, more pepper, more paprika—or, Jesus, no paprika at all. I'm making it all sound very interesting."

She smiled. He looked at her and tried to break a habit of judging by what he saw. Beauty is just symmetry.

"You definitely are," the intern said. "I got so fascinated by the GPs in my internship. I mean, these are literally the most successful people on earth. Everyone talks about them. People run for president to defeat them. They are the winners in our current social structure, and understanding them better seems—"

"I understand the epiphenomenon—is that the right word?"

She nodded.

"The epiphenomenon of finance is interesting," he continued. "When I was twenty-three, I started working at an investment bank after a year of graduate school. Credit Suisse First Boston: a crazy string of random words, right? And I found *everything* interesting. The people were funnier and edgier and taller and more alive—the hunters on the plain—than the gatherers of nuts I had just come from. But that was thirty years ago."

She smiled at him.

"And I still can't help speculating on why money management is debated by the wannabe leaders of the free world. Is it the amount of money nowadays? Or is it just that people have always been fascinated by the occult power to make money out of money?" The CIO spun up his hands, signaling, sort of, occult. "But if you get nothing else from this interview, if you decide that it is better to bolt to Palo Alto or Austin or wherever the hunters live nowadays and invent something tangible and great, remember what we're trying to do in this little office: 264 million dollars is *not* about being a witness to the winners of late capitalism. And it doesn't care if we are doing good. Two hundred and sixty-four million dollars is about being the responsible party on campus, to keep fed this experiment of intellectual freedom and exchange. Even if the art historians and the scholarship kids don't know what we do. Even if they hold what we do in contempt. I have neither the time nor the inclination to explain it to a man who rises and sleeps under the blanket of the very freedom that I provide and then questions the manner in which I provide it."

No reaction.

"Jack Nicholson? *A Few Good Men*? I got to get newer references."

Her walnut brown eyes widened, hopeful and never unconfident.

"Emily says you did a good job on the PMD project." Emily had actually said a touch academic and maybe useless, but it was his duty to guide these kids out of the abstractions of late capitalism. "She also says that, with Edgar off to Makena, we could use the help."

"Because we had a very bad year?"

They were looking at each other, and yet, somehow, she was avoiding eye contact. He squeezed hard his chin, trying to avoid moving his hand upwards.

Who *are* the people who get to be the disproof, who are not the lies and hypocrisies we adopt as purpose, who get to lecture us on the realities?

Weren't those lectures his job, with the x-ray secret talent of a chief investment officer?

He hated—hated—to lie. Not lying is the secret talent of a chief investment officer.

He couldn't give her the job.

"We did not have a very bad year."

Lower-middle market private credit manager
Conference room
August 14

The CIO interrupted the credit manager's pitch. "Please help me." He paused: stupid. "Help me understand why this 8 net—that's 8 percent net to us," he said to the analyst on his team. "Help me understand why this is so easy."

Calvin, the endowment's head of public markets, didn't react. The analyst was taking extreme notes. Across the table, the boy founder of the lower-middle market credit firm bit on a smile, bland and without fear. "I didn't say that it was easy."

"But it's not impossible, is it? I mean, you have this list on page, uh, page—"

Calvin: "Seventeen."

"A pipeline of thirty-four first-lien loans you can make directly to businesses." The CIO's glance paused on a row in a table on page seventeen, which apparently referred to a dental chain in Phoenix.

"That's an illustrative pipeline," Mount Mitchell's investor relations bro said.

"*Loans Illustrated.* I love that magazine. Have you ever seen a loan in a swimsuit? Anyway, math time." He grabbed a pencil from the cup of a dozen sharpened number twos. He offered one to the fleshy IR bro, who didn't take it. The CIO looked at the proffered pencil and flipped it until it was eraser out. The bro took it this time. "Thirty-four loans issued by you guys. Ten to 30 million dollars per loan. Gross interest rate of?"

"Seven to nine."

"And with all the goodies you guys get, origination fees to even get the loan, et cetera."

"Another 2 percent."

"Giddy up. And you could close these all this month?"

"More or less."

He should stop having meetings in August. No one wanted to discuss private credit in August.

He should stop having meetings.

But he went on. "Let's say you make fifteen of these loans at the middle of your range, an 8 percent interest rate with another 2 percent in year one. That's, like, 30 million dollars coming back to the fund annually?"

"That is the math." As the boy founder sat back, his monochrome blue tie ricocheted out, in exclamation, before blending back into the dark blue suit. Midtown standard.

"That's fascinating. On this side of the table, we wake up every morning trying to generate 8 to 10 percent total return from this endowment. That's because the folks out on the campus there get 264 million dollars to fund their Highly Selective American University." Why couldn't he stop? "But 7 to 10 percent cash interest, with another 2 for being kind to small animals... I mean, if *we* could do that every year, I'd just jet off to wherever is cool right now among you guys. The Maldives? I'd 'mal dive' in the Maldives and see tropical fish."

The IR guy was smiling now, widely. What was this Sam Adams-fattened frat boy even doing in this office? In this world? Before the meeting began, he had asked if the CIO knew Michael Hermann. Because, apparently, no one in finance who came to this campus could ever stop talking about Michael Hermann. The frat boy had scanned the conference room as he asked the question. The CIO had followed his eyes to the scratched table, to the chairs too big for the room, to the unremovable photograph of the campus facing the very same campus—none of which blared the presence of the ninety-seventh richest person on earth.

The CIO addressed his own analyst, who had finally come up for air from her own note-taking: "This is the part of the meeting in which I, without being a jerk, try to poke holes in their thesis and in which they, valiant defenders of their return-generating idea, parry the hole-poking with grace and conviction. Did I explain that right?"

The analyst looked at the boy founder, who was closer to her age than to the CIO's. That never stopped being jarring.

The founder said to the CIO, "I am prepared for valor."

"Great. Thank you. Sincerely. Two questions. First, why would anyone take your money?" Neither of the moneylenders were writing this down. Maybe only the powerless took notes. "And second, why does it never seem to work?"

The founder: "Those are excellent questions. We get them all the time."

The CIO swallowed hard and then bit down on his upper lip, a tic he seemed to be picking up from Emily. "Well, I'm glad I'm not being too original. That'd be bad for my self-image."

"I didn't mean it that—" the founder said.

We did not have a very bad year.

"Don't worry about it. Your answer added to your particularity."

The founder looked confused. Or was that just a function of whatever had happened to his right eye, off-focus somehow? He rallied with the prepared answer: "To your first question, think about the debt alternatives for the companies we target. Syndicated term loans? The borrowers we talk to are too small to tap bonds or Term Loan Bs. Bank loans? Since 2008, commercial lenders have gone materially risk off. That leaves a credit with a third option: let some warrant-greedy mezz shop or private equity firm tell you how to run your business and/or fire you from your own company."

The CIO smiled at the shadow of anger crossing the pitch. It was at least non-standard. The CIO had taken the founder for more of a math guy than a deal hustler, the natural progression of the fifteenth-best student at the best school in any mid-sized American city. He addressed him as he spoke to the room. "I'm going to translate this into English for the benefit of everyone here. I would translate it into German next, except I don't speak German. What"—the CIO looked at the business card—"David is saying is that if you're a big enough company, you can sell bonds to lots of investors. If you're a mid-sized company, you can sell what are called Term Loan Bs to hedge funds. Everyone can just try to borrow money from banks like in the olden days, but banks now want to loan only to people who they're 100 percent sure will pay them back. And, yes, you can get investors to buy equity—a stake—in your business, but—"

The founder broke in: "Growth equity is, in many ways, a systematized adverse selection process of providing capital to businesses not profitable enough to use leverage. And so, if you don't want to dilute yourself, can't access bonds, can't access banks, what do you do?"

"Fat Clemenza?"

"We looked into this."

"Now I'm enjoying being at work. First time all summer. Who loaned more, Clemenza or Tessio? I bet it was Tessio. Tessio was always smarter." The CIO looked at the analyst. Surely even a tadpole would get a *Godfather* reference.

"We didn't find much data."

"Well, that was exciting while it lasted. I still bet it was Tessio."

"But you have great companies, companies generating real income—"

"Not vaporware, VC-backed bullshit," the IR guy added on cue.

"—in need of expansion or working capital. And that's where we come in."

"Easy peasy lemon squeezy."

"Sorry?"

The CIO yawned. Was he actually tired? Or was the yawn strategic? "So why doesn't it ever work?"

The founder didn't seem to hear the question. Where did they get this confidence? As if the endowment was *their* money, by right, and the CIO was an obstacle to an allocation. "Our first fund has zero impairments," the founder answered. "Every credit has serviced their debt as expected. The fund has already returned 40 percent of invested capital. And the credit quality of almost all of the investments has improved. Our investments' aggregate operating cash flow is 4.3 times interest coverage, with none worse than three times. I don't want to be a jerk, but I'd say that is working."

The CIO did not say that you are talking about 108 million dollars under management, a nothing amount of money compared to the years-long, billions-deep track records the endowment usually analyzes. He said (maybe wrongly), "You're not being a jerk. But I want to test out two theories on you. Humor me. I don't know how to underwrite loans like you and Tessio. All I see is what comes across my desk, and in the last year, even here in the countryside, we got—Calvin, you calculated this—fifty—"

"Almost sixty."

"Almost sixty incoming pitches from direct lending funds like yourself. *Sixty* firms screaming at us, 'Pick me, pick me, I'm incredibly unique.' And that doesn't even include, what did you call them, warrant-greedy mezz shops or 'product' from the mega firms that don't even bother to pitch us anymore." God, he loved mirroring their cockiness, their fronting, that essential business of Wall Street. Mirroring was his job, a tool to find their vulnerabilities. As a reason to dismiss. And sometimes a reason to fall into hope. "Those sixty strategies covered every imaginable loan type to every type of company and every return target. Except, I guess, negative. And they are all very proud that an Unnamed Cosmological Authority has declared their particular micro-niche to have the holiest risk-reward. Everyone else, the pitches claim, is basically a fake. But my guess is that there are dozens—hundreds—of overlapping strategies in every single micro-niche—"

"If you look on page eight, you can see that private credit is still less than 2 percent of the total U.S. non-syndicated loan market."

"But you just told us that you make first-lien loans to companies that *can't* get loans from banks." He looked at the analyst. Did she get it that the CIO was at check, if not yet checkmate? Did he need to explain to her that first-lien was the first to be paid back in a bankruptcy? "So your addressable market is not the guy going to George Bailey, or even Mr. Potter. So, we have to ask, on this side of the table, why? What would bring a good company to Mount Mitchell?"

The founder started talking about "my" sources of deal flow, which were "mainly proprietary". Dear God, why couldn't they understand that *everyone* has three degrees of random contact from *someone*? The CIO's job was to weigh hunger, system, input. Did that soft-focused, Mr. America eye mean raw hunger now, before being ruined one day, in the success case, by private planes and believing his own bullshit? Was hunger from his strange anger about private equity? Was that anger enough even if his strategy wasn't interesting? Was there, as Isaiah Berlin said, a priori reason that truth, once discovered, had to be interesting?

And really, the CIO thought, his face moving through Expressions of Engagement, who are these people? Yes, Mount Mitchell—

this undifferentiated but potentially sufficient strategy—needed him more than he needed it, but the CIO would give his left hand for truly no-risk 8 percent returns.

We did not have a very bad year.

He wanted to pause the meeting to ask Calvin, even if Calvin wasn't Emily, his opinion of giving this firm 30 million dollars to make hard money loans to dentists. With his capital under management, why was the founder pursuing a national strategy versus a regional one, where presumably he would have more of an edge? More to the point, could this flesh and blood—with an eye condition and, odds are, three children and a wife who spent too much and Instragrammed the ways she spent too much—have really found a key?

The founder stopped talking.

The CIO said, smiling, "You don't need to claim you have no competition. There is too much capital everywhere. Wall Street's greatest talent is to throw way too much money at any good idea and make the returns go away. This has the effect if not the purpose of achieving as much bloodshed for the late entrants as possible. I accept that. This is the business we've chosen, Michael. All I need an answer to—and I'm open-minded—is why you guys never seem to last. We don't have the time to underwrite strategies that aren't going to be around in a decade."

The founder responded, immediate and sharper, "We are going to be around for a lot, lot longer than a decade."

His IR bro wasn't smiling anymore. Why was this pudgy nobody not selling Hondas?

"There are venture capital firms and your archenemies in private equity that have been around for forty years," the CIO pressed. "There are mutual funds that have been around since your grandparents' time. But among private credit firms, the granddaddies were founded in, like, 2009. Maybe except Beal, but I'm not even sure what *that* is anymore. And it's not like charging high interest rates to dentists who can't get bank loans is novel. Even Tessio was in on that action. But it seems like every decade, strategies like yours come around, in some shape and compelling-seeming form: 'safe' debt with high returns. Then, every decade, an extinction event comes—"

"At the next recession—"

"Yep. And we're talking"—the analyst was still writing as if she were a court reporter charged to not miss testimony—"not just about firms going under, but whole strategies, whole neighborhoods of Wall Street emptied out. 2008 redux."

"And we all know how ours will end. If even a few of the borrowers default, the returns get very skinny. I do the math."

"I'm glad you're not the stegosaurus who didn't know the meteor was coming. But even if the smartest stegosaurus had a PhD in astropaleontology from Stegosaurus State, what would he be able to do about the meteor?"

"I'll tell you why you're wrong."

Why did the CIO like that surfacing anger? Did he still, God help him, despite all his self-work, associate some capacity for rage with some capacity for life? His stomach rumbled. He responded, "As long as you don't try to extend my stegosaurus metaphor."

"For you to be right about Mount Mitchell, you have to posit two things. One: that advances in data science haven't improved the ability to underwrite. Two: that commercial banks are not excluding any safe credits."

The CIO asked, in lieu of disputing either, "How old are you, David?"

"Thirty-three."

"Let me see here," the CIO said as he turned to the founder's bio in the pitch deck. "Duke, Morgan Stanley, Apollo, Wharton, Apollo. And now the soon-to-be-legendary Mount Mitchell Capital. Which, by the way, is?"

"The tallest peak in North Carolina."

"I guess that's better than the deepest ditch in Louisiana. For the record, I'm not asking your age to give you a lecture from an old Wise Head of Finance." Jesus, stop performing. "I'm asking your age for context."

They stared at each other. The CIO was trimmer. The founder was custom tailored. The CIO had the money. The founder had an idea what to do with it.

"Why do you want to do this?"

"What?"

"Why do you want to do this? Humor me: I'm trying out my best David Swensen here." The CIO knew that Calvin would start gossiping about this question. Terrible Calvin was certainly already gossiping about the numbers.

"When I was at Apollo," the founder answered, "I thought they—we—had a tremendous infrastructure in place around a differentiated understanding of credit quality. But when they went public, they abandoned the lower end of the market, which I thought was a huge mistake, with all respect to Leon."

"Okay, let me rephrase for this side of the table. You learned a better way to make loans at your previous job. But that better way wanted to make bigger loans to make more money, and thus abandoned making smaller loans that still generated good returns. All very reasonable, but you just answered why *we* should want to do this. I get it: loan money to companies at high interest rates and get it back every time. This is, without exaggeration, the original form of investing. The *Bible* has opinions on this. But why do you want to do this? Why do you want to make people forget that Mount Mitchell was the tallest peak in North Carolina before it became the tallest private credit shop in the lower-middle market?"

The CIO stopped. To generate returns he needed ideas, ideas

that came through distracting vessels: nurture-nature-ego accidents that caused them to believe they could beat the market. The CIO was tempted to give Mount Mitchell a 30 million dollar commitment to re-loan to random companies, even if the strategy might not work, *if* this boy could reveal a sharp personality—and a cause.

The founder said, "I really think there is a market opportunity we've already proved with our sourcing."

"But why? Why you?" How many more ways could he ask this? Was this guy actually any good? Was anyone actually good?

"You have to believe me," the founder said, "that the market is mispricing credit risk for certain companies that deserve non-dilutive financing. We are here for that purpose."

"But why you at all?"

Be a person.

Confidence was not the only game.

"I guess I don't understand the question."

"I guess you don't understand the question."

Trustee (call)
Office
August 20 (unscheduled)

"Marty made clear that it was another dumpster fire at Harvard last year. How the fuck can they be so bad?" Maybe the answer was that they had twenty Ben Wirbins as trustees on their investment committee, guys who also never insulted you by pretending an introduction was needed. "But you should have heard how fucking smug he was when he was telling me this. It's as if their shitty performance is somehow a virtue, a tribute to the unique challenges of managing so much fucking money. As if there aren't a hundred pension funds in this country that have more money and don't embarrass themselves every year."

The CIO loved to think about being better than Harvard, too. The turnover, the strategy shifts, the CIO who made quadruple what he did, the other senior guys with mid-seven-figure salaries who shat the bed. Before, he would have joined Wirbin in the feast, except now that would accelerate—

"What are our numbers looking like?"

The CIO gripped the edge of his laptop then torqued it, slightly, to test its tensile strength. He looked out of his open door, where Emily was standing at an analyst's cube.

"I'm still waiting for some illiquid stuff."

"I'm not Corso, dude. I know you have your little tracking sheet, and I know you can hold flat whatever you need to hold flat—which is probably the best we could have done last quarter."

Wirbin wasn't the CIO's boss. And yet, the investment committee on which short Wirbin stood tall, *primer inter pares*, approved the investment strategy and the asset allocation and the CIO's employment.

"We could end up at 6 percent."

"Are you lying to me?" Don't answer. Don't dignify that. "I don't see how we do better than four."

The CIO let go of the laptop before his test succeeded. He tried to hold his breath, to quiet his heart. Wirbin couldn't have just said that.

"Where would that put us?"

The CIO exhaled. "I don't know. Baseline is that major endowment returns will be all over the place, like a family portrait with a Mexican father, a Chinese mother, and little Swedish kids."

"What the fuck are you talking about?"

"Yale has this golf thing around now every year. That's when the rumor mill starts."

"You golf, dude?"

"No, and I don't even go. Ginning up bonhomie with my peers is not exactly my strength." The CIO could feel Jane's smile. "And I find it hard to imagine anyone in the endowment community having a handicap below thirty. But after that boondoggle, relative performance rumors start spreading through the air as a pollen. Calvin annoyingly reports every tidbit like he's on Twitter. Maybe he is on Twitter. My best guess is, for the second year in a row, we'll not only be America's Twentieth-Largest Endowment but America's Most Middling Endowment."

At least that could be a truth.

"Fuck me."

The CIO heard Wirbin typing, probably sending an email to Pascarella that the CIO was not just a loser but a snake. The typing stopped, probably so Wirbin could text Pascarella private emoticons to convey an ass-fucking. The CIO suddenly regretted, with a sharp cardiac pain, that he didn't hire the intern. She was lovely and kind.

"And this year so far?" Wirbin asked.

"You've seen the market. It's not like we shorted it."

"Fuck me." He was typing again. Could Wirbin be firing him? After two plus years of this performance, the CIO would welcome professional death. Maybe the primary form, too. "The five-year track record is still awesome, right?"

"As long as anything starts with 2014, it'll look good."

"I told you the story of what Blankfein said to me, right?" Wirbin had told him the story four times. "I've had a good career at Goldman. Everyone knows I'm an effective guy. But I'm a relationship banker in the land of wizards. On top of that, I have no eccentric hobby, like being a DJ or starting a charity to teach Bangladeshi girls to code. And my entire educational pedigree is an undergrad degree connected to America's Most Middling Endowment. We'll have to put that on the home page, by the way. So as I'm making my bones by making the firm obscene amounts of transaction fees that the fucknuts love to look down on but love to have, I've always known that there is an asterisk by my name: Ben Wirbin, effective buuuuuut—the all-pro offensive lineman of Goldman Sachs.

"Then, October 2016: bam! The *Times* article comes out about our three-year track record at the endowment. And His Royal Baldness calls me on my cell at six o'clock at night. I first panicked that he had read my emails. I had emailed the article to 106 people. I emailed my personal fucking trainer. And I'm fielding hundreds of other emails, like half the people I've ever worked with, emails from three separate people I didn't know *could* read *The New York Times* because I thought they were dead. Mostly it was real congratulations. Some, of course, had a certain dickishness because that's how you congratulate people in this business. I got two emails from Princeton assholes with their permanent Golden hard-ons. Check in in twenty years, that kind of shit. But overall, people were genuinely amazed and happy for us.

"I pick up the phone and was like, 'Hey, Lloyd, what's going on, man,' as if it's my personal trainer calling. I assume Blankfein is going to be like, 'Do we pay you to email your personal trainer about your investment committee side thing, fucknuts?' But he is calling to congratulate me. And at the end of the call, he said, 'You should seriously think about doing something with GSAM.' I'm speechless for, like, the fourth time in my life. I'm a fucking banker. I give M&A advice, I get IPOs done. I get paid a fuckload of money to bluff. But put me in charge of Goldman Sachs Asset *Management*—actual investing? Is he shitting me? It never came up again, but I don't think it's a coincidence that I became co-head of the investment banking division that year."

"I enjoyed it too, Ben."

"Then what happened, man?"

"Oldest rule of Wall Street: when you do well, you're a genius. When they do well, they're lucky."

"Who fucked us?"

"No one fucked us. I mean, two years ago we fucked us by prematurely going risk off—Jesus, 'risk-off.' In defeat come the clichés. We lowered our relative allocation to investing in straight U.S. equities because I was too stupid to realize that the federal government borrowing 1.9 trillion dollars on behalf of U.S. corporations tends to be good for short-term corporate profits. And now that that call seems to have just been early, with the market throwing up on everything, it's heads they win, tails we lose. I don't know why we were playing macroeconomist. But that's not even it. That was like a 3 percent shift of the total endowment away from U.S. stocks. It's just annoying. It's, like, cut number 832 in a death by a thousand cuts. Hurst Street had a horrible year—"

"I always thought those guys had the most obvious reputational bubble." Wirbin didn't always think those guys had the most obvious reputational bubble. "Did I ever tell you? The one with the skinny pants smokes."

"Maybe he quit and lost his edge. Anyway, let's see: the energy portfolio was just disappointment after disappointment with no land windfalls to break the gloom."

"Why did you say gloooom, dude?"

"I don't know. I was being a contrarian?"

"You sounded like Jerry Garcia strung out on heroin."

"Well, that's good to know. I'll keep that—"

"Go on."

"No exposure to private credit because I'm still suspicious of an asset class that consists of blue-eyed Wharton MBAs loaning money to the dental kingpins of Phoenix." The CIO hadn't told the investment committee about Mount Mitchell. It wasn't the committee's role to know funds he passed on. "Venture capital was dead money this year."

"I thought we were in Mittens with that Asian guy."

"We are in Mittens, but it sold 20 percent below where it was marked."

"Well, you wouldn't know that fact from the press the motherfucker is getting."

"The motherfucker's name is Brian Park, and he and his partner, this Brad Pitt lookalike named Laurent Mast, are coming into the office in two weeks. Everyone here is lobbying me to be in the meeting as if Brad Pitt himself is coming into the office . . . to take off his shirt."

"Do you need a moment alone with your fantasies?"

"The only other person I could imagine coming in that could cause—" The CIO caught himself. He didn't mention He That Cannot Be Named to Wirbin. If he were a braver man, he would have mentioned the name and then matched temper with temper.

"I was joking about the moment alone, dude. I hope to fucking God you haven't put down the phone."

"I'm still here."

"Do you or do you not know the fucking number? Because I really want Marty to eat it for, like, the sixth year in a row."

"I don't know their number." The CIO paused to sense whether Wirbin caught the shift. "I don't know anyone else's number. The horse-race aspect of this business—we are pathetic and they are Warren Buffet if they beat us 8 percent to 6—turns my stomach. And anyway, the primary way I get to learn about anyone else's book is by whatever gossip that Calvin or an analyst bring back from GP annual meetings. So I'm just guessing. If we're at"—he could be correct, maybe Wirbin would have forgotten, Wirbin wouldn't have forgotten—"whatever"—*whatever*?—"between Harvard sucking nuts again and This Year's Geniuses appreciating 12 percent, there may not be any great lessons. I say that, and the next day, you know, Rice will report fifteen and be, um—"

"Us."

"The guys who have permanently (this year) figured it out." He heard Wirbin typing more, probably emailing some Rice trustee to ask if they had a number two who'd make a good CIO. But the CIO didn't even know if Rice had—"You know what looks like it's curdling? PMD. The private equity firm. Have you ever met Mark Polansky?"

No response. The Whirlwind must have shifted to text. The CIO wondered if he had had bespoke emoticons made for him to convey fuckme, fuckyou, fuckthem.

The CIO looked around his office: nineties cherry veneer cabinets, a mismatched round table he used only for reviews, the large picture of Jane and Hannah laughing, the smaller one of Peter, the finance textbooks molding on the shelves beside unread behavioral economics sub-bestsellers from annual meetings. He wondered how much he would miss it. He swallowed a sigh and then continued. "Polansky came in for his newest fund a year ago. These guys have been a machine for us, in an incredibly rational way. Good strategy, good returns. They, Tolemy, Stone Cap, Willfors Reynolds, and, I guess, Brian Park and Lauren Mast are the GPs that made—make—me want to get up in the morning to witness, and believe in the possibility of, the application of human intelligence to market inefficiencies. PMD, remember, invests in private industrial services businesses in the Midwest and South. Asset-light businesses, easy to reset in a recession, almost all sold to strategics, so boring that I can barely tell one company from the next. The crazy thing is that Polansky, the founder of a firm that prides itself on doing boring deals, is Mr. Personality. Six-three, must weigh over 250 pounds, and always emitting *noise* about the Federal Reserve or restaurants or the joy of cheap watches. He makes me look consistently on point."

"That's a talent."

"I guess that schtick works with some dude in Indiana whose family business has been distributing meat slicers since the invention of sliced meat. PMD's first three funds have returned basically everything, with very little left, 2.1 to 2.4 times return on investment, *net*, solid. We were in Fund II and Fund III, but we are also in two subsequent funds that are all at a DPI—"

"What's that?"

"Distributed to paid in. How much actual cash money we've gotten back, not just the paper ROI. And PMD has returned, in cash, a pitiful 20 percent in their two latest funds. So Polansky comes in to pitch us Fund VII, and Emily becomes the Black Sheryl Sandberg and presents a line showing our net exposure to his firm. It has ballooned to 110 million dollars with another 30 million undrawn."

"Jesus, dude."

"That's 2 percent of the endowment. We want that number to be much higher, with actual investment appreciation. Frankly, we should probably be even more concentrated if we had any guts. The meeting was in the late morning, and Emily figured out that that meant that he had flown private. Polansky—I wasn't exaggerating—was talking about Swatch watches, and ballsy Emily interrupts him to ask if he could give us *his* best guess—ballpark—expectations for year-by-year distributions in the next few years." How, the CIO wondered, had he gotten himself here? "A junior partner at PMD starts to answer for Polansky—very transparently. Emily glares at Polansky making it clear that another commitment is dependent on him providing the numbers. That giant tumor of self-confidence never looks back at her. But he finds a way to add needless precision to the junior partner's portfolio walkthrough. The junior partner would say something like 500 to 550 million dollars, and Polansky would say, 'You know, I think there is a case for it to be as high as 600 million.' And you know what we did?"

"Kicked him in the balls?"

"That was the right answer. *Our* answer: re-up for another 30-million-dollar commitment. My job is systems, inputs, hunger. It's to know if the apparently successful are lucky or real. It's to figure out at what point the once successful start to get fat, sloppy, and lazy. And it's still like 50 percent gut calls. And that's—"

A memory grabbed him, seizing his tongue. It was more a physical imprint, on his body. He was sitting in the office of his graduate school adviser, almost thirty years ago. He was telling her facts about John Brown—facts that made his brain tingle. Her short, cropped hair, lesbian of the old school, always made her neck seem ostrich-like. He thought that her jugulars were becoming pronounced in anger at the facts.

Then he realized that she was yawning.

It had hollowed him out.

"Hello?" Wirbin said.

The CIO swallowed and continued. "I still don't know if I should be looking for more mature firms that have moved from the charismatic phase to the bureaucratic phase or if I should *aim* for returns that are 'good-enough' and should have, à la Karen Kahn, lower risk."

"And?"

"And this year, the three active PMD funds are down, like, 10 percent. Not a disaster but not helpful. Emily walks me through the companies they own, and there are so many explanations that none are explanations. Their numbers are like our numbers: everything is understandable and bad luck and win-some-lose-some, not permanent except in a few cases, tariff-related in other cases. It's depressing. A cynic out there, if Wall Street could ever conceive of such a point of view, *could* suggest that PMD pumped up their numbers during their fundraiser. So, shame on me. I want to call up Polansky and ask him what he was doing on his private plane over here. Was he working hard on implementing his quote 'eighteen-step value-adding process'? Or was he just reading *Cheap Watch Fancier* magazine with a feature on the new hundred dollar Rolecks, one c, one k, one s?"

"Why the fuck don't you?"

"Because that's pretty demotivating for Emily, who is alert to these sorts of power dynamics to a mind-blowing degree. It's hard enough to get someone not-white out here in the pastures. And, anyway, what do you think Polansky's going to say? If he was honest, he'd say 'That's for you to figure out.' And, also... And, also—"

"You don't want to know the answer."

"One is required to have faith in human beings, including Wall Street greed machines that occupy the skin and bodies of real-looking human beings, or else endowment management gets very bleak very quickly."

Wirbin was typing again. Probably to get his Goldman buddies to opine on PMD.

The CIO didn't have anything else to say. He checked his computer. Market down 1.8 percent. More joy.

Give yourself a reason to not quit.

Take the kids and Jane out West. Take Peter away from computer games. All the science and nostrums of modern American childrearing had been applied to that boy. And they were mist against computer games.

The CIO shifted his body forward and failed to get comfortable. He then pushed his chair back and leaned his forehead against his desk. It was doing well by doing painful, the wood creasing his head, blocking him from the markets.

Wirbin stopped typing. "Okay, man. Six percent isn't a disaster. Harvard probably lost money on stupid fucking Brazilian land deals again. But just do better this year. Okay?" Wirbin drank something. "Did I ever tell you about what happened after the *Times* article came out?"

Was this a joke?

"Not about Lloyd's call, but about a week later. You see, my wife and I have a very good marriage."

"What?"

"Stay with me, dude. My wife and I have a very good marriage. We laugh, we talk about everything, we're still attracted to each other, even if I swear I'm getting shorter and she's getting taller, thank you very fucking much, Joe Pilates. But we have good, grounded kids that have not been completely ruined by Manhattan. It's fucking ridiculous how lucky I am. But two things are very clear in my marriage. First, my wife does not want to be bored into offing herself by war stories about investment banking. Can I fucking blame her? Six months later, even I can't remember which technology we pitched to a company or whether it was Millennium or Fidelity that was necessary to get the price some private equity asshole wanted on an IPO. Funny stories are fine, because I'm a short Jew and that's really all we have. But, honey, don't go into the fucking details."

The CIO lifted his head. Panic was spreading in his chest. He needed to tell Jane about the numbers.

"The second thing that is clear is that she thinks my attachment to this school is a quirk to be tolerated. Like *I* am into cheap watches. Which, by the way, is the dumbest fucking hobby I've ever heard of. We should have cut the fatass off just for mentioning it. My kids go to Dalton. Already in middle school, they are a bit embarrassed to mention that their dad is a trustee of a safety school. A rich, very good safety school, but whatever. To my wife, this school is a put for the kids, good to have if necessary, *not* an embarrassment, but *Columbia* should be their safety school.

"The week after the article comes out, the four of us, miracle of miracles, are all coming home from somewhere at the same time. Our doorman is standing there in the lobby with some African guy in a worse suit than the one you wore at the last IC meeting." Wirbin had told the CIO, with affection, that he made too much money to look like he'd bought his clothes in the Auschwitz section of Men's Wearhouse. "He's wearing a shirt with the most missized neck hole I've ever seen. He had room for a second fucking neck in there. I'm not the kind of guy who needs to chat up the doorman about Real Fucking Madrid every time I come home to prove I'm a man of the people. Nor am I a dick who demands they genuflect before me because I have reached the pinnacle of human accomplishment for having five bedrooms in a building whose *outside* my great-grandfather would not have been allowed to touch. So, we're walking towards the elevator after a quick nod when the doorman—our guy Winston is from Ghana—says, 'Mr.

Wirbin, can I introduce you to my friend?' I look at my watch instinctively, a total asshole move, but I'm like, okay.

"Winston's guy is Mr. Yeboah or something. And this Yeboah guy tells me that he read the article in the *Times* about the endowment. I'm wondering if he thinks that's *my* fucking money and he's going to ask me for a million dollars to free up the 50 million dollars left to him by his uncle in a Swiss bank account. My wife and kids are watching this all go down. They were wondering if this Yeboah dude is the representative victim of whatever Goldman Sachs supposedly does to people. But then Yeboah explains that his son goes here, on full financial aid, and he was mentioning the article to Winston and Winston said he knows me." Wirbin stopped. "I've never told you this story?"

You would have thought that amid the four tellings of the Blankfeiniad, Wirbin might have had time to diversify. "No."

"Weird. Anyway, Yeboah says that he and his family want to thank me. Because their son is a junior and already has had an internship at Google. And he's getting an extraordinary—that was the word he used, *extraordinary*—education thanks to the generosity of me, 'Mr. Wirbin.' Yeboah apologizes that his wife couldn't be there. He reaches into his bag, and I fucking flinch as if he is going to hit me in the face with a pie. But he brings out a Tupperware dish wrapped in like five bucks worth of tinfoil. He says his wife made us some kind of famous stew. My family is watching, still as fucking statues. I thank Yeboah, hand the famous Ghanian stew to my son, and my family takes the elevator up. And then my daughter, who was ten going on seventeen, hugs me around the waist like she hadn't done in years. My wife brushes some hair out of my eyes. She then kisses me in such a tender way I don't even recognize how soft her lips still can be. You get all this?"

He got all this.

"So no more '6' percents, okay?"

Jane's lips, he guessed, were slightly chapped right now, the grain detectable beneath the wax she used to deal with the fact that they were usually slightly chapped.

She spent a lot of time gardening.

The market was down 2 percent.

The only solution was to quit.

The silence was getting personal, thick, too much.

So the CIO asked, genuinely curious, "How was the stew?"

"Infuckingedible."

Asian long-only public equity
Conference room
August 21

"You have to understand the particularities of the market," the Australian took every vowel, bullied it up to the roof of his mouth, and torqued it. "First, you have your Alibaba and Tencent, which you don't need us to own for you. Then you have your family conglomerates and ex-SOEs that are governance nightmares we wouldn't advise you to own in ehny"—any?—"context. Then you have your straight frauds aimed at, what'd you call 'em, Dan? Wang the Plumber."

"Woah there, man," the CIO said.

The Australian raised an eyebrow.

"You're going to have to translate this into English."

"B'cause of my accent?"

The Australian and the quiet American placement agent for Ledo Road looked at Calvin and three other members of the endowment's team. The CIO had stuffed this meeting as consolation; not everyone was going to get to go hear Laurent Mast and Brian Park. "I wouldn't say that your accent is *helping,*" he answered, "but no: it's because some of us on this side of the table have been working in finance capitalism for all of a year." The Australian narrowed his eyes. "I'm talking about me. I was a middle school gym teacher until last summer."

The Australian laughed, and the CIO smiled back.

"Well, in that case, mate," the Australian said. "I'll break it down. To succeed at investing in Asian shares—you know, public stocks"—he looked at the CIO, who nodded appreciatively—"you need a partner. I'd advise anyone to own the big cap names like Tencent and Tata directly. We could even put together a list for you. But if you want to buy shares in smaller companies, you have to be extraordinarily kahfil"—careful—"and choose an active manager. And a large part of our work is to help you avoid so mehny of the things that are ripe in the small and mid-cap universe in Asia: public companies that are effectively controlled by state-owned entities—which is sorta mad—family conglomerates, and outright frauds that are playing Chinese day trading gamblahs."

The Australian paused, and the CIO nodded; this was all explicable.

"My guess is that the SMID—sorry, 'small and mid-cap'—market is about 10 percent investable in China and about 5 percent investable in India. But it *is* investable." The word in its Australianish repetition sounded like *invegetable*. "On page seven we lay out what you need to make it invegetable. You can do a PIPE—a private investment in a public company—to establish some governance. You can be there in a pre-IPO round if you expect a Wistuhn"—Western?—"underwriter to be involved. Or you can have prior history with management. Everything, *everything* else is suicide."

The CIO was trying to concentrate. He wanted to look at his phone. He wanted to forget what he had told Wirbin. He wanted June 30 to not have already passed.

Calvin, trained, asked, "And what's your system for this?"

The Australian took off his suit coat to reveal a flawless white dress shirt sheathing a muscled torso that squeezed out his shaved, oversized head. He now seemed to take up even more space in the conference room. "Like everything," he said, "it's process and people and experience. Listen: there is no question of long-term mahket growth. One and a half billion more people still to rise into the middle class. Incredible engineering talent. The two most populous national markets in the history of the world. Within this, the most invegetable themes are affordable housing, protein consumption, tech exports, mobility, and health and safety services. And in each segment, we have delineated thirty risk factors and a direct and indirect competitor map."

The Australian turned around his own copy of the pitchbook and narrated the main matrix and the sub-matrices around each theme. He rolled his sleeves halfway up his forearms as if the forearms were sweating with so much proximity to truth. The CIO and the analysts, taking cues, leaned forward. Calvin remained upright.

The CIO daydreamed of a way to freeze the scene to talk to the analysts, over Calvin—scientists sifting through physical evidence. Did these words and shapes and boxes mean a system? Look. Decide between Mount Mitchell and these guys by solving perpendicular decisions around risk and reward. The Australian was smarter with an edgier view of the market. The boy founder was duller but more rigorous and hungry. Did it matter, though, the personalities of yet two more suited white men? Or did the essential ideas of their strategies matter more, the fish or the fowl? Was it better to defy God and go full usury in the U.S. or invest in liquid stocks of small companies on the other side of the world that sell things to people desperate to consume more? And, if so, do we do it with someone smart as fuck or just buy an index fund?

The Australian flipped the pitchbook back, like spinning a tennis racket after an ace. "Our competitor map is not infallible," he said. "But I'd rather be playing in five segments I know are going to grow than have exposure to, what have ya... Japan."

"You're not into sub-replacement fertility ratio?" The CIO and the Australian looked at each other, eyes twinkling, bald man to bald man. That rush was dangerous. "I completely agree with you on what's invegetable," the CIO said. "I mean, what is our competitive advantage as investors?"

"I would say, our processes—"

"I know *yours*: people, processes, 'technology,' the whole McKinsey Triangle of Power. I meant ours, the endowment."

The Australian thought and then: "Your time horizon."

"Bingo. We are investing on the assumption that this university will be around for a thousand years and eventually educate space aliens. We will offer courses on protein consumption—of humans. Also on Toni Morrison. And so we need to find strategies that capitalize on short-term volatility caused by the limited patience of other investors, due to structural factors or character flaws. End. Of. Story. And if you take a step back and ask what are the global sources of take-it-to-the-bank growth, of course it's Wang the Plumber and his brother from another mother, Sanjay the Plumber, eating Chick-fil-A, living in an air-conditioned ranch house, driving a personal hovercraft, building hovercraft parts for Joe the Plumber, who's now addicted to first-person shooter games and/or opioids, and... What did I miss?"

"Health and safety services."

Shouldn't the Australian's quick intelligence win an allocation, the slot machine's *ring ring ring*? Or was this just assortative mating, as Jane once diagnosed second-hand: about men who love men who also think the world is about being right? "There you go," the CIO said. "Sanjay the Plumber spending on improved healthcare rather than buying kidneys on the black market. And I completely agree with you: if I look at it through a decadal lens, how can I not have confidence in *that* growth versus the entire Japanese population declining to three old ladies lighting memorial candles for the Sony Trinitron? Or, for that matter, the U.S. turning ex-growth. I can't. I have confidence. Wang the Plumber the Third is going to be driving a 2017 Chevy Malibu as a hipster affectation. He'll come here for his semester abroad and think our Gothic towers were the native architectural style."

The Australian laughed, his bald head—that topmost, oversized third bicep—roaring back. The CIO sensed the youngest analyst alternatingly watching the CIO and the Australian. Was the CIO's own approach to baldness—the consistent three millimeters across the entire head and beard—a failure of confidence?

"The point of all this being?" the Australian asked, the laugh lingering in his voice.

"The point of all this is the reason Calvin brought you in—and two other groups, to be frank. We are trying to replace our current Asia small-and-mid-cap public equity manager who, in a two-year period when the GXC doubled—" The CIO stopped, caught short by an analyst flipping back in his notebook, seemingly trying to locate GXC. "That is an index fund that gives you exposure to all Chinese shares and is available in any online brokerage account. Anyway, the GXC doubled, and our Asian-focused long-only manager delivered us 18 percent over two years. And our incumbent manager's pitch was also about highly quantitative risk management. They left out the consequence that we will miss out on the earth-shattering equity value creation at Alibaba and Tencent, but they also wrapped us in comforting themes, like profiting from health care systems that don't involve the black market sale of kidneys. And so while I agree that we need all this—I mean, if you can't count on growth and richer human experiences in China and India, just pack up—I need that to translate into alpha—outperformance. That means dollars and cents for this university, which is all I really care about and which is—these things are not completely overlapping—what I am paid to care about. Is what we're talking about *too* obvious?"

"Or maybe you picked the wrong manager."

"Option A: I picked the wrong manager. Option B: I was wrong to pick a manager."

"I like you, mate. You're a little more Bondi Beach than most of your type."

"I have no idea what that means." He smiled. "But I'll take it as a compliment."

"In most of my meetings in the States, LPs just look at me as if I'm some animal. 'Can this little mouse pahform?' But you approach things a bit in the joke, as we say back home."

He looked at his team and then at the Australian. "We're oh for two in knowing what you mean."

"You're having fun."

"I'm having fun?"

"You seem like ya are, mate."

"It seems like I am?"

"Now it seems like you're having a bit a fun at my expense."

The CIO liked the idea that he was having fun. He wanted it to be true. He and the Australian could do push-ups together. A year ago, Jane had asked him, "Why are you doing this job if it's no longer fun?" The CIO was offended by the question, another clunker proving that he and Jane had gotten out of tune. The CIO had answered her, "Why do people live if it's no longer fun?" He thought he had meant that as a joke. His father would not have meant that as a joke.

To the Australian, the CIO said, "Let me give you a little context on the carnival here to explain this huge smile glued to my face. You see, we don't buy individual stocks directly. Because what do we, on this side of the table, know about anything? Also, that whole efficient market thing. We can't even do snoozy fixed income anymore because safe bonds offer no real returns—and because Swensen maxes out at, like, 4 percent as a cash equivalent. Swensen is David Swensen, as someone may have told you, the Chief Investment God of Yale and Father to Us All. Yale is a university in Connecticut known for triumphant parents, a cappella groups, and David Swensen. Because of Swensen, if I tried to go 20 percent into old-fashioned fixed income—corporate bonds, not these new, snazzy private credit funds loaning money directly—all the CIOs at the CIO Summer Jamboree would call me Fixed Income Fatty or Bond Boy Barry."

The CIO reflected back the Australian's smile. The CIO felt his own stomach firm up as if he were defining abs. "And so we do all sorts of wacky stuff to get our targeted 9 percent through-cycle returns. Remember that number: 9 percent per year, not a do-nothing market rate but also not a number that requires miracle workers. In that quest, investments in Indian companies before their IPOs are super-vanilla compared to some of the stuff our GPs do. We give money to guys to give to *other* guys to build pipelines or develop hiring apps for babysitters or 'turnaround'"—the CIO twirled his finger like he was spinning a dish—"companies that need to be turnaroun-ded. Or maybe don't need to be, or can't be by guys whose primary point of view is of other Midtown offices, but why not try? We give it to hedge funds hoping that time won't reveal that their brilliant, swashbuckling contrarianism resulted in owning the same ten stocks as everyone else. We give it to guys to build distribution centers in Tulsa even though they only dimly recognize that Tulsa and Wichita are not the same place. Sometimes I just want to clear the decks. You think I *like* trusting money to Greenwich dads who finance buildings in Tulsa/Wichita to fill the hours before honing their sons' lacrosse skills?

"Technically, I don't have to do anything. I could just maintain our existing allocations to our current managers and run on autopilot. But I do have to"—Christ, stop talking so much in these meetings and so little at home—"do something, *existentially* speaking. For the only thing preventing this school from charging even higher tuition than the unconscionable tuition we already charge, the only thing allowing us to dream of an ascending reputation to become the Yale of the Thirty-First Century for Toni Morrison-studying space aliens, is having exposure to the *right* rising markets, however you predict *those*, and someone delivering alpha somewhere. Then 6 billion dollars will rise steadily in value and spread even more money"—the CIO moved his hands as if scattering bird seed—"to the folks out there. So as much as I'd like to keep this super-fun and Bondi Beach, and just accept that the Chinese and Indian markets are going to have awesome growth over the next twenty years, I have to find someone who can translate that, year in, year out, into performance."

"We do."

"You *did*, and *maybe* you will. But the reason for the serious demeanor of my brethren in the endowment world, a demeanor I should have more of if I—" The CIO stopped. If I wasn't saying we didn't have a very bad year? If I was honest about my abilities? "The reason for that serious demeanor is the selection bias. Everyone who swaggers into conference rooms much shinier than this one has had good performance, in some format. You should see the pre-meeting analysis these guys do," the CIO said, laying his hand out in the direction of the analysts. "Us LPs rely on some past investment returns, over some period of time, to prove the people we even bother talking to don't suck. So you are not alone in coming in here thinking you have the answer. I've given you the wrong impression, though, if you think I find this all fun."

"I think I'm still right," the Australian said, and he actually winked.

"Maybe you are right. Let's pop open the Foster's. Go surfing. That's not a knife. This is a knife. But first, let's cut to it: why do you think you can beat the market?"

"Experience and processes."

"Everyone talks about experience and processes. Why you, though?"

"We have a market niche that others don't fully understand."

"Everyone has a market niche that others don't fully understand. Why you?"

"Because we're not bullshitting about this."

"I believe it, but the market doesn't care if you are. It just cares what goes up and down."

"What d'you want me to answer, mate?"

The CIO didn't say anything. He found his fingers rubbing hard on his high forehead, digging into his temples. His eyes stayed locked on the Australian's as he fought his hand's instincts to circumnavigate wildly over his eyes and beard.

University President (call)
Office
August 23

The CIO paused on cell J7 in Excel. Under Calvin's direction, the analysts had put together a more clever analysis than the CIO figured they were all capable of, tracking Ledo Road's ten largest holdings against various sub-indices. The math was flattering to the Australian. In cell J7, the CIO was trying to calculate how thin the line was from proving that the Australian was just lucky. With an Emily recommendation, he would have called her in to talk through the math.

At the start of 2009, when it became clear that the value preserved at the Eckmann Foundation during the Global Financial Crisis was notable on a national scale, Jane was his co-conspirator, more thrilled for him than he was for himself. There had been a quality of attention. Once, he had caught her looking at the United Way of Central Ohio website, studying how the proceeds were well-used. So, fuck it: last night, the CIO had brought up Yeboah as a non sequitur to Jane asking Hannah what she was most excited about for the new school year. As he told the story, Hannah tried to be interested and volunteered that she knew where Ghana was. Peter had been Peter, head down, twirling the tomato salad around his plate as if enough motion would turn it into an Xbox. Jane and the CIO's eyes used to be, at times like this, in a conversation of what-can-you-do and what-did-we-do and doesn't-Hannah-absolve-us-of-all. But last night, Jane, biting on her fingernails, looked at him with a fake but otherwise inscrutable smile. He asked her if she was listening. She said she was sorry; she was just very hungry.

He tasted his own lips. They felt dry. He rubbed his left hand all over his face, with his family as the only witness.

Maybe he and Jane should follow the lead of the Wirbins and keep the details out.

But isn't life the details? And isn't this our detail: that neither of us has the right to be embarrassed that we both got rich this way? That these are decisions we made together? That this was how we could contribute to the world?

The phone was ringing, each ring cruelly louder.

Lisa, the office manager, eventually picked up. It was Meg Corso, the president of the school, on the phone. He nodded. Lisa knew that he knew that.

The CIO began—why?—Wirbinishly: "Usually it's September before I get this call. Which students are first with the petition this year? The McKibbenese? Private prison divestment? Hashtag BoardToo?"

"All very funny," Corso said.

"I liked hashtag BoardToo. I'm still not sure how putting Martina Navratilova on the board of directors of a reinsurance company is going to change the world, but it's better than a nineteen-year-old explaining to me the Zionist colonialism of farm equipment."

"Are you done?"

The CIO swiveled his chair and looked out on campus, fresh with new students. He couldn't see the main administrative offices, but his gaze still tried to unify him and Corso across space. He measured the pace of his own drivel, counting breaths. "Where is the dark-humored college president I've come to know and respect?"

"She's a bit distracted."

The CIO inhaled; she was working up to it. He inventoried his books. He regarded the picture of Peter—as if the office's new occupant could ever want it. Maybe Jane had just been embarrassed by a simpler thing: her husband telling a story of his glory from three years ago.

Corso continued: "I'm trying to maintain some pretense that I'm still a scholar and not just an administrative cog and fundraising mannequin. My entire summer has evaporated with all of one-quarter of one draft of a new book done."

He exhaled. "Christ, how do you have time to contribute ideas to the world? I barely have time to clear my inbox of all the fund managers telling me how they would 'love' to separate the endowment from some management fees."

"I'm getting some mixed signals."

Who had told her? Sneaky Calvin? Emily, gunning for the CIO's job? The CIO had always thought that Wirbin would be the one to do it. Or would want to. Maybe he would bring in Mr. Yeboah with a conspicuous lack of stew.

"How bad is it?" she asked.

He calculated. He used to be too good to need to calculate. Even though his job was calculating.

"I think it could be 5 percent."

"Which would be above the 4.6 percent payout, right? So that's good."

He didn't say anything.

"And what was Marvin's donation last year? I can't keep it straight." Marvin Trotter was the richest of the trustees. "Hello?"

"Yes, sorry. The final tranche came in, uh, June, and to the endowment because Marvin understands how universities work. Of the 200 million in other cash dollars that Melinda's pit bulls got their jaws on from the best-years-of-my-lifers, the endowment got about 20 million bucks because it's more fun to put your name on a Center for the Study of Interdisciplinary Studies. I wonder sometimes if the endowment should sell naming rights: the Joseph and Eleanor Herlands Allocation to Asian Mid-Cap Public Equity."

"And this means?"'

"Asian mid-cap public equity?"

"No. Your numbers."

"Five percent"—fuck, how could he get out of—"would mean, roughly, that the endowment appreciated last year by 300 million dollars. You then subtract the 264 million dollars paid out. And then add about 120 million dollars in donations, which would mean you are *up* about 150 million dollars."

"That's good, right?"

Was candor, his self-image, just a luxury from when he had performed? "Well, that's Ted's"—the chief financial officer's—"department to say if it's good. But when you have to ask for money to have real returns over inflation, then, you know... not good."

"Oh," Corso said.

The CIO's life, in its Pleistocene era, had had a different trajectory, to a conversation on a campus about ideas other than how to make money out of money. But he didn't want Corso to hang up. He wanted time. So he asked, "Where's tuition going to be?"

"The list price is $47,000 per year. No room, no board."

"Amazing. You could get your kid a new Audi every year. A snazzy one with heated back seats."

Corso was typing. To Emily, to confirm the number? To Wirbin, that she was still working up the courage? She stopped. "Did something bad happen?"

The CIO didn't speak. He saw his computer flying across his office, crashing into the picture of Hannah and Jane. He saw himself on bent knees, hands cut by the broken glass. He saw the computer unflung, on his desk.

Corso asked again, "Is the 5 percent because you made a mistake that someone is going to write about?"

"Nothing bad happened other than dozens of decisions that stack into a pile of mediocrity."

"I don't think I'm ever going to understand any of this."

"Well, I basically understand all of it, only to be reminded that I can figure out none of it."

"Sounds like my job: cocktail party small talk asking a faculty member about how her work is going while I keep a frozen Nancy Pelosi smile on my face as she says something about a LIGO detector or the application of affect theory in autobiography studies."

Why were they being so fucking cool-headed and polite? "I'm sorry, Meg."

"Don't."

"I'm sure you're looking forward to this year's student Woodward and Bernstein taking the opportunity to mention that I'm the second-highest paid person at the university. Which gives them the opportunity to mention that you're the highest paid person at the university."

"My favorite day, after commencement."

"I wish we had a really high-priced basketball coach to take the heat off."

"The last thing in the world I need is a really high-priced basketball coach."

"Maybe I can do both this year, with the basketball thing as a freebie to justify my salary."

"Do you know anything about basketball?"

"I think I can shoot a ball in the general direction of a hoop."

Why, the CIO wondered, weren't they talking about what could happen at this pace? At the CIO's "rounding"—he closed his eyes—last year's numbers were survivable, with the last of Marvin's donations. But this quarter, my God, the incessant negative momentum had one end: the destruction of the university's financial health and the collapse of the funding model of a school that spends 750 million dollars per year. For what? On what?

On him: the most absurdly paid person on campus.

He couldn't breathe. He *wanted* to see the computer flying across his office, to recreate the family failures in physical form.

No. But, no: be the kind of man who is deeper in consequence.

"The reason I called," she said, "is that Marvin mentioned something to me."

Christ, she had already talked to Marvin.

"It was about Michael Hermann."

The CIO closed his eyes. He practiced the three-count nose breathing exercise from Jane's app. Was Michael Hermann finally replacing him? It'd be the most newsworthy move in the history of endowment management...

The CIO opened his eyes to look at the rainstorm of red tickers on his screen. Maybe Hermann should replace them: 1.6 million was bringing them nothing.

"Are you still there?"

"Yes."

"Marvin didn't have any specific ideas, but he thinks it's silly."

"Two or three times per year—it happened last month—some kid will come in here. Not a kid, but a twenty-five, twenty-six-year-old man. It's always a man. He works for some investment firm that we already invest with or who wants us to start investing with it. And he asks about Michael Hermann. These fanboys look around the room while they ask, and you can see them confused by the visible disconnect as they take in the nicked furniture. They desperately want to know if Michael Hermann sat in that chair, or donated this entire room, entire building, entire *campus*, and left his finance genius fingerprints somewhere. I'm considering buying some relic for them to pray to, a Splinter of the True Bloomberg

Terminal. Because I never know what to say. I just smile in-on-a-secret, lips closed, as if Michael Hermann at that very moment is hiding in my pants."

"I don't know why I'm trying to be the seven hundredth voice on the sociology of inequality. Someone should study these boys."

The CIO had long suspected that success at the knowledge worker game made sense only by its own rules, that the nullity of anyone's real contribution could *not* be disproved by how much one makes, that the contributions outside of finance, too, were also nothing but the shape—not the scale—of a con.

But this didn't seem true for Meg.

"I think you'd get satiated very quickly studying hero worship in Finance Bro Culture. But it is something to see these dudes light up when they mention his name and imagine they are on a Planet Krypton of hedge funds. I don't have the heart to tell him that not only has Michael Hermann never been in this building, not only did this building—or an investment office—not exist when Michael Hermann went to school here, but that Present Conditions mean that I've never met Michael Hermann."

"I can sense how that would be disappointing."

How badly, the CIO wondered, did he actually want to meet Michael Hermann? He had never measured that ache because it was a priori unaddressable. How badly did he need to know if there was life after death? "So what are Marvin's non-specific ideas as related to the Famed Ghost Alumnus?"

"Marvin was being Marvinish. No pushing. 'Just sleep on it, President Corso.'"

"He calls you President Corso?"

"Every time. And non-ironically."

The CIO closed his eyes, one after the other. "Did you tell Wirbin about this?"

"Are you kidding me?"

"Are you asking *me* to do it?"

"You'd definitely deserve to be the second-highest paid person at the university on that day."

"Just imagine."

Corso paused to tell her assistant that she'd be right there. "You know, I printed out Wirbin's resignation letter from the incident. I have officially filed it."

"You have?"

"Your dark-humored college president didn't rise to this exalted position solely on her ability to occasionally laugh at your not-quite-as-scandalous-as-you-want-them-to-be jokes. I have my pedantic and rule-following side, too. So, yes, somewhere in my office, there is a printout of the scanned PDF—"

"On Goldman Sachs letterhead, no less."

"On Goldman Sachs letterhead: 'This letter is to inform you that I will hereby resign from my role on the board of trustees and'—what was it?"

"'And from all other support for the University in all contexts whatsoever....'"

She continued: "'If the school ever consults or seeks advice from that sociopath—"

"*Selfish* sociopath, as if there are the generous, charitable sociopaths."

"—Michael Hermann."

Him: "Yours in dead seriousness..."

And then her: "Benjamin Wirbin, '89."

Venture capital firm
Conference room
September 10

Everyone in the office had feared missing out. Consumer-focused VBV was the best performing venture capital relationship they had, over three funds, other than Founders Fund. But Peter Thiel was even more unlikely than Michael Hermann to come to their conference room. The CIO had sort of understood that Brian Park and Laurent Mast were known in the investing world. But until a month ago, he didn't realize that they had risen to whatever was the investing equivalent of celebrities. Even with Sous and Mittens. Maybe because of Sous and Mittens.

All three analysts had separately stopped the CIO to lobby to attend VBV's fund four pitch. And now, this morning: one analyst was in obvious makeup, another in a black track jacket that seemed a compromise between a Zuckerberg hoodie and a Jobs turtleneck. It made him look like he was dressing as a break dancer for Halloween.

The CIO pretended to watch the market move on his screen, then flipped back to his inbox, then back to the market. He understood anew that these kids—twenty-three and twenty-four—couldn't imagine a world in which steel or oil was power. And so *what* was visiting today was the theology of their medieval Europe: startups, apps, gadgets, less friction, less privacy, less isolation, omnivorous attention, eroding attention, the reduction of everyone to data. What was visiting today was the prime movers of nature and thought.

And so what was *investing*? What were the analysts doing *here*? Were they proud that the endowment, through VBV, was the funder of the funder of tech? Or was the joke reversed? Had endowment management become a game, almost physical, of figuring out ways to catch a few buckets of water before a Niagara fell shamelessly to Page and Brin and Bezos and the rest?

What a small life was predicting the bucket that would get you the most water.

The CIO turned off his monitor. He closed his eyes and breathed quietly as if trying to stay submerged.

He opened his eyes and turned the screen back on.

The CIO had told an analyst once (or all of them, too many times) that our job is not to bet that the world turns out how we want it to be. Our job is performance: buying the right shares of small and mid-sized companies that were selling stuff to Asians, avoiding the sectors crushed by Amazon, making sure our own ventured capital was not missing out on the Way Money Went.

Mast and Park were here. The CIO watched them go into the conference room. Everyone on his team was unsubtly ogling. This was not helpful. Laurent Mast, too good-looking to fully place, was wearing a logo-embroidered fleece vest. They all wore vests, in all seasons, as if vests were the one item of clothing suitable for drinking cocktails at the Rosewood, sparking human innovation, skiing in Patagonia itself, and asking college endowments to give you 30 million dollars. After Mast and Park were settled in the conference room for seventy-five seconds, the CIO stood up, packed up his pen and notepad—and rubbed his tongue across his teeth.

Doing a seating chart at a state dinner would have been less draining than managing the lobbying to be at the meeting. He had told one analyst that Mast and Park would be back. He was sure that that was untrue. But he couldn't rouse himself, this year, to lay out the truth about power; the meeting had to be attended proportionally. With an allocation likely in play, the CIO didn't want to feed Brian Park's ego with any more evidence that he was known.

Also, the conference room couldn't fit that many people.

Emily was leading the meeting. The racial politics if he had not let Calvin attend had given the CIO a headache, even though Calvin was Chinese-American and Park presumably not. So he awarded attendance by seniority: Calvin, Emily, and the two most senior analysts, including Josh—his favorite.

The CIO avoided the hungry eyes of the left-behind as he walked into the meeting.

Five, he realized immediately, was still too many on their side. Power would have been meeting them alone.

"Do you want to talk about Sous first?" Emily brought to a conclusion Mast's filibustering of how the summer went by so fast. The CIO liked Emily for not caring how venture capital spent its summer. Before the meeting, she had told the CIO that she wanted Mast and Park to know that the endowment was paying attention.

Mast smiled, too used to admiration from investors and girls. "Clearly, there are lessons learned from not delivering in the first quarter after the IPO. But let's talk about the accomplishments here for a second."

Park angled his chair back to give Mast room. Emily looked up from her notes at the sound of the chair, turned to the CIO, and wrote something down.

"One: 600 million dollars in annualized subscription revenue and 150 million dollars in annualized hardware revenue from sous vide sales. Two: nearly 300 thousand customers with customer acquisition cost behind us with the hardware purchase. Three: a user experience that is literally off the charts in terms of positivity." Each accomplishment was being delivered faster as if the curtain was coming down. "Just look at the numbers on Instagram. We are empowering people to cook the best meal of their lives. You're never going to play basketball like LeBron, but you can cook like Suzanne Goin or Andrew Carmellini at home. And not by being some Blue Apron automaton, either." His three fingers were still up, a permanent statue to the market's idiocy.

The CIO couldn't remember if Mast's beard, and the gray climbing into it, was new; maybe he could set a daily level of attractiveness on an app.

Mast continued, "To be completely honest, Sous has only one problem: short-selling losers who have never had a socially productive idea in their lives. That Barclays report, which I'm sure you saw, has not been helpful these last six weeks. You don't have to worry about Barclays ever getting into one of our syndicates again."

But *still*, the CIO thought, the worst performing IPO in four years cannot just be short sellers.

The endowment had two sides it could be on: as a 40 million dollar victim of VBV's optimism in pushing a premature IPO, or as the co-owner of this Icarus fall. The CIO glanced at Emily to see if her face displayed a preference. The CIO's own silence was becoming an answer. He needed to check his phone, hungry for some good news elsewhere in the portfolio. He needed to go back to his office, to bring his laptop into the meeting, to be able to surf the Internet away, away on a raft of death. He needed anything but to be part of this ritual. He didn't want any more excuses.

"As a literal point of law, that report was libelous. Because we are so far from 50 percent customer churn, it's laughable." Mast chuckled to himself.

Was Mast an actor, the CIO wondered—not in the baseline sense that all the pitching GPs were acting but an actual actor hired by Brian Park to play the role of VC co-founder, as a tech bro experiment in disrupting appearance-based judgments? It would explain the good looks.

Emily caught her upper lip in her teeth, chewed it a bit, and asked Mast, "Is that true?"

How conscious was she, the CIO wondered, of being the only Black person here? Did that matter to her question, which she wouldn't have asked had she not done the research to know the answer? Or was asking the question just a super power, to be able to call bullshit, from some cultural reserve of authenticity and suffering and owed respect?

Mast wasn't dwelling on owed respect, it seemed. He answered, as if from a script, "Barring whatever is happening in this market bleeding into consumer discretionary, Sous is not going to run out of liquidity or slow capital deployment to the Sous 3. This is a full-stack, 600-million-dollar revenue business en route to being a 2-billion-dollar revenue business. The Sous 2 is the most well regarded, most coveted piece of home design since the original Nest."

The CIO wanted to crack the old joke: We're losing money on every sale but making it up in volume. Even in today's tech world, combining negative gross margin hardware sales with negative gross margin recurring revenue was the high trapeze.

But then Park said—and this was what had muzzled the CIO, what had drawn the scrum for seats at this meeting—"Even if you assume Sous goes to zero, VBV II is still at 5x gross in year five."

Five times their money before fees, four times after fees and carry. One percent of total positive endowment performance from one fund, of one manager. And the fund still held positions that could theoretically double its value, or more, again.

Park let that fact perfume the air.

Why, the CIO wondered, wasn't this making him happy?

Emily apparently was at no risk of that. She said, "I would want to know how your valuation approach feeds into that number."

Park looked at a text on his watch. Had he heard her?

The CIO should call him racist. Koreans and Blacks. That history.

Park exhaled, then looked at Emily, then Calvin, then Emily again. "Mittens," he said, "was sold at an incredible price."

Emily flipped three pages back into her notebook to confirm something. She said, her voice rising a half-octave, "But at your annual meeting, you guided to a double from the year-end valuation. There was no ambiguity."

The CIO could feel Calvin slink back in his chair.

"I absolutely stand by that," Park answered. "But we got a 3.2 billion dollar cash offer. Do you know how many non-biotech cash strategic exits there have been greater than 3 billion dollars in contemporary venture in the United States? Eighteen. We've now been in three of them."

Emily bent over her pad, writing harder. The CIO wanted her to draw blood.

"Maybe it'd be helpful from a clarity perspective to level set the Mittens exit?" Park asked.

Emily looked up. She had not worn her contacts today—to foil Mast's handsomeness? She seemed to be biting her upper *and* lower lips. The younger members of the team watched her, their own mouths slightly open, seemingly wanting her and not wanting her to be a badass.

She nodded.

Park began, "When the board gets the offer from Jobful, we convene an emergency Saturday meeting at the Four Seasons in Beverly Hills. While we are discussing the mechanics—and, frankly, there is little to discuss, it's a cash offer—Evan Byrne is in his chair, bouncing as if this meeting was a nuisance to him. And then he stands up and says, 'This has been a fascinating exercise in human rationalization,' and walks out of the room. After we vote without him, because we don't need him from a governance perspective, Scott from Tiger Global says to me, 'The winner of this fun task is the Series A.'

"I really want to get home, my kids are annoyed because I canceled plans to go to our place in Healdsburg for the weekend, but I do my duty and drive to Byrne's place in the Hollywood Hills. I text him three times to let him know I'm coming. I'm wondering if Emma Watson is going to be there and can talk some sense into him. While it's not clear what my daughter thinks VCs do, I once heard her tell a friend that her daddy knows Belle *and* Hermione."

Calvin's eyes widened. The team had, of course, joked about Byrne and Emma Watson before the meeting, but maybe the fusing of dreamworlds, to Calvin, became real only when heard about first-hand.

"Byrne had not texted back by the time I get to his place. I ring the bell, and eventually he opens the door. He's wearing these kung fu pants and a tight t-shirt. I have no idea where he had the time to transform his body while working eighteen-hour days running Mittens, but I guess you don't get to date Emma Watson by being the 140-pound beanpole I met four years ago." Park was not wearing a vest as if to separate himself from the boy games of his now less successful partner. The sleeves of his soft gray button-down were rolled up, exposing his own toned forearms. "This is the first time I've been to his house. He has the most child-unfriendly home, from a safety perspective, I have ever seen. It's as if he's trying to prove how indifferent he is to children despite being the founder of the 'Uber for babysitters.' His balcony hangs over a hundred-foot canyon. The only thing stopping you from falling in are these thin, nearly invisible wires between posts. And there's a huge open fireplace where you can light a fire on the floor to give children a non-zero chance of being incinerated before they tumble to their deaths.

"Byrne and I sit down." Park looked at Emily and then bestowed eye contact on the two other senior members of the team. "I'm blunt with him: 'I can just tell you how this is going down, or I can explain to you why this is the right decision.' He says, 'Your choice,' his face making it clear that everything I could possibly say from an explanation perspective has already been eviscerated by him. But I'm in a patient mood, so I list the reasons this is a killer outcome, even at a 20 percent discount to a no-consequence, 200-million-dollar investment round from J.P. Morgan's private bank." Park looked only at Emily this time. "I make it clear to him that what he's not taking into account is the market. First, independent of his company's trajectory, the market after Uber and Lyft had already peaked in terms of exit *and* valuation sentiment. Trees do not grow to the sky from a growth perspective. Second, even if you ignore WeWork, it's unclear how long Masa and Mohammed bin Salman have for this experiment of theirs, but their hundred billion feels half real, half PR stunt. The people who cash-sell into that reality early are going to be remembered as super-smart from an exit perspective. I go on with three, which is that even if it was 2016 again, are mid-sized companies winning?"

As Park continued talking, the CIO shifted in his seat. The CIO *needed* to check his phone, needed to get back to the market. Had he picked this up from Peter?

He had told Jane to look at Hannah; Peter obviously wasn't learning this from them.

And now, here: Brian Park was the direction of history, pulling him against his will.

The saddest part was that the discussion of portfolio companies—their universally unique Sustainable Competitive Advantages—used to be the most soul-awakening part of any private capital meeting. We are, all of us, merchant bankers bringing ideas into the world. Mittens had returned thirty-four times VBV's investment. That return was more important than wondering what the gray French shirt—it had to be French—thought of his LPs, specifically this Black woman in a blouse so aggressively uninteresting that it had to be making a point.

Shockingly early on in his time at the endowment, Calvin had argued that that the investment team should have bespoke offices designed by real architects, far off campus. The CIO knew what he was talking about: electric whiteboards everywhere, nooks in which an endowment's own Vest People met visitor Vest People. The CIO could have one. A few trustees were embarrassed to not have one. But he had never considered it. It seemed unseemly. Also, when he had had first-rate numbers, he was vain about the shabby office, his thin beard, and his skinny-fat non-physique. Looking like an anthropology professor—sort of being an anthropology professor—made his first-rate numbers seem effortless. With an attractive wife, stylish by college-town standards, the CIO had won the Revenge of the Nerds, unlike the Brian Parkses who paid someone to make them over by prescribing forearms exercises, gray-on-gray clothing, and wool shoes.

Yet now, in the wake of Mittens and deXt, Brian Park would have rich great-grandchildren. Part of the CIO didn't want to know how the reorganization of American life, American money—American morals—came down to the returns to be captured by intermediaries to intermediaries to intermediaries. Because where did this leave the CIO? With his second-rate numbers, his 6 percent to Wirbin, his diversified fucking portfolio, the school itself (frustratingly close to the super-elite), how was he not the presiding officer of the University Department of Post-Graduation Fallback Plans?

Park was still talking. "And Byrne tells me, 'That's the problem with you finance guys. Possibilities to you are defined by noise inward. I measure potential from ideas outward.' I don't say anything. I didn't tell him that at our annual meeting, I showed a slide with the TAM"—total addressable market, the CIO translated for himself—"for Parent Tech larger than for mobility. So we sit there silently. He hadn't offered me anything to drink. He is nursing something in an old-fashioned milk bottle with nothing on it from a labeling perspective. Unlabeled water has become this whole thing in LA." Park looked at Mast, presenting an investment theme. "I'm certain Byrne's had three extra milligrams of magnesium or something in it. And then he asks me if I want to know why I'm wrong. Thinking from noise inward had apparently only been the lead-in.

"I tell him that I *always* want to know why I'm wrong.

"He doesn't talk about the market, or other buyers, or even how *he* can be a better aggregator than Jobful, which has a non-zero chance of being true. He asks me if I'm familiar with Joseph Campbell's *The Hero's Journey*. I tell him I know it. I can't remember if it was Elon or Chesky who started it—I have to look this up—but it's become a touchpoint for every founder. One of Laurent's jokes is that Campbell combines their four passions: *Game of Thrones*, Burning Man, microdosing, and bottomless self-regard."

Calvin laughed with his whole body, his head actually thrown back. Even Emily vocalized something as if she had learned third-hand what laughter was supposed to sound like. The CIO wondered if Park had paid someone to write Mast's jokes.

"Byrne explains it to me anyway, at length, and then says, 'This is so clearly the apotheosis, so clearly Yahoo-Zuck, that it's laughable. We just got an offer for 3.2 billion *cash,* and we've scaled to only eighteen markets.' Then he stands up, walks past his child-incinerator, and gets another bottle of placebo water. Just one. I mean, I'm used to these guys being"—he looked at superfan Calvin—"jerks from a personality perspective, but that is classic Evan. He sits down again, stares at me, and is apparently waiting for me to leave. I say, 'Evan, I have to be honest: I'm more of a science guy than a humanities guy. I don't do narratives.' I let that sink in and explain that one of my hobbies, as a failed evolutionary biologist, is following the punctuated equilibrium debate. It is savage. Just when you think someone from the Dawkins crowd has settled it once and for all, some Gould disciple comes up with new physical evidence. I deliver this as a preamble to what I'm about to make clear: that tech valuations, in *our* evolution, are not linear. Yes, we sold Mittens because timing is everything in everything. But there are bigger things at work from an exit perspective."

Park stopped, seemingly to give the CIO a chance to take notes for a five thousand-word LinkedIn post. "He doesn't say anything. This whole scene is surreal from a reality perspective. It's as if the Warriors, after they win the NBA championship, are sitting in a conference room like this"—Park looked around at the chairs made of leather that could possibly be leather, a quarter smile on his face—"to talk about a loss in week three. So, I tell him how punctuated equilibrium works in tech. There are four basic phases, and each phase gets you a non-linear step-up in valuation."

The CIO pushed his feet against the floor and lifted his seat a half-inch. He held the pencil tighter. He couldn't look at Park. He tried to look at Mast, but all that male beauty was too much. So he looked at the door, his ass pressed deep into the chair. He calculated that the more he stared at the door, the more he could remain seated. How much longer was he going to have to do this? His body needed to leave. He stared just at the dirty brass doorknob, dented asymmetrically. How does a doorknob get dented? He tried to assess the void space of the biggest dent. This was working. This was a quality of attention, even if his chest felt gripped to him, aching, as if his pecs had ripped due to his body's own effort to both escape and not escape the room.

Park was still talking. "The first phase of our evolution is

Stake-Claiming the Obvious. You will get a valuation from *someone* for being the first person to own the problem: eyeglasses are too expensive, international texting shouldn't be metered. For us, it was that a huge informal market was price inflexible, devoid of data, and not inducing its true demand. I congratulate Byrne on figuring this out from one 10-minute conversation with his sister, which if true, is genius. But that's one valuation level, one equilibrium. Being the first technically functioning solution to gig-economy babysitting is worth 50 million." Park held his hand low. "The next jump up is Flipping the Flaw. I remind him about those early articles about Mittens. If Laurent thinks that that Barclays report was ugly from a criticism perspective, I can show him some clips from that *Daily Show* episode that asked why police weren't arresting parents for using Mittens. But people tried it because they spent seven hundred dollars for *Hamilton* tickets that would kill them to throw away because the teenage neighbor girl, whom their kids never liked anyway, is a catastrophe from a reliability perspective. And afterwards, those parents joke with friends about how they could barely enjoy the show because they left their kids with a stranger. But you know what? They actually enjoyed *Hamilton* immensely. And then their friends try it two weeks later, on the spur of the moment, just to go to dinner. And they all start talking about how, if you think about it, it *was* weird that people *used* to use neighbor girls with no real references, random pricing, no data on performance, no insurance, no accountability, and sketchy certification. And now the girls become self-selecting, with anyone with a brain realizing you make more on Mittens, even without the sign-up bonuses. And the most super competitive girls love the gamification of the rising Mittens levels.

"I tell Byrne, people who think 15 percent higher annual revenue next year gets you a 15 percent higher valuation know nothing about tech. It was Flipping the Flaw that raised Mittens, in, like, two months of execution and good UX"—user experience—"from here to here, to a new level, to a company worth 750 million dollars. And then I tell Byrne that we're *starting*, in our core markets, with the third phase of equilibrium: Redefining Deviancy. You see it in everything social and mobile. Millennials arriving in an airport will walk by ten cabs in a line to wait twenty minutes for some guy in a Camry because they consider it gross and weird to be in a highly regulated vehicle purpose-built for the exact service they need. And for Mittens, well, there are markets—the Bay Area is one—where the husband will point out to his wife that a random babysitter is Mittens14 as if it's an accomplishment of his own child. And if he and his wife are talking to some acquaintance at the school auction, and the other mom mentions that she still uses the neighbor girl, the Mittens customers will ask something passive-aggressive from a conversation perspective, like, 'So how do you control sitter screentime?'

"And I tell Byrne, it wasn't scaling to Denver or San Diego"—Park rolled his eyes—"that got us an extra billion dollars in our valuation in a year. It was starting to Redefine Deviancy in New York and San Francisco. Byrne's condescending smirk is starting to unwind as if I'm making the case *for* him and we're rejecting Jobful's offer. But I tell him that the fourth phase doesn't come from ten more markets or *any* of the things we had talked about in board meetings. From a valuation perspective, 3.2 billion dollars accounts for three years of perfect execution in a perfect environment. And I mean perfect. No drop in consumer spending. No regulatory issues. No fatal accidents, which we have avoided incredibly well from a luck perspective, given the non-zero chance that those will occur. Byrne interrupts—he's always been hypersensitive on this—and tells me that we're prepared for that. I remind him that I'm the one that's been obsessed with the cert protocols and brought AIG in. We're not Series E here."

How had he gotten here, from a luck perspective: two tech dudes arguing about the valuation hit of dead children? He had to get out of this room. It was only a matter of getting out of the chair, keeping his eyes locked on the doorknob, and turning the knob.

The CIO had followed the evolution of Mittens as it was happening, or at least he thought he had. But now Rip Van Winkle woke up to a different colored sky. And beside him, awaken, an app—however the CIO doled out attribution to the VC or the Journeying Hero or Emily—that had produced 50 percent of VBV II's gains and made the endowment 40 million bucks. And so was Park a genius? Was this speech what is genius today, in a world in which the measure of all philosophies was money? Had 40 million bucks made the CIO complicit in redefining deviancy? Does 3.2 billion dollars allow them to redefine deviancy as if they know the face of God?

The CIO could point out the nothing productive they built but their arrogance and wealth. What is that but deviancy?

Jane might approve, or at least be interested, if he said that at dinner.

The CIO couldn't, though. Because, at night, he didn't ache for sex with Jane, or Emma Watson, or both in some gymnastic group. He ached for a time machine to allow the endowment to have been triple-weighted to the right VCs, to have gorged on Amazon and Apple and Facebook shares at the start of the boom, to be a bucket brigade of ways to take what money was there.

To be a Brian Park for a day, with a win like Mittens.

Park had not stopped. "Byrne takes another swig of his Hero's Journey potion. I suddenly wonder if it's the salt juice Dorsey drinks, and I am tempted to just walk over and taste it. But instead, I finish up. I explain that the next phase of evolution is Independent Viability. Even if you reach the market penetration necessary from a free-cash-flow perspective, can you really see Mittens as a public company, reporting every quarter on the volume and margins of arranging babysitters? Analysts writing reports on it? Long-only investors having opinions on it? Who would want to be the CEO of a company like that? You? Anyone you could respect? Look at what happens to every independent dating app. If the market can smell that you are not independently viable, you never—no matter if you're in eighteen markets or fifty—get to the next level of equilibrium. It just doesn't happen.

"Byrne looks at me and tells me that I'm basically defining Amazon as a bookstore.

"I guess he thinks that I'm going to ask him to explain *that* to me because, you know, he's the first person ever to use it. They all think that the lesson of Uncle Jeff is that you can lose money for twenty years and end up as the richest man in the history of the world. But look at what happened to Neumann. And so I don't say anything from a response perspective. I just tell him, you know why species die. They die because they didn't adapt.

"Byrne takes another swig and puts the potion down so hard that I'm still not sure why the table didn't shatter. Maybe it's gorilla glass or something." Park looked at Mast as if there was another interesting idea to explore. "And then he 'explains' to me why the VC model is broken, why VCs are the ones that are going to be extinct. Because VCs have 'one input and one output—greed,' and so habitually destroy businesses by forcing them into a narrow lane to protect the VCs' other companies and by selling them to stupid myopic buyers who don't understand the opportunity set.

"I think, whatever, dude. I'm tired. I'm also really thirsty. So I level-set it for him from a governance perspective. He had left the board meeting. His absence was recorded in the minutes. The board voted without dissension to take Jobful's offer. I tell him it's happening in two hours.

"He puts his head between the knees of his kung fu pants. At first, I wonder if he has nunchucks or something under his couch.

But finally it dawns on me: he is crying—not just whimpering but full-stack blubbering."

The CIO's ribcage shuddered as if he too was about to cry. Six percent? Why?

"Another one of Laurent's jokes is that tech founders pretend they have Asperger's because they think it will get them Zuckerbergish valuations. But Byrne, still crying, spit coming out of his mouth, starts yelling, 'Everyone told me it was a huge mistake to go with you. I should have gone with Benchmark. They don't do this drag bullshit.'

"He catches his breath and wipes his face on his tight t-shirt. I couldn't take it anymore. So I reminded him of a few things. When it comes to not showing emotion, wannabe Zuckerbergs have nothing on actual Koreans. I remind him that Sameer didn't even sit in on his pitch to Accel. I remind him that Jim Goetz walked out of his pitch halfway through, saying that they were in the business of disintermediation, not pointless intermediation. I remind him that our old boss Ben Horowitz told us that he told Byrne that his baby-killing idea would go down as the shark-jumping moment of the gig economy. And I tell him that if he imagines *Benchmark* would have done something else, go ask Travis.

"He stops crying, scrunches up his face, and looks at me.

"I try to be nice. I didn't remind him that he's dealing with people who take their duty seriously from a fiduciary perspective. I didn't remind him that we are talking about cash, real cash, your cash, UVA's cash, the Hilton Foundation's cash, the Carnegie Corporation's cash. I didn't remind him that he is twenty-seven years old. I didn't remind him that he is dating Emma Watson. I tell him that in about ninety days, he is going to get a check for 480 million dollars.

"He looks at me and says, 'A year from now, it could have been a billion.'"

Investment team
Conference room
September 22

Calvin covered a gasp with his hand when the endowment's director of investment operations revealed last year's performance.

The mission of the CIO's life was to uncover which of *them*, the GPs, were slippery.

When he told Wirbin six, he thought some lucky breaks could bring them to 4.5 percent.

It was 3.8.

Emily said, "I would say that the investment committee can't expect better performance."

Calvin said, "We are below the benchmarks."

"Benchmarks," Emily answered, "are crude instruments that don't take into account our risk positioning within asset classes."

The CIO looked at one of the analysts. She was dressed in pencil pants and a Victorian-seeming navy blouse, buttoned up to her neck and probably unaffordable on her salary. Her scent—lavender and fresh laundry—mixed with the musk of someone else's—everyone else's—pit odor in the packed room. Like the rest of them, she was not looking back at him. They were all watching Emily versus Calvin, unsure of who was right. None of them but Emily seemed to be taking it personally that 3.8 percent had been the product of *their* rigor and diligence, too.

Or was it not really theirs?

Emily stopped talking. Why couldn't he be more appreciative

of her? He *was* appreciative of her. But why couldn't he summon—what did he call it?—the authenticity and suffering and survivor-respect—to break the growing silence.

The CIO moved his hand to rub his forehead, his only comfort, but after two circles he moved his hand to the back of his head, rubbing, flea-bitten. His stomach felt empty. His stomach felt food-poisoned. He wanted to put his head between his legs.

From that position, he could tell them about Wirbin, Corso, 5 and 6 percent.

No one spoke. The CIO had to get out of the room. He had to take both hands to his face and rub it completely off. Even Josh, his favorite, looked neutral. Couldn't Josh at least measure the gravity of the numbers? Or did the numbers just mean a rich school not getting richer for all of one year. Or, in fact, still getting slightly richer because rich people gave the rich school millions of dollars just for being rich, and maybe to help their rich kids end up more rich.

But 3.8 percent was a miracle of capital appreciation compared to what had happened since the fiscal year ended.

He looked again at Calvin. Eventually, he had to. He was wearing a vest given to him by his best performing GP. His face was broadcasting that he was still bemused to be here instead of at Stanford Management.

The CIO began quietly, as if to himself. "During the Global Financial Crisis, I was the CIO of the Eckmann Foundation in Columbus, Ohio." The kids looked back at him, finally. He stopped and swallowed. What did his team see in him? A sage investor? A breathing human being with prior jobs and disappointments? An office fixture, like the nicks on the table and the 6 billion dollars on a spreadsheet? "We were on regular calendar-year reporting, like sane people. Our September meeting was historically held by phone, so December 2008 was the first time we had gotten together in person in six months."

None of them showed interest. Or non-interest.

"The foundation was a textbook of poor governance. One trustee was—I'm not exaggerating—an eighty-eight-year-old retired stock broker at Edward Jones, who was on the board because his wife had been the childhood playmate of the late Mrs. Eckmann. Another trustee was a retired executive at the trust company that had worked for the also late Mr. Eckmann. He looked like a pudgy George Peppard. The A-Team? Mr. T?" No reaction. "The best show going in Columbus was to watch which of the two would fall asleep in meetings first. Their eyes would flutter, heads droop, pop up again, then droop again—all to a tune no one could hear."

The CIO demonstrated this to giggles. Why am I—?

"Then there were the Eckmanns' three kids: the butcher, the baker, and the candlestick maker. The older daughter wrapped herself in so many layers of cashmere and silk that you wondered if the goal was to become drapery. She was always baking one of her 'famous' this or 'famous' that. I would wonder if they were famous because, regardless of ingredients, each and every one tasted like sandpaper. Once she brought a 'famous' berry cobbler but no spoons. This somehow ended up with Pudgy Peppard eating it with his hands. The younger daughter—she was in her early seventies—never married and lived on a farm in Vermont, where she raised alpacas and honeybees. She would bring in gifts to thank me for what I was doing for 'the family.' These alternated between alpaca knitwear—if anyone needs an XL-sized asymmetrical poncho, see me after the meeting—and beeswax candles. I assumed she gave me these gifts because she was lonely and my qualifications were being A Person She Saw. Or maybe she was thankful. In hindsight, in the 2000s, it was not all that hard to make money. Or maybe, just maybe, it was I who encouraged low interest rates and the urbanization of three hundred million Chinese peasants to allow for pleasant secondary impacts on the global equity markets. And so at the board meeting... Yes, Josh?"

"Who was the butcher?"

The CIO smiled. "Ah, the butcher: he was the Eckmanns' son. Now, he wasn't actually a butcher. But calling him the butcher is more fun than saying the duffer, the baker, and the candlestick maker. The butcher kind of fits, though. Because the son acted as if each board meeting was taking him away from incalculably more important things. Which, from what I gathered, were a) making investments with dubious logic in his buddies' real estate schemes and b) traveling to high-end golf courses to discuss said investments.

"The CFO and the executive director of the foundation were also on the investment committee. Those seven, mind you, had oversight of a 2-billion-dollar pool of capital. A pool of capital, by the way, about which it was never clear to me if anyone really cared how we performed. The charities that got 100 million dollars per year cared, of course, but the foundation had only two grant officers—and Gayle and Cherie were not venture philanthropists, paving new modalities of result measurement. Three quarters of the money, year in and year out, went to the same institutions that the Eckmanns had always supported: the Lutheran Church, Ohio State, the United Way, food banks, people in Columbus doing low-glamor, little-appreciated, necessary work. The rest of the money was informally earmarked to the butcher, the baker, and the candlestick maker to allocate to causes that were often at cross-purposes, usually via the underwriting of overly fancy themed benefits.

"So, it's late 2008, and"—the CIO looked at the kids—"how old were you then, Josh?"

"Um, thirteen."

"Well, in 2008, while Josh is entering manhood and his parents are panicking about how they are going to afford those little baseball helmet ice cream dishes at his bar mitzvah—"

"It was actually football-themed."

The CIO nodded approvingly. He should hire only by the speed of wit.

"While Mr. and Mrs. Kaufman are dealing with Josh whining about wanting *real* NFL helmets and Bubbe demanding *real* hydrangeas, they are looking at their brokerage account and wondering if the centerpieces are going to have to be crabgrass in paper bowls." He paused for a quick, private relief at having instinctively picked Josh for this riff. He had once found Josh's dad, and socioeconomic status, on LinkedIn. "The S&P 500 is down over 30 percent with a presidential election going on, Congress unable to get their act together, the Federal Reserve throwing shit against the wall to see what sticks, banks going under, people demanding prison time for poor investment decisions, pundits speculating on whether *capitalism* still works. Some of you know this, but my investment team at the foundation was one Canadian guy, Ian, incredibly skilled and talented across asset classes. He is now the CIO of The Orange-Carlin Trust in London, which has more money than we do, a fact of which I'm strangely proud.

"I know that I tell you that rule number one, two, and three of endowment management is *never* try to time the market, but there were signals out there that were uniquely out of the norm. So we had gotten crazy nervous earlier in the year and, thank God, were basically as defensive as one can be and still have a pulse. I suspected we were going to come out okay, relatively speaking.

"I gave the trustees a few lead-in slides on how world-historically catastrophic the markets had been. I am going asset class by asset class." He nodded at the operations director. "I didn't bother to explain to that audience that had we been allocated as we had been a year earlier, we would have had to question the very logic of the endowment model. It seemed to have become unglued. The stock broker, God bless him, stayed awake for half of the slides because the collapse of global capitalism was *kind of* interesting. But not so interesting to prevent"—the CIO horse-headed his chin down—"good night. Pudgy Peppard kept on scarfing down the baker's dessert as if he was going to survive the Second Great Depression by pre-eating brownies made of sand.

"Three slides before I finish the market update, the butcher barks out"—the CIO did his best patrician voice—"'Just give us the numbers, goddamnit.' I present the slide. The candlestick maker—this woman, mind you, inherited 300 million dollars independent of the foundation—looks at it and says, in her Joni Mitchell voice, 'Oh, but 11 percent is very good. I heard that the market was down.' Ian and I look at each other. It's not clear if *whom* she heard that from was me, ninety seconds before, or from her most market-savvy alpaca. I want Ian to say something, but Alberta Einstein is silent. So I eventually say, 'That's *negative* 11 percent.'"

At the room's laughter, the CIO thought, Fuck you, Brian Park, We can all tell a story that puts us in the captain's chair.

At least mine feel human, in the lightness of the absurd.

The CIO felt lighter, too—numbers once gravity-bound and important were now effervescent, through the popped top of the truth. He felt dizzy from the pressure change. He said, "That negative 11 percent, by the way, is why I'm here. I was considered either a genius or the luckiest son of a bitch in the endowment and foundation world."

The director of investment operations asked, "Do you want me to put negative three and a half for our Q1 estimate?"

Was that the lesson she had heard in the story? He gripped his hands, trying to push through whatever arthritis prevented a hard fist. He tried out, "These numbers seem to be moving around all over the place."

She stared at her work on the table.

He didn't want to scare these kids. For many, this was their first adult job. But numbers are always moving around. Numbers exist to move around.

The CIO caught Emily's eyes. She had tied her center-parted hair behind her.

"How about," he said, "if we just *describe* the performance, with clip art of very unhappy looking cats?" He showed his own sad face.

But what were Emily's eyes saying? He *was* appreciative. She was the one who wanted to hire all these people because she had heard his John Bogle story already.

"It's fine. Put the numbers in." He had put in the interim performance estimate every quarter for nine years. If he was going to be shot, he was going to march straight-backed towards the enemy line, waving the flag of his own mediocrity. "But let's talk about stuff we can control. Let's talk about Actual Investing. Calvin, do you want to present Ledo Road?"

Everyone had read Calvin's investment memo on the Australian's Asian public equity strategy, a paraphrase of the Australian's pitch with basic analytics and some market commentary. The younger team members asked nothing and even Emily, with dignity, was silent. Calvin was not an idiot, so everything he presented was unassailably right. It was hard to argue with Ledo Road's numbers, or the strategy's logic, or the need to maintain exposure to Asian public markets. It was hard to argue with the gut call the CIO had made before the Australian had left the room.

Still, the CIO wanted one of them to ask if this was all too tidy.

The CIO should have asked if this was all too tidy.

The agenda moved to VBV. Josh asked Emily, "Did Park explain what happened with Mittens?"

The CIO couldn't remember if Emily had ever before not previewed a decision with him. He would support her decision whatever it was. Because he had to. Because he still trusted her, despite PMD.

She tried to smile as she answered, "It was like he was giving an effing TED Talk."

"In his defense," the CIO added, trying too hard to be jovial himself, "it had to be long because he gave us at least three explanations: one, that Evan Byrne had gone insane because of magnesium water, Emma Watson, and poor domestic architectural choices; two, that the tech market had peaked and it's all deunicornization from here; and finally, an exceptionally spontaneous analogy about punctuated equilibrium."

"Even though he doesn't 'do narrative.'"

"But a narrative that mentions the words 'evolutionary biology' is not narrative. It's science."

The kids mocked non-zero level-setting UX tech clichés before catching themselves, each silent in turn, maybe collectively recognizing that they had all been jealous and approving when Edgar posted a picture on Instagram with Evan Byrne at VBV's last annual meeting, that those happy few allowed to attend the pitch this week had texted friends that they had met Brian Park and Laurent Mast, that none of them had ever come close to directly making a venture capital investment.

The CIO asked Emily which way she was leaning on the recommendation.

At the end of the VBV meeting, Park had checked his watch as if he could measure his virtue on a pedometer. He then looked for the last time at Emily and told her that he was closing the new fund in six weeks.

"I would say that I doubt that VBV has the systems, unique intellectual framework, or super proprietary deal flow that Brian Park claims he has. And Fund II, from Sous at its IPO price and Mittens at its pre-sale mark, lost half a *billion* dollars in value. Fund III was deployed really quickly"—one of the analysts added "like, twice expectations"—"and has no real performance data. And their diversity and inclusion metrics are near the bottom. Brian Park is the only non-white male professional of any type at the entire firm, and he is, you know." The CIO had to strain to not look at Calvin. "But they are showing the best performance and DPI of any of our venture managers except for Founders, for which our 10 million dollar allocations don't move the needle. We looked at the volatility too, and it's hard to conclude from the loss ratio that VBV has taken on measurable additional risk to achieve this. So, if we want to maintain our allocation to top decile venture, I would say that we don't have a choice but to make a 30 million dollar commitment."

The CIO was proud of her. That was the right answer. VBV's decision to sell Mittens was ballsy and clean, and—with no alternative life from which to measure—probably right. So grin and bear it. Don't punish the self-important. Don't overthink FOMO.

The CIO didn't have time to linger on his internal approval, though. Calvin had prepared an ambush.

"Is there any way they are going to give that to us? I heard that Penn told them that they'd take 100 million."

Emily seemed to be taken aback by the news. She looked at Calvin and answered, "I don't know what we can get."

Calvin's primary investment insight, transparently jealous of any GP glamor that didn't fall into his mandate, seemed to be this: that because great managers were oversubscribed and could choose their investors, stiff and slightly bitchy Emily would never optimize the endowment's allocations to great ideas. "Do we have a strategy for getting a bigger allocation?" he asked.

The CIO wanted to intervene for Emily, even if Calvin had asked a sensible question.

Emily didn't need him. "I would not say that there is a 'strategy' except to ask."

Calvin: "So, basically no."

The CIO interrupted. "I can handle this." Was that the right answer? "I can see if Ben Wirbin's new best friend, and our own newest trustee, Anil Ghosh, can help us with the request."

Emily looked at him, blank-faced.

The CIO pushed his chair back. He could pretend he was being ironic by putting his head between his legs. Instead, he closed his eyes, for too long. He needed the darkness. Could Emily see a captain, he wondered as the darkness flowed down from his forehead, a cold, a release, a blankness, an end?

Could she see what was left?

And what was left?

A brain—not even a person, maybe just a thought in this now dead silent blackness? And maybe just *the* thought, the one metastasizing through every midnight when the numbers were bad: that I am not a genius investor, that I'm not even a good investor, that I have only been lucky when good, and that if I am not a good investor, what am I, what am I, what am I—and what happens (to the pay, the purpose, the status) when They find out?

He opened his eyes and looked at his team, his neck working too hard to keep his head straight, chin up, looking at the world straight on.

Trustee (call)
Office
September 24

Anil Ghosh said, "I finally reached Brian Park. It took him four days to phone me back. He said that he was very very busy." It sounded almost like *wery wery* busy. "The rumor in town is that he is part of the group trying to buy the kings."

"The kings?"

"The Sacramento Kings."

"I guess it's better than buying, like, Richard II."

"Park was very very curious about the board, about how I became a trustee. He asked if Michael Hermann was involved."

The CIO would not go there.

Ghosh went on: "I do not know him so well. I am probably twenty years older than he, but there is some recognition that *not* being a Stanford white dude"—almost two syllables, *dew-id*—"we are in the same pea pod."

"And you told him?"

"I said be careful if you ever talk to a Goldman Sachs banker at the parents' weekend, as you may get a call from Ben Wirbin."

"And Ben Wirbin is not to be resisted."

"My daughter is very very self-conscious, lest the five people who know that I am a trustee assume she got into the school because of that instead of it being spun around."

In another life, for confirmation and curiosity, the CIO would have guessed-and-googled how trustee-level wealth had otherwise lighted Ghosh's daughter's path to admission. But he said, upbeat, as the help: "Tell your daughter that we approve of her sacrifice of reputation in helping her school have a greater insight into the Asian and Californian venture communities. In addition to however much Ben Wirbin extracted from you directly." The CIO knew roughly how much Wirbin extracted. What a business, trustee sales: you get someone to pay an uncomfortable amount of money to then provide free advice. "And so what did the Kings-buyer say about our allocation to VBV's fund?"

"He said 'in consideration of our friendship'—this is quoting him—he could 'squeeze' out a 20 percent higher allocation."

"Okay: so 22 instead of 18 but not the 30 requested."

The CIO was not sure if Ghosh was trying to be blunt: "He said 21.6."

The CIO went blind. He was suffocated by a blocked scream. His hands grasped air, needing something to throw.

Do not talk. Do not throw. Do not be him.

The CIO should call up that basketball-team-buying asshole and tell him to take his 21.6 and shove it up his self-assessment as the second coming of Sequoia because of three fucking deals. Seriously, how the fuck had the school, before the CIO's time, managed to be the only top-twenty endowment *not* to have gotten a toehold with the real Sand Hill Road kings, where at least the egos were fully built?

It was the duty of the Mount Mitchells, Ledo Roads, even the Brian Fucking Parks to beg the endowment for money, regardless of the realities of allocation supply and demand. What did anything matter but that?

"What a prince," the CIO said eventually. "A prince to buy the Kings."

Ghosh didn't reply. The CIO didn't know if he had lost him. He was still trying to get a read on Ghosh's point of view. The

CIO's only reaction on hearing of Ghosh's appointment was befuddlement that they were still in the league that had non-alumni trustees.

At Ghosh's first meeting of the investment committee, he had worn a gray pinstripe suit, creases sharp. The incumbent male trustees had all been in blazers.

The CIO now sighed, pointlessly calmer. He explained to Ghosh, "The worst of them flatter you, and the best of them see you as a problem to be solved. I appreciate you putting in the call. I'll have Emily follow up."

He wasn't sure if Ghosh wanted to end the call. The CIO opened his browser to check on the market. The S&P was down 6 percent for the quarter, but at least the red days had paused.

Ghosh finally spoke. He must have been texting. "I found the meeting very very fascinating. The way everyone leaned in, at the same time, whilst Marwin—uh, Trotter—was speaking. It was quite like a film. I cannot even remember his words."

The CIO needed to be careful; the other trustees were chatty as ducks on the lakeshore. "I find that Marvin radiates authority with what he has accomplished more than with what he says. But if he had thrown a coaster at my head, all the other trustees would have done the same, in some endowment version of the stoning scene in *Life of Brian*."

Ghosh didn't respond to his reference. No one responded anymore to his references. "It is quite a power, no?"

"Well, he's given more money to the school than the rest of the investment committee combined and as a greater proportion of his net worth—which, at 2 billion dollars, is also probably greater than the rest of the committee's combined."

"But is he interested in investing per se?"

"That is the question. The man has built a fortune by expanding his family's brutally low-margin business and by refusing to even consider an IPO. And yet he has an unusual pain threshold for the Olympic margin grabbers in the investment business."

Ghosh had a higher-pitched laugh than the CIO was expecting. "People love his shops, no?"

"Most people love their children, many people love their spouses, a few crazy people even love their parents, but there are some people who use the word love only to describe buying groceries at Trotter's. There was an article in *The Wall Street Journal* about how the Trotterheads in Pennsylvania—and, yes, that's what they call themselves—held a vigil for the first store to open there. It was like North Koreans looking over the DMZ and praying for liberation, except in this case it meant no longer having to drive seventy miles to buy Trotter's cheddar biscuits."

Ghosh's high-pitched laugh came again. "It was very very fascinating how personal everything was at the meeting. To be frank, I could not quite believe we were talking about that apartment."

"On the one hand, it's indisputably inane that an investment committee overseeing 6 billion dollars would spend five minutes talking about a 10-million-dollar loss on the *personal* apartment of the manager of"—the CIO scratched the math on his notepad, for himself—"about 1.2 percent of the endowment. On the other hand, if a guy who lost the money is supposed to be focused on investing institutional capital in multi-unit residential housing from North Carolina to Texas, it brings up legitimate questions: why had he decided to buy an apartment on Oligarch's Row in Manhattan, how had he that much money to burn, why had he told us that he lives in Charlotte, and—oh yeah—is he a good real estate investor? But the primary reason to talk about it is that it was in the *New York Post*, which to Ben Wirbin and Jim Pascarella provides unrivaled credibility in asshole-revelation. Generally, what you'll find from these meetings, if we have not scared you away already, is we convince ourselves that we have found the good guys, or at least the 65 percent good guys—good in the sense of generating accretive performance, not doing completely gonzo stuff, coming to work every day in Charlotte rather than buying an overpriced apartment between Ivan the Aluminum King and Sergey the Embezzler—and give them rope. And if they subsequently have a mediocre run, well, we decide that our assessment was off, and they must have been, you know, reputation bubbles. The old joke is that it's the anti-two and twenty. For hedge funds, two down years in a row or one year down 20 percent. For private equity and venture, it's two down funds or one fund below a 0.8x net return."

"But that is only after—"

"Exactly. It's a compassionate form of justice. To prove *your* guilt, you have to lose *our* money."

"But what did Trotter say about the performance? I did not catch this part."

At the start of the meeting, as he revealed 3.8 percent, the CIO had looked only at Pascarella. He hadn't previewed the number with Wirbin. As the meeting progressed, Wirbin's face was all contempt—as if sipping from a tea cup only to taste burnt coffee. It was unclear if the contempt was directed at the numbers or the CIO.

It was possible that Wirbin had forgotten 6 percent.

"Well, I think that the minutes will record Marvin saying, 'Well, 3.8 is not the worst.'"

"And is that true?"

"Do you ever watch competitive figure skating on TV?"

Ghosh chuckled. "This is not something I have done."

"Maybe I should hire you to babysit my ten-year-old daughter. I'll book you through Mittens."

Ghosh laughed. The CIO smiled in a small, warming victory.

"After a figure skater completes her routine, she sits down, hyperventilating next to her mannish aunt in a track suit. Viewers know if she *completely* wiped out. But in most cases, there's considerable tension of what the score will be until the judges rule. In endowment management, it's the same thing except, for us, the judges' scorecards are flipped on the Internet starting next month. And we learn, in slow motion, what our returns are relative to the thirty other endowments we care about before we get judged by our formal benchmarks. And we can judge ourselves against a generic stock-bond portfolio in the near term, although that is not that relevant."

The CIO paused to consider whether to continue that line. He also wondered how he could deliver this speech so coolly, without endless, spitting Evan Byrne tears of his own? He said, "But given how much of everyone's strategy nowadays *has* to be weighted to idiosyncratic, hyper-specific, 'market mitigated' strategies, like direct first-lien loans to dentists and countertop frozen chicken warmers, your question is Schrodinger's Cat: Is 3.8 percent the worst? The best? Middling? Or is Marvin's wisdom all we have?"

"I see."

"That being said, as we were talking about at the meeting, the absolute performance is below the payout. And I don't think we're going to be surprised that it is great, relatively speaking."

"Better than Harvard?" Ghosh offered.

"As Ben will tell you, the amount of braindead pools of capital who can say 'better than Harvard' over the last decade does not allow much pleasure in that compliment."

"You know, the whole time through the meeting, a little incident kept playing throughout my mind. In the late 1990s, the company I was working at, Sequent, was acquired by IBM. This is a few years before I got into venture"—*wenture.* "I had made the most money I had ever seen. Two million dollars. I am an engineer, and I am used to numbers, big big numbers. That number, though, seemed fantastically high to me, like numbers did not really go so high. I did not know anything about investing, I could not imagine the *skills* needed to touch a hot fortune of such magnitude, so I followed the lead of a colleague at Sequent. He introduced me to his 'guy.' A month later, I am talking to my friends, this crowd of IIT graduates who all did okay-okay in the 1990s. And I mention that my Merrill Lynch"—Meralynch—"broker had put me into this biotech stock, and they should look into it. My friends are eating their laughter until one of them shouts '*Chutia bunghi*'—which is sort of like, 'You stupid bumpkin.'"

Ghosh waited for the CIO to interrupt. The CIO knew where this was going.

"Well, it was six more weeks until it was goodbye Meralynch. Now, independent of what I invest in our own funds, I have been sixty/forty stock-bond index funds."

The CIO held his breath, closed his eyes, and twisted the edge of his laptop. He tried to know what was on the browser *through* shut eyes, to see the news, to see nothing. Maybe a war of mild humanitarian but important financial repercussions had started, requiring him to get off the phone.

"And I don't make time for bullshit anymore, an attitude I am very very interested in bringing to the problems of your endowment."

GP stake acquisition fund
Conference room
October 2

Why couldn't he get angry, the CIO wondered as the two Alderine partners delivered their pitch with rehearsed confidence. The CIO was not his father, whose life had been dominated by a thesis that he never rose in the traffic department at Briggs & Stratton because of this guy or that guy or antisemitism. Even if the supposed Nazis managed to tolerate him for a quarter century. To his father, everyone who had more than him in life was a faker, a schemer, a moral cheat. Everyone who had less deserved it. Even though *he* didn't deserve the less that he had. The CIO couldn't remember when his childhood pride that his father was part of a company that made something everyone knew became a realization that his dad was stuck low-ish in a public company's bureaucracy while all the other Jewish dads were doctors, lawyers, teachers, business owners, free men.

The two guys were droning on about their existing investments, partial ownership stakes in *other* hedge funds or private equity firms. They detailed the unrealized gains in value, every deal skipping down the yellow brick road.

Imagine that, he wanted to say: when you start paying a lot of money for things, things are suddenly worth a lot of money.

He returned to ignoring the pitch and tried to remember how long his father had been a widower when he took the buyout in that particular downsizing of American manufacturing. Eleven years? (The CIO didn't need to calculate the year—his sophomore year in college—when his mother died.) Afterwards, his father set out to show the world that he had a knack for money: he began buying stocks. Neither the CIO nor his sister, a guidance counselor, wanted to press too hard on why his father decided that he, too, was an investor only after his son started working on Wall Street. Neither believed for a day that their father would be any good at it. (The CIO has been eager to tell Ghosh all this before one-meeting Ghosh had announced that he, too, was the solution to the problems of the endowment.) For years, his father wanted only to talk about the market when the CIO dutifully called every three weeks or visited every year because his sister's guilting him had worked. Or, more likely, because he had to be near Milwaukee on business.

Mainly the CIO didn't listen to his father. Yeah. Uh huh. Sure. But occasionally he'd say that an individual investor had no chance. He would try to keep the advice to the market and not to the specifics of the case. Because the specifics? Every old person in America seems to find the cable channel that tickles and cripples his soul, and the CIO's father had found CNBC and the squawk-box power-lunch dopamine drops it dealt to sell ads.

As an investor, his father was lazy, volatile, reactive. He could never shake the idea that a stock was "cheap" because its share price was three bucks. He would ask the CIO for tips with a forced bonhomie that demanded his son ignore forty years of direct observation of his father's true personality, a mirthless carp. (The exceptions: decent taste in movies and a gentleness toward a series of orange cats.) His father's approach to investing had one constant: rewards without work. Was that why he never rose at Briggs & Stratton? Had he never been good at *anything*?

But the CIO never went there, because when he laid out how truly efficient the market was, how one in a million stock traders would become someone like Michael Hermann, his father would explode.

You know everything, don't you? You got a lock on all the tricks? You think I believe that crap for one second?

A slammed door. Or something broken.

He'd died at seventy-one, with a home equity loan on a house that he had lived in for forty years. His brokerage account had $21,000 in it.

In the meeting, one Alderine partner had triathleted away all his body fat, which accentuated an Italian nose whose bridge's angle changed its mind halfway down. He was one of those guys who always addressed the best looking woman in the room. So the CIO's female analyst was benefiting from a mentor's lesson on an unbelievably well-timed recent purchase of a stake in Busken Capital, right before it hit the home run with Zonner and raised its next fund at twice its targeted size.

He expected mechanical braggarts like this from Calvin. But why had *Emily* brought them in?

Why wouldn't she protect a young woman from their charms?

The short, fleshy Indian-American partner delivered his script with such self-love that the CIO needed, for rescue, to break his one life rule. The rule, after all, was nothing but his deal with himself.

"Do you guys find this hard?" he broke in.

"Find this what?" the triathlete asked.

The Indian-American looked at his watch. Really, there was no reason *not* to be his father anymore. The endowment up only 3.8 percent last year was his father.

"Do you find this hard? This divining the Truth of Individual Manager Performance Persistence. Because that's the same thing that we are trying to do. And we find it hard. Isn't that right, Emily?"

Emily's smile was pained. He needed to get her back. But first she should explain, to the entire team, *why* exactly she brought these guys in for a meeting. The point of the experiment of advancing human thought and human character by delivering 264 million dollars a year wasn't to make money however you could.

"I wonder if investing is actually getting harder," he said as he glanced at Emily again. He wanted her to like what he was going to do. He wanted her to run the world someday.

He took a sharpened pencil from the container and ticked through points as he spoke. "Correct what I have wrong. First, you value acquisitions at around seventeen times current cash flow, which yields only a percent or two more than we could earn through corporate bonds. Second, you don't underwrite a real exit plan for any of these positions except hold and hope. Third, you kind of don't care how the acquired managers perform as long as they perform sufficiently. I understand the dark logic behind this. Private equity firms and hedge funds are not the Sisters of Infinite Charity. Their businesses have sticky customers and high gross margins—even when they are delivering rude service, as measured by completely average investment returns. I am also aware that equity investors spend every moment dreaming of high-margin, sticky businesses immune to true differentiation in the delivery of their service. So maybe you should be commended for grabbing the opportunity in front of you. It's Dick Cheney at the head of the VP search committee.

"But the crux of your pitch doesn't seem to be to invest in annoyingly good businesses. It seems to be that you are going to generate money by charging *us* to get a cash back refund from every private equity or hedge fund investment we've ever done by owning, through your fund, a small piece of the firms themselves. I guess this is a hedge against the lie when PE firms and hedge funds look us in the eye and say that they absolutely need 2 percent annual management fees to support their business, their salaries, their incredibly intensive value-adding operations. Because they seem perfectly able to sell 20 percent of that 2 percent for you to a) collect, b) charge 75 bps on, and c) distribute."

He turned to Emily and spoke to her, eyes locked. She was not afraid to dress the CIO down with her particular no-nonsense. So was she on his side now?

"Our friends here are also apparently a hedge against the lie that private equity as an asset class can return 15 percent net to us. They have what I hope to be the best data imaginable, and they don't seem to underwrite any carry when they buy stakes in PE firms."

He turned back to the triathlete. His father had lived in a world, in a market, with injustice.

"Carry is just 'upside,' right?" the CIO continued. "Upside: the word that has led more sheep to slaughter than any other in the investing dictionary. But in your case, what I have to conclude is that you guys, who have seen the GPs' books, bet in aggregate that no one long-term generates much above the 8 percent preferred return. And I guess you're a particular hedge against *our* strategy—what we're really, sincerely trying to do—of finding systematic, edgy, hungry differentiated niche managers, because your strategy works if, by buying stakes in groups at peak reputation and asset aggregation, they continue to hoover up assets. Through you"—he spoke as he wrote numbers on a piece of paper—"we can see the world's excess liquidity: the too-much-money-chasing investment ideas because too much capital is desperate for returns. So through you, we can—"

It was painful not to say it, but he couldn't say it with Emily, with his life, in the room.

Through you, we can see into the counting house, to the world, as a grift.

He looked up. They were all watching him struggle for the next words except for Emily, whose eyes were fixed hard on the Alderine business cards in front of her. He had to finish the sentence—any sentence. He cringed as he felt his words go milder. He wanted to embrace these guys in correction and forgiveness. "Through you, we can see the world's excess liquidity take bodily form in a Japanese capital allocator buying a management fee stream from the Louis Vuitton of PE and the Gucci of hedge funds."

The triathlete looked at him blankly, almost bored. The short Indian-American seemed to be savoring tomorrow's gift of smugly telling the story of a snob CIO in nowheresville.

"Part of me admires the logic, like what LBJ said about J. Edgar Hoover: 'I'd rather have him inside the tent pissing out than outside the tent pissing in.' But frankly, I'd rather put the entire endowment in the Vanguard Total Market Index fund and call it a day than own 20 percent of fifteen different private equity and hedge fund managers partially cashing out, to say nothing of paying people to do that for us."

That hadn't been as satisfying as he had expected it to be.

Lower-middle market private equity firm
Conference room
October 5

All three of the firms' managing directors smiled, their printed pitchbooks facedown in front of them. They were the CIO's age, by the graying at their temples. Then why did they all still have hair? Because of the hope?

Emily, scratching the bottom of her pen against her notebook, seemed anxious. The CIO would not repeat Monday, with Alderine. (The middle one asked if they should begin with personal introductions.) The analyst on his team was typing into a Surface. About what? Couldn't even he already tell that thousands of others just like them had been through here? *Why* did these guys deserve his attention, given everything already stacked in their favor? In his favor, too, but he was on his side of the table, advancing human thought and human character.

If you want to take notes, kid, this is what you're going to hear. They are going to talk about edge, opportunity set, and track record. ("I think it makes sense to walk you through how the presentation is organized," the middle one was saying now.) They are going to mention the team's experience and relationships. They are never going to say that they are a bunch of really smart guys who know a lot of people, but the essential point of why we should invest with them is that they are a bunch of really smart guys who know a lot of people. They are going to mention proprietary deal flow. They are going to use the word proprietary so much that the word proprietary gets a restraining order. They are going to show a pie chart with the fattest slice of pepperoni proving how proprietary their deal flow is. That pie chart will also prove that pie charts are pointless unless one is raising money from innumerates or babies.

They are going to discuss the portfolio company investments that came to them from a chain of events that can be called proprietary. When discussing the competitive positioning of those companies, they are going use the word moat so often that the word proprietary will worry that they are cheating on it. They are going to mention their proprietary processes to measure risk. Most of these processes will be spreadsheets. They are going to brag about how they use leverage wisely. They will say leverage because it sounds more sophisticated than debt. They are going to mention a few portfolio companies that could have gone bankrupt. They are not going to mention any that did.

They are going to talk about how they add value to the companies they own. They are not going to talk about a zero-sum world. They are not going to talk about people they fired. They are not going to talk about competitors undercut.

They will not be Gordon Gekko. They will talk about an advisory board or operating partners that will make their portfolio companies flourish. They are going to tell us how amazingly connected *their* one-term senators are. They are going to convey amazement at *their* retirees' former titles at Fortune 500 companies. They are not going to mention that none of them would have been caught dead climbing the corporate ladder of those bureaucracies. They are not going to mention how much time their operating partners spend on Nantucket golf courses or napping at three in the afternoon. They are not going to admit that plenty of private equity-backed companies, despite the advisory boards and operating partners, end up in a worse position than before.

They will move on. They always move on. Slide after slide after slide, PowerPoint never dwelling, PowerPoint never changing, PowerPoint telling the same sensible archetype, the same causes and effects.

It's the only story they have to tell. Isn't it, by definition, too conventional to generate alpha?

The one who went to Harvard was talking now. And here it goes: they are going to talk about the opportunity set. They are going to express delighted surprise that their targeted industries or stage or size has, by the Will of God, the fewest private equity and strategic competitors of any size or stage or industry. They are going to show that chart with a lot of names on the edges but none in the middle.

They are not going to know that we see, on a slow week, that chart once a day.

They are going to "prove" to us how disciplined they are. They are going to show us a funnel because we've apparently never seen a funnel before. Being familiar with funnels, we will now become much more adept at pouring things from big bottles into little bottles. (The CIO chuckled, causing the new presenter to stutter.) The funnel will show how many deals they look at versus how many they have done. They will imply that their competitors, ignorant of the invention of funnels, invest in every deal they look at as a chute.

They are going to give us case studies of their newest babies, the ones so proprietary that even *they* don't know the source, the ones in which the moats have their own moats, the ones that are too early for proof that the future will not unfold exactly as predicted in their investment memos.

They are not going to talk about the deals that were off-strategy. They are not going to tell us that they, deep in their dull hearts, believe that all *we* want them to do is to make us money.

They are going to show us their track record, closing in for the kill. They will describe their investment performance as top quartile. They will define top-quartile by whatever funds or deals make them top-quartile. They will prove that their being top-quartile was a direct function of deal selection, of operational value-add, of price discipline. They will show a stair-step chart, attributing return on investment data systemically to valuation arbitrage, EBITDA growth, and leverage. The charts will prove that they are company builders, not financial engineers.

There will be footnotes qualifying all this in seven-point font.

They will, in forty-five minutes, prove that being top-quartile came from proprietary deals, from being smart, from knowing a lot of people.

But mainly from virtue.

That's why the CIO shouldn't be able to stand any of this anymore. Because even his analyst, the CIO thought, watching him type, can do the math to prove that these guys are actually second- or third-quartile. Middling without consequence. (There is the name for someone's memoir. For every white finance guy's memoir.) Yes, these three weren't yet private-plane guys, or Davos guys. But still, houses in Telluride or Quogue aren't third-quartile, nor kids at Brown or Vanderbilt, nor a table at a fundraiser, nor a liberalism insisting everyone, everywhere should have the same opportunities.

But what did he do with his opportunity? Made a life of needing to care whether these three dull neckties could deliver him 15 percent annual returns? Made a—

"What?" he said.

Emily, through a pained, pulled smile, said, "They asked you a question."

Sometimes, the CIO found, it helps to get through these meetings by observing them as if they were happening to someone else, as if *that* CIO was going to have to squint and see whether this, too, could be a good investment. Observing *that* CIO allowed him to accept that maybe this was an interesting life.

How long had they been waiting?

"Salad, no fries," he said. "Unless you think the fries are worth it." He put his hands on his belly.

Emily looked straight ahead, her lower jaw tighter.

"Sorry. What was the question?"

"Did you want to hear about another deal in their new fund or more about the team?"

"I would like to hear it all: everything, everything new."

Managing Director of Private Markets Office October 6 (unscheduled)

Emily shut the door behind her. The CIO studied his screen and continued to type as if the email to one of the analysts doing work on Hurst Street required bomb-squad concentration. He had left the office immediately after the meeting yesterday; its rhythm had never recovered.

She sat in his guest chair, her loose hair spiraling outwards in waves from the centerline of her scalp. His office felt like half the size it should be; some gravity-at-short-distance was causing his knees to sense hers below the desk. They could have moved to the table crammed to the right of his desk. But the team all seemed to fear it as The Review Table.

He had an open door policy. He apparently also now had a shut-my-door-if-you-want policy. He wasn't going to talk first.

"I am here to ask if you realize that this is my career, too."

He turned off his monitor and began stacking the risk reports into one pile and the Hurst Street quarterly letters into another. He had to work.

"I guarantee you," she went on, "that no one will ever come here ever again if they are going to be lectured out of cynical amusement."

"Cynical?"

Emily chewed on her lower lip as she cracked her neck sideways, left and then right. "You don't think you were being cynical?"

The CIO had no words.

"What did you think you were being?"

"I don't know." He looked at her, finally. "I may not be David Swensen, but isn't it okay for me to want us to have access to uniquely talented investors rather than three, you know"—he never knew whether he had the right to talk about his own race—"perfectly adequate, well-rounded, well-educated boiled potatoes? I get it: they are not assholes. But their unmitigated blandness is what world class investors foam at the mouth to bet against. I mean, what was the firm's name again?"

"North Meadow."

"Are you kidding me?"

Emily didn't speak.

"How do they expect us to believe in them if we can't even remember their name? We should invent a drinking game. Private equity firm, Indianapolis subdivision, or nursing home? Walnut Grove. North Meadow. North Hill. Hill Valley. Valley Valley."

"Are you willing to acknowledge that we talked about them before and that I said it would be a good idea for them to fly here? You are the one who reminds us *not* to confuse personal presentation with investment edge. Can you acknowledge that I respect your time and you should respect my judgment on how I call on that time?"

The CIO needed to turn on his computer, to read the news, to continue his work on Hurst Street.

Or he needed to move to the small table, to not be imprisoned by her knees. He reached his right hand to his head but brought it down, sitting on it, to not invite any accusations.

She asked, "What markets are they targeting?"

"Lower-middle market growth?"

She waited, for specificity.

"Health care?"

"Do you even see yourself?" she asked.

He thought about that for a second, with respect. "Does anyone ever see themselves?"

Emily heaved a single laugh, immediately pulling down her upper lip over her gums.

"So what do you see about *my*self? Please tell me, Emily."

"I would say I see someone who's becoming shifty."

Did she know about 5 and 6 percent? From Corso? From Wirbin, insanely?

"I thought," the CIO started and then stopped. "I thought that you were going to say that I was cracking up, or having a midlife crisis."

"I don't feel comfortable speculating about causes; I do outcomes. And no matter what names GPs choose, they are busy people who inconvenienced themselves to fly here on *my* invitation."

"And?"

"And I have to say that you are embarrassing me."

The CIO bent back the corner of one of the risk reports, focusing on the quality of the crease.

"Am I to take it that that's how you're going to respond?"

He continued to look at the crease as he spoke. "I don't think I've actually responded."

"This profession is barely tolerable as it is with all the mansplaining. Do you understand how bad it gets if I also have to apologize for wasting people's time?"

The CIO needed to face away, to look at the leaves just starting to turn, watch the students gliding along the pathways, backpacks hiked high. What sounds were out there? Kids stopping to let the witty carillon bells wash over them? Or just the reporting of what was on each other's phones?

He straightened two stacks of reports into one stack, looking in unfocus in Emily's direction.

She wasn't speaking.

Where are my senses?

He asked (because she was challenging his decency, because he guessed he still had decency, because he liked and needed her), "Then why do you stay in this barely tolerable profession?"

"I would say that it's because things used to be different here. You used to run an office in which that type of ego-tripping was discouraged even if—"

"Even if Calvin."

"I don't have time to get into his latest effing monstrosity." She almost smiled at the CIO, bringing both lips between her teeth. "But, yes, this used to be a place where I could do the work."

The CIO scrubbed his face hard and then blinked his eyes clear. "I want this to be a place to do the work. What other goal could I have than for this to be a place to do the work. My father—"

"I would prefer not to hear about that."

"What?"

"I would strongly prefer not to hear another overly long story about something that once happened to you, with roundabout lessons on endowment management."

"That is really narrowing my field of discourse." He smiled, waiting for the reflection in hers. Didn't she understand the sacrifice he was willing to make to be open, and vulnerable, talking about the calming quality of irony, about succeeding over your genetic animal? He had not been about to tell a happy story. "So, what do you want from me?"

"I would prefer for you to apologize."

"My behavior was inappropriate. I apologize. To you, sincerely. To North Meadow Soprano, sincerely. I apologize to Alderine maybe less sincerely."

She was considering it. The "maybe" had been a life preserver tossed to his own sense of self. "I suppose that I can accept that."

They stared at each other. Was this going to be a passing of power, with her bringing up 6 percent?

She said, "Do you know that my father is a dentist?"

"Are my teeth that bad?" The CIO licked his tongue over them, wondering if recent performance had corroded them from what they had been for years: the color of yesterday's newspapers.

"I was curious if you knew that my father is a dentist and that my mother is the vice principal of a junior high school."

"Maybe?"

"I have been working here for four years, and I have always wondered if you were curious about what they did, if you hadn't listened when I told you that, or if we *had* talked about it and I forgot."

"Those are all very good options."

Emily was trying not to smile. "You get away with an incredible amount with your innocent professor persona."

"Well, it's not meant as protection. It's not *meant* as anything."

When they first moved here, Jane had teased him for liking this town so he could claim there were too few people to find new friends, because he was already too old to make friends.

Why do I need friends when I have you, he would answer.

It'd be nice.

Love don't make things nice, Loretta.

She used to smile to that.

But it could have been nice. Could Emily be his friend now? Was Emily, partnerless (he suspected), childless (he'd have to know this), more lonely than he was? She had come for the work, too, to this cold alone.

The CIO asked, "So what does a dentist and a junior high school vice principal think about their daughter working in endowment management in the provinces?"

"One of my cousins figured out how to read the Form 990, which got to my auntie, which got to my parents. And so they understand the compensation part."

"Do they think that's why you're not part of Orlando's best father-daughter dentist team?"

"My father—I am going to assume he wouldn't mind me sharing this—is a Certificate of Deposit type. We still have in-depth discussions on a twelve-month CD at 1.3 percent versus an eighteen-month CD at 1.6 percent. When the 's' hit the fan after the Form 990, I tried to explain our comp system relative to benchmarks. I wouldn't say that he totally followed me. But I think he understands why I want to do this."

"God bless him. Maybe it's because you're an adult. All I do is project what my kids are going to be, alternating between approval, disapproval, and discomforting jealousy. With my son, the best-case scenario is that he becomes a mid-level software engineer grossly overestimating his own importance at a series of companies. Worst-case scenario: mass shooter in a shopping mall. Base-case: he leaks government secrets and blames it on 'late capitalism.' The only thing that gives me hope—or, conversely, total dread—is that all his fourteen-year-old friends seem to be on similar trajectories." The CIO tried to make her laugh by Chaplining his hands into trajectories. "Maybe my ten-year-old daughter's cohort will take over the world. I guess singing 'Let it Go' one billion times each trained them for that." Nothing. "But where *I* stand, in the light of day, is being intensely impatient about how she's going to make the world better, safer, fairer, more beautiful. And not one molecule of me yearns for her to do that through a career in finance."

He had never said that aloud, not even to Jane. He had never asked himself if Jane's fingernail-chewing look at dinner was her accusation that this *could* be what he wanted for Hannah.

"Because you don't think it's an honorable profession?"

"I think... it's honorable enough?"

"I have to be honest and say that I find it pretty insulting for you to tell me that your daughter should not do this kind of work."

What did she think he did to *survive*? No one is excused from defending himself to the mirror. "Listen," he answered after a pause, "I want her to responsibly earn enough money to make rent, pay bills, and be a productive citizen. But there is no part of my imagined future for her in which she spends her days thinking of money as her mission, as her measurement, as her profession, as—I don't know—her identity. Can I say that?"

"*You* can say that."

His shirt had dampened, he realized, even before he knew he was sweating. Didn't he get *any* credit for hiring Emily? For liking her despite her irreversible seriousness? For believing that her race was an asset rather than a box to check? For entrusting her with the decisions that would determine whether this school got its 264 million dollars a year?

She was staring at him, biting her upper lip, waiting. He rubbed his eyes quickly.

He tried from this direction: "It's pretty much consensus that a—maybe *the*—major problem of America is the financialization of our economy, our society, and the ambitions of too many young people at places like this. So I don't think it's a radical idea that I don't want my daughter to do it."

"I would prefer to say that it is just privileged."

He knew how stupid the idea of himself as a white savior was, bestowing jobs. She had earned her job after a national search. She was no better nor worse than he was, lately, as measured by performance. But it wasn't stupid to want some thanks for tolerating her failures of judgment, too. PMD? We *really* have no access to better venture capital innovations than babysitting apps? Was this because of her brains? Her contacts? As Calvin diagnosed, her aloofness? Or was it more accurately apartness?

He asked, "How is this different than if your father didn't want you to clean people's teeth?"

"It's incredibly different. Wishing that your daughter doesn't have to think about money is also super patriarchal. We live in a winner-take-all society, and there are *no* winners who are not also thinking about money. Politicians, athletes, musicians, scientists, authors, actors, you name it, everyone that is part of the American elite, anyone that is relevant to America today, is also wealthy. I would ask you if you could imagine the Clintons or Beyoncé or Michael Jordan or, I don't know, Reese Witherspoon as just well-off, driving themselves to the grocery store? That world doesn't exist. And that world didn't happen by accident."

"I'm not sure how I'm the cynical one."

"I would not say that I am being cynical at all."

"So your working here, and my daughter's future yearning to become the Elsa of Endowment Management, is to be a self-directedly relevant part of the American elite?"

"In my case, I would say that I'm just being totally effing honest about what doors are open to me. I am very aware of how hard it would be for me to land at a private equity firm, given that there is, more or less, no one who looks like me in any senior positions in the investing world."

The CIO looked at his screen, away from her eyes. How did he answer for that uneradicated fact?

"But when I'm the one who controls the purse, that's something they are going to have to respect."

"And that's it?" He looked at the corners of the reports as he straightened them. "This is just about power."

"I am not asserting that at all. I am asserting the context of a job in which the work and the people and the challenges are interesting. It's a job in which I can do well by doing good." Let it pass.

"You are not the only one here who cares about contributing to the university. And that is why it would be catastrophic if you make GPs refuse to visit us."

"I don't think two meetings with assholes and/or completely undifferentiated managers who were called out for being assholes and/or completely undifferentiated managers has had a catastrophic effect on our ability to locate investment opportunities."

"But that is your privilege."

The CIO wanted to wave his hand to dismiss the obvious: the pale head, the pale face, the graying-brown beard in a mouse-color of no color that made everything boiled potato here, too. He looked at her instead, imploring her to say more.

She took pity on him: "How you behave. Everything comes naturally to you, so everything can be a joke."

He had to say something. He had to do something. He stood up and felt himself crowding Emily, towering over Emily. She put her hands on the opposite side of the desk and scooted back. Her face was impassive as if she had been prepared for this her entire life. But this—whatever his body was doing—was the exact opposite of what he had wanted to do.

He walked back towards the window, the two steps allowed, and put his own hands behind him, as safety. He was still standing, though. He wouldn't sit down again. He needed to turn around, to look out the window, to Corso, the campus. No part of his body ever did what it was supposed to do.

So he looked at Emily and said the truth: "I like my job."

Mineral rights acquisition fund
Conference room
October 8

Focus. For Emily.

The one from Houston was saying, "We've been doing this business for a long time, but the shale revolution changed everyone's math. We're"—*wuhr?*—"buying undrilled minerals we absolutely know are gonna be drilled. And the sellers know it, too, but they can't grasp what three-four zone development is gonna be like in terms of production. It's just a whole different deal. For a lot of reasons, we want them to participate, but you gotta accept the risks of timing and oil price and the operator."

Emily and Josh had already been to Midland and Houston to visit the offices of the manager, who wanted the school's money to buy oil and gas mineral rights in their new fund. Emily had been pressing the CIO on a market that, she claimed, both needed liquidity and had a rare information asymmetry advantage to the buyer. She now asked the Texans whether they share their underwriting case of 3x plus returns with the sellers.

Does anyone, the CIO kept to himself, ever say, I want to triple the money I paid you?

The one from Midland answered the planted question: "Wuhr honest with people that wuhr buying from. We tell 'em our deal is to make money. But you gotta remember that a lotta these people inherited positions that, twenty years ago, were worth a hundred dollars an acre and are now worth tens of thousands of dollars an acre."

The CIO was trying to not take anything lightly, to not be "shifty." If a personality could change, a personality could change back.

But the *Wall Street Journal* article had come out that morning.

The one from Houston said, "To most people the idea that the Permian Basin is gonna produce more oil than Canada or I*raq* in a year or two—it dudn't even make sense."

"We were in Scarsdale, New York, this week—near Josh's stomping grounds," the one from Midland added, smiling at Josh. "There's this older gal whose grandfather was patented a lease in Howard County back in the twenties. Her mother had moved to New York City in the fifties, and the woman didn't even know that her mother was getting royalty checks, itty bitty ones for most of that time, until her mother passed two years ago."

He listened to these stories. He understood non-correlated assets classes. He understood system, inputs, hunger. He hired smart, level-headed people.

And he was twelfth out of the twenty-largest endowments. Duke had delivered 10 percent.

"She wudn't poor, but we couldn't get a sense of what her financial deal was. And it's not clear that anyone in the oil business had ever been in that house. She offered us lemonade. I was waiting for her to next offer us a mint julep."

He swallowed hard. His heart was drumming loudly as if he had just gone for a run. He understood how Emily was right. He understood risk. He even liked this guy, or at least the joke about a mint julep.

"And then just when wuhr done explaining the whole deal, she says, 'But I don't frack, do I?' I look over to J.T., stumped how to answer her."

The CIO understood U.S. oil production and Chinese equity

markets and private lending risks and value-add from private equity operating partners. He understood cap rates in multi-family and portable alpha and passive investing and momentum trades and the cash burn of Sous. He understood what combination of growth, value, arbitrages, and inefficiencies were being sold to him as necessary to generate the returns he needed. He understood all of it better than the people who worked for him and the lazy CIOs with downloaded asset allocations and Calvinish fanboy decisions. And who was he? Twelfth out of twenty.

"I was about to tell her that we call it hydraulic fracturing and that all her checks came from folks doing a heckuva lot of it. But J.T. says, 'Ma'am, you can't imagine how much more you're gonna frack before it's all done.' She says, 'Oh my.' And he says, 'How 'bout we handle all that for you.'"

But he didn't know his mistakes. He wasn't in the room where the money was being made. He didn't know why he was six points behind Duke. He didn't know how he could be six points behind Duke. The *Journal* included the compulsory paragraph about the sub-Top Twenty Freak of the Year. This time: Reed College, 13 percent on 500 million dollars. *How*? How had the CIO's assessment of the systems, inputs, and hunger of the best and brightest on Wall Street, Sand Hill Road, Hong Kong, even Midland, Texas, become a gastrointestinal loop, consuming knowledge and turning it to shit? Maybe it was all Greek inevitability, nemesis destroying hubris. Maybe the Greeks understood reversion to the mean. Maybe the worst things that had ever happened to him were the three glorious years and the article in the *Times*.

"We went in figuring to pay $15,000 an acre. But J.T. saw something and starts at *eleven*. Well, the gal almost fainted. It was one of the days that you felt like Santa Claus."

Would he stop having an answer for Jane when she asked why he still did this?

Would he stop having the daydream that another life was visible, with an onramp to that road?

Emily and Josh were both looking at him, between them. Christ, how long had the Texans been silent? Were the Texans even silent? Was he doing this again? I think this is a good idea. Do whatever you want. I am being fired. I should be fired. I—

He pushed the chair back, stood up. Oh, again. Fuck *no*. Where had this new habit come from? The CIO looked behind him for an excuse to sit down again. His body had failed him. He didn't know where to put his hands. They tingled with a need to rub his face from top to bottom, rub it off as erasure. He felt his hands starting to shake almost arthritically, as if being jostled by his even louder beating heart.

He should have rubbed off his face. He didn't need a face. He and Emily were beyond ever being able to look at each other again.

Still standing, the CIO looked at Josh so as not to be pierced by the other eyes on him. Answer, Josh, if you can hear me through my thoughts. There is nothing yet in your young life to look back on with regret. *Answer* me: why are we smiling at this fun story of not paying the lady from Scarsdale $15,000 an acre? Why are they Santa Claus for not paying the lady from Scarsdale $15,000 an acre? Because everyone has the right to buy low and sell high? Because they have to promise *us* a doubling of our money to get our money to invest?

Why are we complicit in that if the reward is being twelfth?

University President (call)
Office
October 9 (unscheduled)

"I'm not calling about the article," Meg Corso said. "Or directly about the article. I do wonder why it can't be a *little* different one year. Re-reporting a *Wall Street Journal* article on how we ranked. Paragraph on what the endowment does. Your salary. My salary. And a paragraph about a divestment petition. Did anyone call you for comment?"

"No."

"I guess that's the problem of having no journalism major here. Then again, not charging someone $47,000 a year to learn journalism might be more ethical."

Six months ago—two months ago—he could have made a joke. Now he was looking for clues that she remembered that he had told her 5 percent. Could she calculate the difference between 3.8 and 5, to the school?

Seventy-two million dollars.

"Are you still there?"

"Yes, sorry. No one called me."

"I'm surprised every year by how little of a ripple it makes."

"You aren't worried?"

"About the article?" The headline had read, "Endowment Lags Again."

"No. About the facts."

"That's Ted's department. I have enough to worry about. But I have to believe that a university that still has more than 6 billion dollars, still convinces people to donate hundreds of millions of dollars a year, still has over 50 percent of its student body on no financial aid, and still has loads of grants coming in directly to the faculty—I mean, if we're really going to be in trouble because eleven other large endowments did better than us, I fear for the world."

He knew too well the easy psychology of why he appreciated maternal reassurance. But, objectively, the CIO should have that comfort printed on t-shirts—in Declaration of Independence cursive—to distribute to the team. Or Corso should just do his job, too. He said, "I don't want this to sound sexist...."

"Nothing good has ever come from a sentence that started that way."

"But it's like I came home with straight B minuses and—" He paused. Had he ever told Corso about his own mother? He barely mentioned her to his kids. "It's like I came home with straight B minuses and my mom is telling me I did a super duper job."

"You sure know how to make a lady feel young." Corso was three years older than he was but much more fit. She was a trail runner, maybe compulsory from her University of Oregon days. She had somehow bottled the smell of the trail: juniper and fir. (Wirbin once asked her if she had showered in gin.) The physique, the scent, the practical blond haircut in which the Future is Female—they were nothing like his mom.

"Sorry," he said. "But you know where I was going."

"Actually, I don't."

"I'm tired of being a B student."

"Were you ever a B student?"

He considered mentioning the graduate school rejections from Yale and Columbia, which still confused him. Instead, he joked, "I think I got a B plus once in French. But I didn't go to Harvard and Stanford."

"I can assure you that Bs are the most avoidable thing imaginable at Harvard and Stanford."

"Then maybe finance is the revenge of the B students at the B schools."

"I doubt most people look at Wall Street and think, that's the B team. They think, those men run the world."

"Sure, fine, but run the world how—making a lot of money? I'm talking about really accomplishing something, being one of those people in those old Apple ads, insanely content at a world they *changed.* Einstein, Dylan, Mother Teresa."

"That's a very male way of looking at things."

"I listed Mother Teresa."

"The most desexualized notable woman of the last century."

The CIO smiled. "Okay. I'll trade her for Martin Luther King."

Corso laughed, her mouth away from the phone.

"You don't ever think this way?" he asked.

"That I'm on the B team if I'm not Martin Luther King? I can confirm that I never think that way."

"I'm jealous."

"Well, this has all been a perfect lead-in for the reason for this call." So naked yearning had been permitted as the fried chicken before the execution. This was the day the trustees had decided that, as a non-super elite school, they and Mr. Yeboah could not afford 3.8 percent. "It's about our colleague who still thinks he's in the running to be Mother Teresa *and* Martin Luther King."

The CIO couldn't process how those words were a lead-in to his being fired. "What?"

She gave him time to understand where the words led.

"Ugh. What does Larry Galanos want now?"

Corso laughed. "Larry called Ricardo Budd, who called me. He heard that Emily and Josh what's his name were in Texas, looking at investments."

"Where did he hear that?"

"Who knows. Any flight around here is, what, a quarter-filled with university people?"

"And what does Galanos want me to do about them?" The CIO had given them the go-ahead to start writing the investment memo on the oil and gas minerals fund.

"I think that was just a shot across the bow. He told Ricardo that the Faculty Senate was likely to endorse the 350.org petition this year."

"The trustees are in charge of governance and investment policies." His usual response.

"They also are going to endorse a 10-percent commitment to clean energy investments."

That woke him up and brought his voice up an octave. "That's twice our *total* energy commitment. It's a third of our entire illiquid portfolio."

"Are those bad investments?"

"Ten years ago, they were bad investments. I avoided them because the butcher where I worked thought solar panels were for commies and women—no offense. Emily has had the team look into it recently. Renewables seem to offer better prospects now. Then again, a lot of them seem to be offering 6 percent project finance returns with no risk except if a utility goes bankrupt or power prices go down. And utilities go bankrupt. And power prices go down."

"You're going to have to translate."

"I have no idea if they are good investments. I do know that if I'm told to put 600 million dollars into wind farms and utility-scale solar, it would be all we could do for a couple of years. And just wait until you see our relative returns. Not a single major endowment is investing in clean energy if it involves any tradeoffs whatsoever. But we could make it easy. I could call up BlackRock or, I don't know, Commonfund tomorrow and say, it's your problem, get fatter off us. But it'd be pretty hard to do that with any sense of fiduciary responsibility."

"In addition," Corso went on, "they want a total divestment of all oil and gas investments by year-end. Something about—let me see my notes—'stop, drop, and roll.'"

The CIO wasn't sure he was responsible for telling her that this was not the same old thing. She should be talking to Wirbin. He said, "Truly, I'm very happy to let the Faculty Senate, and an unlimited number of student petitions, dictate our investment strategy."

"I don't think this is—"

"No one has tried that before. What have we tried? We have tried the second-highest paid person at the university following twenty-year-old standard operating procedures on asset allocation to implement an endowment's so-called inherent advantages, regardless of what that allocation's popularity has arbitraged away. We have tried a bag of tricks on manager selection and human behavior. And we have gotten 'Endowment Lags Again.' So let's just have the Mensheviks of the Faculty Senate tell me what to do. What else do they want?"

Corso didn't speak.

"Never mind. I know. No Zionists, no private prisons, no blood diamondeers, no banks other than those that exclusively lend money to people of color at a zero-percent interest rate, no tech companies because they are selling *us* as data and requiring us to watch sequential clips on YouTube, no big pharma, no small pharma, no health care companies that fight Medicare for All, so no health care companies at all. Let's just say no American companies because they are inextricably complicit in racial capitalism. Does the Faculty Senate Investment Team like the Chinese?"

Corso was still silent.

"I think there's a split. Some Democratic Socialists say no to investing in China because of censorship and their nastiness to the Dalai Lama and Richard Gere. On the other side is the whole Fourth International crowd that likes Maduro, Putin, Castro's brother, and Xi for their workers' paradises and adherence to the hammer and sickle, even if just on flags and hats. But let's say no. So, we are left with, um..."

"Female-owned wind turbine manufacturers in Sweden?"

The CIO laughed. Why couldn't Jane be like this, his partner again? "I think there might be some capitalism in there. So only female *co-op* wind turbine manufacturers. In Sweden."

Corso sighed. "I wait for the day we find out that our calls have been recorded."

"They will play them at the Faculty Senate Show Trials. Luckily, I bet Chairman Galanos is really into decarceration. His gulags will be without fences and right next door to the Swedish-lady turbine co-ops. There will be lots of clean energy, lots of wood puzzles, lots *and lots* of time to explore our feelings, and freshly baked bread. I really like freshly baked bread. Maybe it will be that dark rye—"

"Okay."

"Sorry."

"No need to apologize. But still: the joke has been made."

The CIO smiled.

"I am curious," she asked, "why don't you even want to consider it?"

"Why don't I want to allow a man who probably thinks it's immoral for us to *have* an endowment to dictate the investment strategy *of* the endowment?"

"No. Why don't you want to try investing in clean energy? It's been eight minutes since you were telling me that your goal in life was to sell iPhones by being Mother Teresa. I would imagine that this would be a way to start, to catalyze something."

"Become Mother Teresa by listening to Larry Galanos?"

"Or at least be a bit different. What was it? 'We are the crazy ones, the troublemakers....'"

He wanted to be in her office, not on the phone, to discuss this. He wanted their eyes uncomfortably alive to each other, in the way he had failed to do with Emily. He'd smell the juniper and make a joke about Wirbin. He'd invite Jane to the meeting for a sexless threesome of diagnosing a man's life.

Last night, Jane had said "that's nice" when he told her about walking out of the minerals pitch. He told her that that had not been a good thing. She'd said, "Well, then: not nice."

He tried with Corso: "Maybe it's because a large portion of my self-worth is about truly calling out bullshit. And Larry has very glib arguments. Oil and gas investments have sucked for a decade. He *can* throw that in my face. I sometimes wonder if unprofiting from the destruction of the planet puts us in good shape virtue-wise, from our everlasting souls' perspective. But let's be clear: even though the sector underperformance has had nothing to do with my moral failings, it's futile to talk about supply disruption with the campus equivalent of a Scarsdale heiress."

The CIO stopped. He didn't want to explain. He was humiliated to be on this campus, second-paid after her.

Larry Galanos was not embarrassed to make what Larry Galanos made.

"Are you still there?" Corso asked.

"Yes. I'm just trying to—" What? "Is he asking us to sell our private energy allocation in a secondary? If he is, we can get in line with Cal Regents and the rest."

"And this means?"

"If we tried to sell our energy investments, the only buyers are the ones that like the smell of blood. A banker told Emily that the market is fifty cents on the dollar, at best, to clean our conscience." The CIO took out a pen and did the math. "That'd be a 143-million-dollar immediate loss from selling illiquid assets below their value. Which is basically the tuition of, what, three-sevenths of our undergraduates in a year. Is that all of our annual financial aid? I don't need to be Mother Teresa if those kids are the bill.

"But maybe Larry is more reasonable than the 'Police the Police' t-shirt I saw him wearing last month. If he just wants us to never make an oil and gas investment again, would we fail? Could I make that decision and become Mother Teresa? I have no idea. After the last two plus years of mediocrity, it's hard for me to say what is essential to any investment program. Common sense, all the data, and a surprisingly large number of Bob Marley lyrics tell you that there is always sector rotation. And there is no chance that oil, gas, market inefficiencies are going away soon. But if I can't name the month or even the year when alpha *there* could be coming back—and I can't—should our investment strategy just be All Tech All the Time until the singularity? Or was that just last decade's great idea? Is performance just about capturing upwardly re-valuing sector excitement at the right time and getting out at the right time? Which feels like 92 percent luck."

"Oh."

"Which is 100 percent the opposite of what I would have told you when I was The Best CIO in America in the Jurassic period of three to six years ago." Why was he being honest? He had to throw up.

"Well, at least you always do it with astonishing hyperarticulateness." She laughed gently.

Did she know how much he cared? Was he supposed to *tell* her how much he cared? He looked at his hands holding onto the side of the laptop again, testing its strength for what that plastic could prove. "I've probably told you this a thousand times, to pathetically ingratiate myself to a real academic, but I went to graduate school in American history for a year after college. Fear not: I'm not going to tell you what happened with me and John Brown, but it did not end well for either of us. I then got a job as a junior equity research analyst at Credit Suisse First Boston as it was then *in*-articulately called. A friend had told me that they suddenly needed an off-cycle hire. I worked for the packaged goods analyst, which was then thought of as a plum job. I guess we used to spend a lot of our nation's mindshare considering the buying and selling of food in packages. Maybe another topic for sociological study.

"Anyway, an equity research analyst writes reports and opines for institutional investors on whether one should buy, hold, or—once every millennium—sell a stock in the sector in which you are supposedly expert. We did this back then primarily by interpreting information given to us directly by the companies. And companies naturally tried to put the best face on everything. My boss hated their spin—Shia-Sunni level hatred. Often, on a quarterly analyst call, the CEO of a company that had missed its earnings target would say something canned in response to one of my boss's questions. He would blurt 'never mind' for everyone to hear and then—boom—hang up the phone. In those days, you needed to listen to every live answer in the Q&A to do your job. But my boss couldn't help himself. He liked hanging up the phone. Again. And again. And again. 'F you, f you, you lying you-know-what."

"Thank you for protecting my dainty female ears."

"My apologies for being heteronormatively cis-chivalrous. Every two or three months, my boss would actively rip the phone out of the socket and throw it. He was a spaz"—the CIO stopped, wondering if he could say "spaz" anymore—"his shirttail flying out, his hair flapping out of his stupid combover. And the phone would fall clumsily, and dead. CSFB knew about this. But the guy was consistently ranked in the top two by *Institutional Investor*, which was then the ne plus ultra of human accomplishment. So he was given a spare phone to keep in an on-deck circle in a drawer. He would just plug in the new phone, right after, calm.

"I would watch the whole thing, eating my popcorn from the front row. Although I loved—and quoted—mafia movies with the same ardor as everyone else on the Street, I was certain I would never act like that. I was certain that a large part of me was prone to act *exactly* like that, for familial reasons about which I will not burden you. So I would never allow myself to act like that. But this is the point, I think: I *admired* him. I learned from him about a fusion of... the person, the markets, being an investor, and the absolute need for the truth to prevail. And some part of me has been looking, with apologies to William James, for the moral equivalent of smashing phones ever since. I, um. I—" He had turned on his screen as if desperate for distraction, as if fearing where his conversation would lead. To Gordon Gekko and Michael Hermann and Alec Baldwin: third prize, you're fired. "Um, so much for hyperarticulateness." He was stupidly looking at his email inbox. He would have given anything to not have turned on the screen. (Christ, what quant hedge fund was Calvin excited about now?) "Sorry, I have to get back to work. I have to figure out—I have to—I don't know."

"Are you okay?"

He had to get it together. He could find that moral equivalent. He would not go down. Not with "5" percent.

She was silent, as were her fingers, from real courtesy. And then she asked, "Did you ever think about Michael Hermann?"

Trustee (call)
Office
October 11 (unscheduled)

The CIO was ignoring the predictions and masturbatory math in the sell-side reports cluttering his office as he went to the heart of the matter, his focus pressed against the Excel on the screen. He adjusted the value of VBV II with Sous still at the IPO price. He replaced Mulberry's numbers last year with Ledo Road's. He erased the declines in U.S. equity everywhere. Hurst Street: up 20 percent. PMD: flat. He would send these to the investment committee. He would force them to tell him why this, too, didn't make sense. He needed to see what was possible, to be this time Duke, last time MIT, before that himself. Excel made everything alive. The public markets were not going to change, but he could hope for some lagging write-ups or write-downs in Q4. He typed over names. Thoma Bravo instead of PMD. Benchmark instead of VBV. A little Uber for me. A little Uber for you. Just make up numbers, higher-than-even-6-percent numbers.

Peter always had a clever argument in favor of screen life. Peter could argue why the *CIO's* numbers, his higher sense of human activity numbers, were just as true as so-called actual numbers. The CIO sometimes wondered if Peter was an independent person or just his id—or his evolution. But were numbers just his evolution?

Even if actual numbers, real numbers, God's clear judgment numbers had given him as much purpose as Yeboah's scholarship's number, Larry Galanos's salary's numbers, 264 million dollars of numbers.

But the actual numbers, the year-end numbers, were summaries-of-complexity numbers that no quarter-end estimate of value could sand over. The actual numbers were *temporary* values of debt, currencies, options, companies that no one could value permanently—down 15 percent for trade wars, down 20 percent for Emma Watson, down 90 percent for going public. They were numbers that, if he could map it in this spreadsheet, were the sum of economic activity.

Also human activity.

But those numbers were house addresses that told you nothing of how the homes were furnished, who lived there, who was happy.

He should throw the laptop through the window, shattering the numbers.

The phone was ringing.

He would not pick up for a man without regrets.

It was still ringing without regrets.

"Do you know this Galanos?"

Were there any private spaces left? Or was life now just the embodiment of a group text? He wanted another ten minutes and/or a lifetime to work on his valuations—the just numbers—in peace. But he answered Wirbin: "I've met him a few times."

"Bernie Sanders bumper sticker?"

"Well, he has a ponytail."

"Fucknuts probably has a Bernie sticker on one of those three-wheeled bicycles that only douches and ice cream salesmen ride. And he's going to tell us how to invest?"

Even if he agreed with Wirbin, the CIO needed to be on the side of Galanos and ice cream and three-wheeled bicycles, whatever three-wheeled bicycles were. Weakly: "I don't know."

"And why the fuck does he go by Larry? *Larry* Christ? How the fuck would that have gone over? You know, when the students present their petitions, we meet with them. I am a very good investment banker. I know how to stroke my chin super thoughtfully, nod my head, and let the deep, deep bullshit of a counterparty wash over me as a show of respect. But, truth to fucking God, we hear them out. They don't control the endowment, they *aren't* the endowment, but at least they are links in the chain that forms this, this community.

"But what drives me ape-shit is tenured faculty, the luckiest assholes on earth, who think they own the school just because they can't get fired. You know what the fuck they are? Employees with sweetheart deals. And I swear that I will string Larry Galanos up by his tenured cock if he doesn't keep his opinions on endowment management to himself. What is he, a creative writing professor?"

The CIO needed to get back to his spreadsheet. He would submit revised numbers to NACUBO. It must have happened before. Finally: "Philosophy... Bioethics."

"What. The. Fuck. Is that like, 'Is it fair to the flowers to pick them, Professor Galanos?' I should have become a trustee of a trade school, where at least the faculty aren't warping children."

"Maybe he's right. Maybe we should just invest in windmills...."

"Are you fucking serious? Have you been hiding a ponytail, too?"

"That would be a real feat."

"I'll have you know that the last four CEOs of Goldman Sachs *and* Gary Cohn are bald motherfuckers. You assholes just pretend you have nothing to hide."

Was this the—? "It's just. It's just I'm not in a position to criticize."

"Well, I'm in a position to criticize. It's my favorite fucking position. Way better than doggystyle, which I'm starting to think is sort of greasy. And *I* don't care if Larry Galanos is David Swensen and Warren Buffett rolled into a ponytail and shoved in a Subaru. It's hard as fucking hell to manage an institutional pool of capital for eternity being drained 4.5 percent per year by jackoffs like Larry Galanos and more fucking administrators than the UN. And that's before having to deal with the virtue signaling *graffiti* of a) biohazard professors, b) random alumni who have guessed my Goldman email account, and c) nineteen-year-olds who, after three months on campus, decide it's their God-given right to tell us what to do with the 6 billion dollars subsidizing every fucking minute they are here. You want to be a good person? Open a Fidelity account and put everything in resi solar and recycled paper towels."

The CIO upped all the privates on his spreadsheet by 15 percent.

"If we let the dam break here, we might as well give up. Write *it* down: if I'm ever forced to sit down with the Boycott Sanctions Detestment fucknuts on Israel, you are on your fucking own."

Then he halved everything. "What?"

"I can deal with anti-Semites. I'd be jealous, too, if I were them. But if I so much as acknowledge that BDS exists, every alter kocker alumni is going to tell me that he is revising his will to leave the school out. 'I am very disappointed in you'"—Wirbin put on a credible Lower East Side accent—"Benjamin, given that you work at Goldman Sachs.' As if Goldman is the ADL's investment banking division. I do have a fucking job, you know. I can't just respond to Jewish anger 24-7. Luckily, you and I married gentiles."

"Jane is not a—"

"You know what word I fucking hate? Shiksa."

The CIO needed to hang up; Wirbin was already in his mind as a parasite.

"This morning, a Duke Pride asshole, who took an *obscene* guarantee to go to Moelis, called me. He's an 'alumni advisory board' kind of guy who doesn't give a fuck about his school, but he called me about the *Journal* article like he'd been waiting three years to get his revenge." Wirbin suddenly was quiet. He was breathing, quietly, closer to the phone. The CIO wondered if Wirbin had rolled up his sleeves, like the Australian and Brian Park, in calming self-admiration. The silence continued. Then Wirbin said, "Okay, we have one more quarter or we're going to have to do something different."

The CIO zeroed out the spreadsheet: a clean endowment of no endowment.

"Do we throw out Swensen?" Wirbin asked. "Throw out privates? Throw out all the shit and try something new? Get one of those Dalio types with their modern portfolio theory to shake shit up?"

The CIO closed the file without saving it. How did Wirbin know about the portfolio theory crowd? And why, God, was he talking about a new approach with him? "There's no proof from their numbers," the CIO said, with unsteady conviction, "that all that liquidity works better in the end."

"Do you think *this* works anymore? You intellectualize everything, so put your big brain on these facts: somehow, twenty big endowments with the same approach have performance that ranges from 1 percent to 10 percent in a year. I was talking about this with Pascky. If endowments were car manufacturers, it'd be like twenty blue cars came out every year looking exactly the same. Twenty poor schmucks would start driving them for a month. And then, after six months, one driver is having fun with his blue car going from zero to a hundred in six seconds, another realizes he has the engine of a subcompact when he keeps getting passed on the road, and another watches his gas tank spontaneously combust on the way to Applebee's. The next year, same blue cars but with *new* fucking surprises for the drivers. That variability is fucking bonkers. Manager selection can't be everything that separates the geniuses from the numbnuts. Because I know a lot of these GP assholes, and they are not that differentiated or—obviously—that fucking smart if you look at their results. And so if the endowment model doesn't work, we got to find something that does work. Why don't you, me, Jim—what do you think of Ghosh?"

You? Why won't he leave out you?

"Dude, are you there?"

"Yes. Sorry. Ghosh seems smart." The CIO didn't make the joke, to Wirbin, "And humble."

"Okay. You, me, Pascky, Ghosh, Saint Marvin. Let's fly to Aspen, get Jim's place for forty-eight hours, and take out a clean sheet of paper." Wirbin suggested this every other year, independent of performance. "Well, I guess Marvin would probably make us do it at some fucking Trotter's so he can straighten out pickle jars while we're talking. But we're not doing it without him."

"Maybe you should do it without me."

"Because of your 6 percent bullshit?"

The CIO couldn't speak.

"Are you there?"

"What do you want me to say?"

"You don't need to say anything."

The CIO was done. He slammed his laptop and gripped the edges. His heart was pounding for escape out of his chest.

"So are we going to do this?"

Say it. Lie big. Numbers to escape numbers.

"Y'ello? What the fuck are you doing?"

Say it.

"What the fuck is wrong with this phone?"

"Sorry." Say it. "I was just trying to figure out, you know... If you're disgusted by the Heroic CIO Era in endowment management's late decadent period, then maybe you shouldn't have a conventional hero model CIO."

"That's what I like about you, dude. You are not some miserable rent seeker. You also all of a sudden can't invest to save your life, but, hey, no one is perfect."

He said the opposite of what he wanted to say: "The first quarter is going to be ugly."

"Just to be clear: I don't think you're a better person if you're a worse investor." Wirbin laughed.

"Sometimes I think Wall Street's greatest product is jokes."

"Dude, that's its only product. Listen: in every fucking respect, we're not Yale, so let's not be Yale here either. That's what me, you, Ghosh, Marvin, and Pascarella can hammer out."

"Okay."

"You sound very enthusiastic."

"I am extremely enthusiastic."

"Do we need more people on the team?"

"Well, Swensen would say we're delusional for trying to run an endowment with this few people and with the age gap between me and Emily and then between her and Calvin and the analysts."

"Then why the fuck are we being delusional?"

"Have you ever gone into one of these modern endowment offices? Some have thirty or forty people, layers of interns, associates, VPs, managing directors, in huge offices far from campus. You can't tell if you're in a mid-level corporate law firm, an insurance company, or an endowment. And the newest trend is that once you do a physical makeover, you do a personnel makeover. Out with the sheepy allocators of capital to GPs, in with new types who see themselves as peers of the GPs, smarter than GPs, playing them off each other, seizing special economics and deal flow. Co-investments everywhere. I never wanted—did I ever tell you about the time I met Jack Bogle?"

"What?" Wirbin seemed to have been texting again, probably to Pascarella to ask about the availability of his house in Aspen.

"Bogle. The Vanguard guy."

"I know who Jack Bogle is, fucknuts."

"About a year after I started working here, Hamilton Lane was trying to break into the endowment and foundation community and somehow got Jack Meyer to address a half-day event at their offices. I've since learned my lesson about going to those types of things, but back then, I was flattered to be among fellow big endowment CIOs. To make myself feel like less of an asshole for going, I set up a lunch with a guy I was friendly with from, um, business school, who worked at Vanguard's headquarters nearby. The day before, he asks me if I wanted to meet Bogle. Of course, why wouldn't I—it's kind of crazy. So we have lunch on Vanguard's campus, and we talk about what second-tier friends from business school always talk about: losers who really flamed out. This helps us to not delve too deeply into the fact that I'm an asset allocator, he works at what is essentially a consumer products company, and neither of us is, you know." The CIO caught himself before he said Michael Hermann. "But we have a good time nonetheless, as there was one loser who flamed out doing subprime loans in a way that was both entertaining and well-deserved.

"After lunch, we walk to Bogle's office past these boxy red brick buildings that eradicated the idea of architecture. Or maybe they manifested the concept of low fees in every unadorned window. The only human flourish on the campus is a statue of Bogle, with one hand on his knee and the other mysteriously in his pocket, as you walk to his office. I wondered what it was like to see yourself already bronzed on your way to work. Are you tickled by the flattery, or do you just want to crawl into a grave beneath it? I also wondered what's up with Philadelphians and statues of the living. They also have that Stallone one. I mean, is human accomplishment in Philadelphia so sparse since 1782 that—"

"Go on, dude."

"We get to Bogle's office, which is a Wall Street guy's idea of a professorial study, especially if he has never seen how unimpressive actual professors' offices are. Bookshelves everywhere, books on top of a kitchen table-looking thing, books stacked on a coffee table. Bogle's sitting there, writing longhand on lined paper. I presume it's a draft of another book on investing. My classmate and I sit down on this stuffed Chesterfield sofa, and Bogle slowly moves to sit across from us. He's already in his mid-eighties, deeply wrinkled around the eyes, and tiny. But, oh man, is he sharp in this performative way. And I come to realize that I'm visiting Wall Street Yoda.

"Yoda Bogle has *power*. It's power that comes from his certainty, his clarity. It's power that comes from the near impossibility of disputing the exact same advice he has been giving my entire life. And he knows it. But he's not showing off that he knows it. Hundreds of visitors must get the same show every year. And you know what? I agree with him. Everyone agrees with him. But it's like I'm sitting in the confessional booth, admitting all my lustful thoughts to the priest, with penitence truly, *truly* on my mind... while watching porn on my phone.

"Bogle's nice about everything. I don't know if you've met him, but he's like Marvin, with that vanishing Protestant Establishment dignity. Although, unlike Marvin, he talks. Really talks, in unspooling paragraphs. I can't help calling him Mr. Bogle. He mentions that his son runs a hedge fund as if to absolve me for how much I'm paid to beat the market with the strategy of finding even more highly paid people to beat the market.

"I can't remember most of the stuff he said he was putting in the new book, but he said one thing in our half-hour together that will stick with me forever." The CIO remembered why he hadn't told this story before. "He said, 'If investing were just a function of effort—if you think you could be a better investor by putting more people on the problem—don't you think Fidelity would hire two thousand analysts?'

"I like Emily and the team we have. They see what we need to see in this job. They work as hard as any people on campus. They work way harder than Larry Galanos, with his two-two load and Twitter addiction. Some of them even seem to care about our performance. But that conversation with Bogle is why I've never asked permission to hire five managing director types like at Stanford. It's why I've always tried to be humble about what I can do, even before I was humbled. So I'm not sure what could come from convening you, me, Marvin, Ghosh, Pascarella, Warren Buffett, Peter Lynch, George Soros, and the proclaiming ghost of Jack Bogle himself in Aspen or among the pickle jars to try to address a problem—a problem that seemingly more resources and more brainpower fundamentally can't solve."

The Whirlwind had been silent, fingers unmoving, the whole time. The CIO only now realized it.

"Well," Wirbin asked, "if more people don't solve it, how do you solve it?"

"That's what I'm trying to figure out."

Industrial real estate manager
Conference room
October 13

Tom Miller, blow-dried white hair, was a jock in acting class, sulking that the hot girls he had been promised were not there. His firm had the endowment's money for two funds. He mentioned that they still had distribution centers in Memphis, Boston, and Tampa that would be monetized "in a year to twenty-four months." He had already measured time in a "year to twenty-four months" twice before. Now Miller Lamb's IR guy was talking, and talking too much: "Blackstone just has a very different cost of capital than we do when they label something 'digital infrastructure.' And so we're not surprised that they bought three of our last seven exits."

The CIO would later translate "cost of capital" for the intern. He would tell her that Blackstone, by labeling investments lower risk, gets to offer their investors lower returns on purpose. But could he explain to her how subjective, self-appointed, and public-relations was the idea of a cost of capital, even if it sounded like math?

Addressing Miller, Emily asked if the rest of the new fund would be invested more in distribution or data centers. The IR guy answered instead—data centers—and then hacked a liquid cough. Emily wiped her hands on her pants to get ahead of the coming need to pour a bucket of Purell on them.

Miller looked at his watch and said, "I think that's right."

It was Mark Polansky and the cheap watch meeting all over

again. The CIO should tell the intern that these kinds of patterns are what he should learn to see when assessing managers' hunger.

But Miller Lamb had done well. (So, alas, for many years had PMD.) Yes, 10 percent net in their third fund was less than promised. But still, 50 percent already realized, and accretive to an endowment that generated just 3.8 percent last year.

Maybe that performance, in a fallen world, spoke for itself.

What had Emily said that he had taught her? Don't confuse personal presentation with investment edge. Another lesson: don't confuse edge with inputs. Miller Lamb had always built big boxes. Was anything else important? For nowadays, one big box held the server that calculated the shipping from another big box that was together grinding retail into dust. Shouldn't we be proud of having gone with the box guys? Isn't it super nifty that we were right?

The IR guy was trying to brag about relative returns when coughing overtook him altogether.

The CIO looked at Emily. He was going to try to be kind.

"Seriously. I know you flew here and spent the night. And we get the message: you don't take the endowment for granted. And an even better message: we're crystallizing positive returns."

The IR guy coughed again into his hand.

"We will not hold it against you if you need to rest."

He said, "We haven't gone through Fund IV yet."

"It is interesting," the CIO said as he turned to Emily. He could not—*could not*—be that embarrassing. "There are—what?—five hundred institutions in this country allocating capital in a real way to GPs. Which means—" He took a pencil from a cup, to be the him he had always been—"a half-million meeting hours per year, which has to translate into the same amount of colds spread per year." The CIO started doodling numbers on a page, for their roundness. He did not glance at Emily even though his whole body wanted to freeze time to talk to her. "But how many honest hours of human communication are there?"

Miller couldn't seem to rouse himself into defensiveness. In their original diligence, they learned that, when he was at Lone Star, Miller complained every year at compensation time, no matter the millions he had made, how he was floating "losers" who didn't produce. Maybe the eyes of the Man in the Arena didn't register people like Emily or the CIO.

"I think people are honest," Miller eventually said.

"I'm not talking about the blood machines of Elizabeth Holmes." Why was he allowing *himself* to happen again? And why had this failure of control chosen his hands as its puppet? He opened them and closed them, tighter. "I'm talking about the percentage of time in which people are expressing their deepest held beliefs, or lack thereof—rather than talking about the future sale of distribution centers or future acceleration of IRR, which, by the way, almost never happens. Trust me: I've been through seven lifetimes in these meetings. Twenty percent of the talk is about the past. But half of *that* is about what you guys thought in the past, as hypotheses for events that have still not transpired. So maybe 10 percent of these meetings are about events, numbers, realizations that have indisputably, fixedly happened. With a mandatory 10 percent dedicated to discussing air travel and frequent flier programs, this leaves 70 percent speculating about the future. This is a confidence game in the most literal, nonjudgmental sense of the phrase. But just once—"

He moved his chair back to talk to the intern, avoiding Emily. He had not yet stood up. "Just once, I'd like someone to say, we did this because we had money burning a hole in our undrawn commitment, or we did this because Excel said it *seemed* good even though it scares the popcorn out of us, or we did this because we are exhausted trying to count the thousand variables we understand and the million variables that will never move in a way comprehensible to algorithm or person. We did this as a surrender to action, because it's our job, because it occasionally works, because it makes us feel human...."

The CIO still had the pencil in his hand. He put it down.

He looked from the intern to Emily, to test if he was improving, to test if she could finally see the world on his terms.

Emily stared ahead.

So, fuck it: "Why do you do this?"

The IR guy, Christ again: "We think it's important to visit you, given the trust—"

"No, not you. Tom, why do you do this?"

Miller asked, "Visit here?"

"No, this—" He waved his hand around the room, at the endowment made flesh. "All of this."

"I don't understand the question."

Emerging Europe hedge fund
Conference room
October 14

Through with speculating how placement agents—normal-seeming people—could sit so still, the CIO didn't want to know what was going through this mannequin's head. He also didn't want to learn what he had been missing all his life, in what this hedge fund, too, was offering him. Emerging Europe? Hadn't Europe emerged in 1000 BC? One partner of the fund was going on about a Polish convenience store chain expanding into Slovakia.

The CIO just wanted the cancellation of this noise, *all* noise, so he could focus on when existing managers would perform, when everyone would stop peacocking their intelligence and inputs. He wanted to lie again. He wanted to tell the truth again. He wanted Emily and Calvin to turn into different people and be the same people at the same time.

Mostly he wanted to know what was on his phone. Why had he turned out no better than anybody else in always wanting to know what was on his phone? (In the ashes of civilization, will the last man use his final moment to check what was on his phone?) The CIO's self-defense: how could he be expected to remain seated when last year's shit gain could be erased double again in a week, when everyone was uncertain and grumpy and jostled by the turbulence of tariffs and bile at the top? He'd go with Wirbin and Pascarella to wherever they wanted—a meditation center, where meat and Bloombergs were not allowed. They'd stare into themselves for the Inspiration Within. Over rare bourbon and mountain views, they could fake an answer that the smartest people in the world could not deduce.

Or, it was a trick. Wirbin and Pascarella would throw him off a mountain, a sacrifice to the gods in exchange for the 9 percent annuity everyone wanted.

But MIT was invested with this hedge fund. So why wasn't MIT right? Calvin believed MIT was always right. The CIO had not proved that Calvin was wrong.

He blinked a few times and looked around the table to rouse himself to the Slovakian present. He understood that someone had changed the topic to Hungarian fast food. It was even possible that the placement agent had said something. But the last thing in the world he wanted to know about was the return on capital employed that this hedge fund alone had discovered around one and/or all the providers of Hungarian fast food. They had already found a new route—Ledo Road—to late emerging markets growth in China and India. How many more fucking places can we be expected to worry about, Calvin? Isn't our life easier if we don't have to think about the Slovakian appetite for slurpees?

But it wouldn't *have* to be a chief worry, right? It would take up only two or three cells of the CIO's mind. But to what end? Different inputs? A system not available to the lazy and cautious? The lazy and cautious whose ideas were... China and India.

Calvin was speaking. Now Calvin was not speaking. This was when the CIO was supposed to speak.

Couldn't he just acknowledge that he realized that this was their career, too?

But the CIO said, "Why do you do this?"

And a GP, once again, asked, "What?"

Cannabis sector venture capital firm
Conference room
October 16

"So our first portfolio company came out of the Wild West at the start of the sector. We invested in a technology to measure THC and a hundred other cannabinoids in any strain, and it turned out—shame on us—that the technology was basically a scam. Lost 3 million bucks. But in the bankruptcy, we got the busted IP, if you could call it that. We took it to a molecular biologist at the University of Wisconsin, who's basically The Man in botanical spectroscopy, brilliant, brilliant, *brilliant* guy, basically a genius. He surprised us by saying that while effectively nothing worked in what we had invested in—I mean nothing, like the 'on' button barely worked—there was an idea there that could work.

"And so we hired Peng as our CTO, and his science works beautifully—years and years ahead of anyone else's. We now have three first-gen machines, costing us 275 each, that we put on Citation Ultra jets. We are dealing with the growers that are the absolute uncontested leaders in branding and sophistication. And even they have been guessing at the active ingredients. Because it's not just the THC-cannabidiol ratio but how all of cannabinoids interact, counteract, drive healing, drive pleasure, which is the mystery. We're saying to them, give us an hour, we'll blow your minds with *all* the data. You can throw it away if you want. A few of the Humboldt County crazies say no, but even your average Ben and Jerry, fat-hippie capitalist knows this game is not about security of supply and tie-dyed names anymore. The growers think that our business is giving them the data, but the real money multiplier is *getting* the data. We'll be able to monetize that, moving upstream and downstream, basically becoming irreplaceable with 90 percent recurring revenue.

"The killer app is getting the second-gen machines in dispensaries and in doctors' offices, so that end users can understand which active ingredients maximize both user experience and medical success. This gives them total consumer control. They'll be able to root in deep science their preferences in terms of strains and of delivery modalities—and not have to rely on some high school educated 'budtender' making stuff up, especially in the med space. This is a 10-billion-dollar idea at least, commanding a premium SaaS multiple on exit. Cannabis is going to be a bigger industry than spirits or video games within five years. And, to be clear, I'm talking about only *one* portfolio company, one that is already in the fund and one that has a very high potential of returning way, way more than the 300-million-dollar fund all by itself. It's also indicative of the white space that is available right now. I've been in venture for twenty-five years, and I've never seen an industry already this big that, through an inflection point in the legal structure, is going to provide the opportunity to create multiple world-scale winners in basically an instant. In other industries, it took decades—a century—for this to happen. This is literally the most exciting thing to happen in medical and consumer venture in our lives, and there are very few, if any, other credible firms poised to take advantage of it."

The CIO pressed the heels of his hands into his legs until pain electrified his wrists. He held his breath. He didn't ask, Why do you do this? He stared ahead, counted down from a thousand by sevens, and kept pressing into his legs until his heartbeat took over his mind.

Campus
October 16 (unscheduled)

And now the CIO was walking, his phone left behind. He would not acknowledge the market, shouting with news and dopamine and missed chances.

He had waited, thank God, to escape until the meeting was over. He had not provoked Emily this time by asking Cannabis Man the fundamental questions. What would he have answered anyway?

I want to be rich.

They all wanted to be rich. They had all shattered definitions of where rich used to begin.

The CIO *had* waited for the meeting to end. He lingered behind his office door, eavesdropping, a prisoner wondering if the warden was talking about his parole. Even though he was the warden. They had done the meeting as a favor to Jim Pascarella. Had Emily actually liked that sub-institutional roulette wheel—a market opportunity to sell drugs? Or had she just pretended to, as torture?

He had finally understood, maybe, what they meant by late capitalism.

He was now on the campus's original stone-buildinged quad. One maple was already flaunting peak crimson. How could the CIO have become so inside-minded that he wasn't certain if that tree had always been there? How could it have not?

He had fled without a coat. The green sweater, whose neck

hole had been ravaged by the button-downs he wore underneath, was inadequate in the shade of the eastern buildings. There were twenty degrees of sunned warmth to be had on the other side. A few jocks were walking on the sunny side, cocky to the weather, long shorts tight around their thighs, XXL hoodies falling beneath their waists. Everyone else seemed to be wearing puffer coats. The only way to distinguish the he-Taylors from the she-Taylors was whether there were leggings on their bottom halves.

Was he—a middle-aged, white, bald university bureaucrat—even imaginable to these kids? Did they see his work as this education, this place, the purpose of their driven childhoods' end?

To advance human thought and human character.

To determine life's possibilities.

To keep their phones plugged in.

What did they smell like, *she* smell like, he thought about an uninteresting rich girl in a white puffer coat outside Heller Hall. Maybe like lavender and laundry, like the intern he should have been brave enough to hire. (We had a very bad year.) Cheeks drawn in, the rich girl was taking a selfie. Maybe she needed a screen to confirm her beauty was real.

He stepped off the path to walk faster and out of the quad.

Where was he going? To Corso? To ask her why he was objecting to Larry Galanos making the endowment about Galanos, the CIO, the world, their souls. Did a single one of these students consider, in gratitude, what 6 billion dollars meant to the blanket of their very freedom? He knew the answer: the 6 billion dollars was WiFi, 4G, sexual possibility, preprofessional education, the free air of the university that was theirs by right.

The CIO should just give Emily her profession: go, make a new world ruled by people like her. Emily would engage with the GPs from strength, not from a constantly comparing mind. Or, better yet, he and Emily should together distribute the 264 million dollars to people *not* guided here by ambitious parents who knew the rules of the development office and the sports popular at boarding schools. They could triple the pay of the nurses' aides at the hospital, of the Somali landscapers now everywhere.

Could Gabriela, who cleaned the endowment's offices, her salary and paperwork on ABM's conscience, even fathom how much he made sitting in a chair?

I could not believe numbers could go so high.

They all wanted to be richer.

He had wanted to be richer.

At least today, the school smelled of 6 billion dollars. The golden tree on the other side of the quad would inhale applications of any parents walking by. (A puffer coat was resting alongside it, reading its phone.) Even the pathway he was on justified a kid taking Russian math in elementary school: the brickwork was tight, the curve engineered with elegance, the late autumn grass trimmed at the edges. He walked past the Mercein Library with its new Castine Atrium, a glass entrance designed to ensure better "flow." It had been advertised as a metaphor for the innovative mind. Nothing associated the building with dead paper books.

He walked eastward, farther from his office. Breathing this almost-Rockies air could fuel the alchemy he wanted—to be contribution at its purest, to be incremental good. These kids would discover soon enough how unimpressed the world could be. But for now, the atmosphere the endowment bought was the last free air they would breathe.

And he was failing at it, failing at providing 264 million dollars per year to oxygenate this experiment in privilege and grace. Next year, if the negative performance held, the payout formula would call for a declining contribution from the endowment. And even if the payout slipped to 4 percent (30 million less, which enrollment management would have to solve with more selfies and less Yeboahs), the endowment would be 9 percent smaller.

Twelfth out of twenty.

Why did you do it, Daddy?

Because the work was too hard, Hannah.

Like how, Daddy?

Like it turned out that maybe I wasn't any good at it.

But you told me, Daddy, that you have to practice to become good at anything.

Jane, please help. Jane, I don't have—I don't want to take them down with my inadequacy.

You are not inadequate.

Would Jane say that? Despite the bored, inscrutable look at the dinner, despite "that's nice," yes, she would say that. Twenty years of accreted support, by both of them, would leave her with no other instincts.

And what else could she say? What else did she know?

But last week, this: "I'm not going to have this conversation again."

He: "I'm talking about our children."

They were in the new kitchen with subway tile everywhere. She asked him to keep his voice down. He told her that he hadn't raised his voice.

"Peter and Hannah are their own people," she said. "They aren't problems to be solved. They aren't things to be predicted."

"What's this about, Jane?"

"I know you are going through a tough period at work. But *we* aren't defined by your work. *You* aren't defined by your work. You need to turn off your mind when it comes to them. Just let them develop. They are fourteen and ten."

The refrigerator had cost $12,000. He would have brought that up if he wasn't more embarrassed by that fact than she was.

You are not inadequate, he was certain she would say. He

would bet his life on it. He had bet his life on it. But when he left the kitchen, she hadn't given him a Kate Wirbin kiss.

The CIO walked towards East Campus. He was getting hot. But if he took off his sweater, it would pull his shirt out of his pants, revealing the hairy paunch jarring on a skinny man.

And then he noticed a girl reading on an unshadowed bench. She wore purple-framed glasses that beauty could get away with and mid-blue overalls over a tight, long-sleeved white t-shirt. The sun loved her and the small stud in her nose.

He slunk thirty feet away to a tree on the far side of the path, its roots pushing up the edge of the stonework. He considered sitting down but stood instead, abutting the trunk, the overhead branches not fully covering his face. He could tell her that he was there to cool down. He could tell her that he was studying Thoreau.

This is what Hannah can do in nine years, Emily. She would *want* to study the fundamental questions. To find her own faith, any faith other than work hard, do well in school, get a good job, and be tolerant and conscientious as defined by the opinion section of *The New York Times*.

He should move to the bench, to stop being creepy. He would ask her if her plan, too, was doing well by doing good. He would ask her what's she reading, explain that she's his daughter, the vessel to be on the other side from every side he was now on.

To be the opportunity before capital.

To explain that the problem of performance was not just 3.8 percent.

He could do it, too, by *not* being complicit in all that he had. To hate with burning intensity all that was unfair, all the pat answers from guys like him—like Emily—about how we live in the money-world we're given and should be realistic about the world we can make. All the self-satisfied, self-fortifying *lies* about how benign we are. He would tell her that there is not a day in which a believer in capitalism is not embarrassed by capitalism.

The cover of her book tilted upward, showing a slaver's silhouette on the cover, about or by Kara Walker, whose work they had seen at the Whitney on their last trip to New York. (He had suggested the museum; Jane was enthusiastic, Peter did not surprise them.) Maybe the girl had been drawn to the school by the hoopla around the renovated museum. Kathleen Niles-Krulic (always Kathleen Niles-Krulic, '66) and her second husband had the third-largest collection of Dan Flavin sculptures in the world. They'd decided that they should graft a world center of Flavinism onto the university's undersized museum, a storage locker for the masterpieces of forgotten faculty and minorpieces of nineteenth-century landscape painters. At the opening, What's Her Name Farber had talked down to the CIO as if he were a calculator. Sure, the CIO didn't understand how Niles-Krulic, '66 had decided that her immortality was to be found in preserving a stranger's corners of neon light. Nonetheless, he should have told What-*Is*-Her-Name Farber (he should tell the girl on the bench) that he *could* appreciate that light's pink triangular cast on the floor.

For what did *he* do but stare all day at the abstract, the ever-changing, the agreement that 6 billion dollars was true? What had investing become but a search for an edge when all the precedents had been painted? Once, there was beauty on canvases. Once, there was the allocation of capital. Now, there was Steve Cohen, modern art, never get caught. Now, there was infinite equity and the critics silenced. Now, there was a CIO of a major university hiding under a tree from a girl he had never met.

Two students walked past him, one of them doing a double-take at the double trunk.

I accept the humiliation, but please don't cause her to look up.

He needed to ask her if Larry Galanos could be right, if Kathleen Niles-Krulic, '66 could be right, if he could have been right:

that *the* top performance over three years meant that he had escaped the decadence that forwarded too many people to Wall Street, that paid too much to Wall Street?

Or are we all so temporary that we ache in sympathy with whatever beauty there is while the light is still on?

The CIO was desperate to get out of there—to scream with feral hunger. His hands still couldn't grip into commanding fists. (Why? Early Parkinson's?) He pulsed his wannabe fists again and again until the knuckles ached. His fingers were too brittle, too ungripped, too temporary. He'd hurt himself more than the person he punched.

Had he *ever* believed?

I like my job.

He shuddered before he processed that the girl had looked up and in his direction.

I went to the woods because I wished to live deliberately, to front only the essential facts...

He didn't know whether to smile, didn't know if she could understand, didn't know if she was just thinking about Kara Walker. He looked at the top roots of the tree as if he could have lost something there. This brought a confident smile to her face. *Please* be human and curious about the innocent-bearded professor, the innocent-bearded professor persona, the pervert dad in corduroys, the homeless man in a green sweater, neck-ruined.

He could tie his shoe. He could have a purpose. He could be the engine of the destruction of this world by broadcasting *its* destruction. He could bury his eyes into a forearm resting on the trunk and shout, to Hannah, Ready-or-not-here-I-come.

He stepped out into the path, his face composed: a man with a destination. He walked on as if he had never stopped at all. He heard his heartbeat in his steps until he was certain she could no longer see him. He walked faster towards East Campus, the dorms, the students, a purpose, education, the past, his choices, graduate school, escape.

And then he broke into a full run, praying for the first time that no students knew who he was.

Emerging market credit hedge fund
Conference room
October 21

"The entire summer," Karen Kahn explained, "the team was stumped why the Uridashi trade wasn't working. Even as Erdogan was doing his best Putin, these bonds lived on their own planet."

The CIO needed to translate the technical details for the analysts, but he was hesitant lest he humiliate himself in front of Kahn. He understood the big thing: Tolemy had seen something that didn't make sense—Japanese retail investors being promised a suspiciously high return through Turkish bonds—and had found a derivative, wizardly way to take on *less* risk in a bet that the bonds' value would collapse. But he was fuzzy himself on what the wizardly way entailed.

"We may have missed this," the CIO interrupted, gingerly, trying to bring his two analysts into the "we." "You shorted the bonds?"

"No." Kahn glanced at Marcus, her IR guy. "You can't short these bonds. You have to pay swaps because a side effect of the bonds is the swaps go tighter. That being said, all summer, I wondered why we hadn't just shorted something simpler, like a liquid credit or the lira. But we have to remind ourselves of our strategy. I'm not paid to make macro bets. I'm paid to locate inefficiencies and market patterns. As Jeff looked like he was about to throw up for two straight months, I reminded him of the cardinal rule that drew us to the trade. Anytime Japanese retail investors"—Kahn turned one hand sideways, chest high—"and emerging markets"—she interlaced it into her other hand—"intersect, it ends badly for the Japanese. When it comes to yield, they are—and this is a legitimate diagnosis—insane. It's hard to judge Deutsche for this."

"Wait? These Uri—"

"Uridashi."

"Are Deutsche Bank products?"

Again, she glanced at Marcus. "They are. Deutsche or some other fraud factory develops these credits specifically for Mrs. Watanabe. Even though she couldn't, one, locate Turkey on a map or, two, tell you how the yen-lira trades. If she even knows what a lira is. Yet they just go their Japanese crazy when they see a 14 percent yield. And their brokers tell them it's a bond. Which it is. But it's really an emerging market currency bet. Because the local bonds trade at 17 percent and Deutsche has covered itself with swaps at 16 percent."

"What's going to happen to the Mrs. Watanabes?" the CIO asked, not looking at Calvin.

"They can learn to be more careful or continue to suffer. *If* these things fall apart is never a question. As I have explained before, trading against these types of flows always comes back to three elements: one, timing; two, structuring; and three, catalysts."

As Kahn continued to narrate how the trade had flipped into a solid win by late August, the CIO could feel a warmth envelop him as if he had stepped out into the sun.

And just like that, all of it—the 7-percent-down October market, his 6 percent lie to Wirbin, the undifferentiated blue button-down shirts pitching their differentiation—no longer applied. Rested, he could rebuild the track record and finish the work.

He was not responsible for all the problems of the world.

He wondered if he was permitted an urge to kiss Kahn in thanks.

Kahn hadn't given an update in person in three years. (Why

was she in town now? A kid's college tour?) He had forgotten how sexy was that one, two, three. There was beauty in that nose more beak than honker, the tiny double chin, that neck-up nimbus of graying hair barely showing an effort to be composed. But it wasn't as if the CIO dreamed of her in white linen. He wanted to marry her for her reminder of cause and effect.

"You can't imagine what a cool glass of water this is," he said, "to hear about returns following a hypothesis controlled and confirmed. You do not know what the last few months have been like on our side of the table."

Kahn didn't respond.

"What's your five-year IRR for us, again?"

Marcus answered, "Even with 2015, for five years as of September 30th, KK is at 12.3 percent net."

Kahn added, "Which has been dollar-averaged without manipulation."

"Christ." Twelve point three percent total return per year, with only one mediocre-but-still-non-catastrophic year in there, for five years. It was almost a machine. The CIO looked at Calvin with an intention to *not* accuse. But Calvin's job, if one were to bring up inconvenient things like Calvin's job, was to find more almost-machines. "And how many years have you been working with us?"

Marcus answered, "Thirteen."

The CIO didn't know if Calvin was quick enough to grasp that this meant Tolemy had been put into the portfolio before the CIO's time. In the ancient days of Ivy slipstreaming and trustee hot tips.

But Calvin was otherwise occupied, it now became clear, getting up the courage to ask, "Would you attribute your alpha to your gender?"

"My what?"

The CIO could feel the female analyst, sitting next to Calvin, squirm. Calvin up-talked the repeat: "Gender?"

Kahn scrunched her eyes under her black owl glasses low on her nose. "I don't quite under–"

They all watched, breathless. "I'm joking."

The CIO in his soul was on Kahn's side of the table, not Calvin's. He should lean across the table to kiss her with the same chastely passionate kiss he thought of sometimes for Corso. Oh, he loved Jane, never once considered straying, but maybe he loved Jane *and* Corso *and* Kahn because supreme female competence in the world of disappointing, return-bleeding incompetence was the last erotic charge.

"As it relates to *that* topic," Kahn finally responded, "I'm surprised that I have time to invest, as I am daily inundated with, one, requests from reporters to Comment on the Issue and, two, invitations to be on yet another panel."

The CIO was smiling as mild male Marcus, familiar with all the routines, said, "Every conference seems required by law to have a number in its name."

Kahn went on, "One Thousand Women in Hedge Funds, with a stupid TM at the end. Even though there is also One Hundred Women in Hedge Funds, Ninety-Nine Women in Hedge Funds."

The CIO said, "Do you sing Ninety-Nine Women in Hedge Funds on the Wall?"

Kahn didn't acknowledge the joke. "The agenda is always me, Nancy Zimmerman, IR girls–no offense, Marcus–and CFOs. There is not enough to talk about at *one* of them, to say nothing of one a month. Which doesn't stop some hair-dyed Erin Burnett-type, or Erin Burnett herself, from being paid a stupid amount of money to ask me onstage if I attribute Tolemy's alpha to my gender."

The CIO could feel the analyst biting her smile, eager to report Calvin to Emily. So was he, but the CIO wanted to also tell the analyst that there were more important things going on. Take notes on confidence, success, tone.

"But..." Kahn tossed her head to prod Calvin to provide his name again. "Calvin, I attribute my alpha to, one, holding my team together by not being greedy; two, being aware enough to understand the optimal size of these trades and not overcapitalize the fund; and, three, our strategy. Which, as far as I can tell, has been executed by the men on my team without any measurable adverse impact on anyone's level of estrogen. Our strategy is rooted in a simple understanding available to all: China aside, every emerging market eventually finds a not-that-new and not-that-interesting way to shoot itself in the face. So: timing, structuring, catalysts."

This was it. He had won his first night of sleep after two months of insomnia. The CIO pushed back his chair and turned to Calvin. Thinking better of it, he angled to the analyst. "You know what I like? Simplicity. The more years I've been doing this, the more I realize that investing is impossible enough on its own. Not proved impossible, obviously"—he tipped his chin at Kahn *te salut, Don Corleone*—"but almost impossible. And maybe it's because Wall Street's greatest product is adding complexity to impossibility. And if you think about aesthetics, just commonsense aesthetics, it teaches us that simplicity is better. No one wants a building with Roman columns and Bilbao curves and a Mansard roof. So, our task is to find the people with the courage of their strategy, of their self-assessment of their own skills and necessity *to* the market. That's how we are going to outperform. Think about"—after nine years, he still never felt comfortable calling her Karen, and KK seemed reserved for her apostles, and Dr. Kahn too sycophantic—"Tolemy's strategy. Maybe we should have a new requirement that everyone who pitches us gets an index card. They have to submit it through a slit in a lucite box at the front desk, like when you complain to the Burger King about wilted lettuce on your Whopper. And if this index card is comprehensible and simple, only then do we invite them here to add to the world's landfills of PowerPoint."

The CIO was awkwardly angled towards the analyst. He was able to see Kahn only peripherally. His mind stuttered for the next topic. Michael Hermann? His own return to the Trois Glorieuse and 12 percent until death? "I really can't tell you how much I admire the strategy, so different than what everyone else is pursuing because of fidgetiness or asset grabs. I think I literally lost my mind last month when faced with more of the same from some generic PE shop. But there are inefficiencies that capital can address. Can correct. It reminds us what we are here to do: *intelligent* investing."

Kahn smiled tightly and turned to Marcus.

And Marcus said, "It was great seeing you, too."

Trustee (call)
Office
October 25 (unscheduled)

The first principles filled variously shaped and colored boxes on his own PowerPoint slide. They were not yet revealing—describing—sustainable outperformance. But the principles *were* correct. They could—

They could resolve into a breakthrough if he didn't pick up the ringing phone. The Karen Kahn meeting had guided him to the better question to answer. Investing is investing. He just needed more time.

It wasn't a matter of applying Kahn's specific strategy to the entire portfolio: what she did was too niche, the liquidity—the trades—in her markets too small. But what Kahn proved was that the excuses—his excuses—were lies. He just had to be smarter. He just had to work harder.

He had cleaned out the clutter in his office in a frenzy, thrown away years-old reports he'd never have a chance to read and asked Lisa to ask Gabriella to dust. He could love his job again. He could do his job again.

If he could just get rid of the phone.

Through the half-closed door, Lisa told him what he already knew.

"Are you going to this Galanos meeting?" Wirbin asked over the phone. He knew that the CIO wasn't going to the meeting.

"I have jury duty. And a, uh, medical procedure."

"You're a fucking weirdo—and a fucking coward. I've been following this fucker on Twitter. Is *anyone* clocking how much time Professor Ponytail tweets, given how unconscionably little time these fuckers are already asked to actually educate children? Anyway, dude must have been googling his bioethicist fingers to the bone, because fucknuts has gotten off of the 10-percent-in-windmills bullshit. He now wants—let's see—'phased' divestment, a 'quantified,' mission-driven impact allocation 'following the moral and fiduciary leadership of the Ford Foundation', and an ESG screen for all new investments. I'll give the asshole 10 thousand bucks if he can tell me what three letters are in ESG. I'll do that right after I ask him what our mission-driven strategy already is."

"With the answer being...?"

"The motherfucker in charge is asking me what the answer's 'being'? How about generating returns for research and education at one of America's best universities? AKA running a college fucking endowment."

"Where are you calling from? You sound..."

"Sound what?"

"Um. A bit supine."

"Well, you may be a fucking weirdo and a fucking coward, but you're the Sherlock Fucking Holmes of voice assessment. I am in the Ritz-Carlton Shanghai where, yes, it is 10:00 p.m., and yes, I got tired of answering emails, and yes, I may have opened, what is this, a twenty 'c-l', Chinaman-sized bottle of Talisker that the Görings in accounting will insist I pay for. For you see, Dr. Holmes, a Goldman Sachs Man is expected to fly commercial to China, expected to not mind being a sock puppet in a meeting, expected to take seriously some impenetrable government-connected family conglomerate, expected to answer questions from Uncle Liu about buying U.S. Steel and from Auntie Lee about buying Hearst Communications and from Nephew 'Clark'—no joke—about buying Halliburton as if they picked random acquisition targets out of a hat. He is expected *not* to text Solomon to ask if Jho Fucking Low and his see-through piano are going to be at this reputation disaster party too, expected to order some poor schmuck who got straight As at Princeton or, I guess, Tsinghua to stay up all night to run a model on how this mess could buy U.S. Steel, but *not* expected to open a bottle of whisky to have a few glasses of mid-tier single malt."

"Are you wearing pants?"

"What kind of question is that?"

The CIO closed his eyes—

"I'm a fifty-three-year-old investment banker in a luxury hotel in Shanghai, sitting on a bed at ten o'clock at night drinking overpriced whisky, talking to the chief investment officer of a major university. I haven't been wearing pants for two hours. I am wearing underwear, though, if that makes you feel more comfortable. Or maybe less comfortable. And, let's see, I was too exhausted to take off my button-down shirt. So your image of the vertically challenged but still incredibly handsome head of Goldman Sachs North American IBD is now complete. What are you wearing?"

"I'm, uh, wearing—"

"Jesus Fucking Christ, I don't want to know what you're wearing. What are you doing?"

"I'm, uh"—Wirbin wouldn't understand yet, because the CIO didn't fully understand yet—"this project, following a meeting with Tolemy—"

"That's that lesbian Karen Kahn?"

"She's not a lesbian."

"Then how do you explain the haircut?"

The CIO smiled despite himself.

"Dude, you never got back to me on my idea. You, me, Saint Marvin, Pascatastrophe, and Anil the Friendly Ghosh getting together somewhere."

"Yeah, um."

"'Yeah, um?' A very fucking eloquent rebuttal."

The CIO looked at his eleven off-centered, pastel-colored, word-filled shapes. He rubbed his right hand on his baldness and then across his eyes, to see if that would rearrange what he couldn't yet consciously correctly arrange. He scratched at nine years of nicks on his desk where the chair's armrests rubbed whenever he brought his face closer to the monitor to stare at noise. How had he let this all accrete: the furniture from campus services, the random photographs on the wall? Why hadn't he chosen what others had? Clean lines, Aeron chairs, nooks for spontaneous collaboration. That would have been the right setting for whatever he was doing with this slide.

Wirbin was still on the phone. He asked, "Do you know how important the endowment is?"

The CIO couldn't talk right now. He needed to work on his slide. "More important than Jho Low's piano but less important than world peace?"

"I'm being serious, dude. Did I ever tell you what happened after the *Times* article came out? Not about Blankfein. I know you know that story. But a week after the article comes out, I'm coming home to our co-op. And there's Winston from Ghana—he's our doorman, a super positive motherfucker—and *another* African guy wearing a shitty suit and, and, and, like a shirt without the right buttons or something else that's causing it to be fucked-up collar-wise. And then Winston says to me, 'Mr. Wirbin, may I present to you Mr. Beyobah.'"

"Yeboah."

"What?"

"Yeboah. You told me the story this summer, and you said the guy's name was Yeboah."

"Yeah, yeah. Excuse me, it's been a very long day, a very long day ending with a very short bottle. So I told you this?"

"You even told me about the stew."

"I did?"

"You said it was bad stew."

"It really was. It was very bad stew."

"I'm sorry to hear that, but I have to—"

"Hold on a second, man. I want to talk to you. That's why I called you. I've been doing some thinking. I want to talk about the big picture for once and not about fucking tactics. Think about schools in this country today, not Harvard and Yale, which are like fucking Stonehenge. Think about Duke, Emory, Northwestern, Michigan, Rice, Vandy, Wash. U., USC. Think about when we were kids. Who ever thought about those schools outside sports, unless you lived nearby? They were rich kid schools for regional rich kids—not idiots, mind you, smart regional rich kids. And, okay, for clever fucking parents from Edina who knew that Minnesotans were pretty rare shit in Nashville in the days before the Internet. But when you think about those schools now, people really admire them academically. Even jerkoffs at Goldman are impressed if someone's kid goes to Duke or Rice. And why? Because of the advances made in Rice's philosophy department?" Wirbin began laughing. "No one knows a fucking thing about what goes on in the classroom. Which is probably for the best. No, these schools are admired because they are filthy fucking rich.

"Look at *U.S. News*'s algorithms. Look at the campuses. You can feel the money in all the diversity you need to buy nowadays. You can smell it in all the new buildings that look like Apple Stores because every new college building, by law, must now look like a fucking Apple Store. And the schools with the most diversity and the most Apple Stores are winners *not* because they started with Coke stock or tobacco money, although that helps a whole fucking lot. The winners are the ones that have endowments that manage to grow even bigger and get more respect because of donations and investment performance. But that shit also works the opposite way. Think about—I don't know—BU. Why isn't it Rice? Money. Think about Chicago. Their endowment has stagnated. In 2007—I just looked this up on Wikipedia, of all random places—Chicago, Penn, Duke, Northwestern, Notre Dame all had 6 billion dollars, what we have now. A decade later? Those Catholic football fuck-nuts have 13 billion and Chicago has 8. Milton Friedman is lucky he's dead so he doesn't have to find that shit out. What's crazier is that because annual tuition has gone up at most places from, like, $35K to $50K, an endowment increasing from six to eight actually has *less* money as measured by student-tuition years. The numbers are fucking fascinating. The fact that we have to contribute a quarter-billion dollars a year to the school is mind-blowing. And the bottom line is *I'm* not going to let underperformance happen here, and not going to demean the education of every person with our diploma, by letting our reputation sink because of endowment performance or lazy fucking development. Do you get it?"

The CIO had to invest better. He had to reverse the numbers. He had to find more Karen Kahns. He had to be Karen Kahn.

"Hello? China calling...."

The CIO looked at his shapes. The answer was to get back to his shapes. But he spoke. "Do you think that I have hobbies or interests other than calculating the compounding effects of 1.5 percent annual outperformance? In twelve years, that would add 30 percent on *top* of the base performance and Trotter windfalls. That'd be 2 billion dollars—BU's endowment, right?—attributable to very small outperformance. I *know* that the school—the world—would be better if we had that. Yeboahs would outnumber kids from Exeter. And that outperformance should be possible, given the conventional people using conventional wisdom managing capital conventionally. *But*—and this is what I have to remember—conversations like this are happening at every endowment in the country. Well, maybe not with people asking each other if they are wearing pants, but how many Goldman Sachs bigwigs are on an investment committee of some pool of capital somewhere? Every one of them?"

"Fair."

"And every one of *their* conversations is probably the same as ours: aren't the benefits of modest, non-piggish outperformance so cool, so awe-*some* that we would be idiots for not getting us some of that? Please, Lord, I'm asking for only 1.5 percent more per year. But do the math. The only ones who have a tight strategy to increase their performance by 1.5 percent per year are, well, the Bogle purists who say, well, we used to pay more than 2 percent in aggregate fees and carry. So if we just cut *that* crap out... Yet, that has its own complications. You have to shoot the moon and call up Vanguard. You can't go halfway like CalPERS and obsess over who will provide you with petty discounts, leaving you adversely selected into less expensive active management with already obscenely rich firms. And so if getting that outperformance is *not* connected to the sincerity of your non-piggishness and not connected to the goodness of your use of funds and not connected to your *will* to actually get it done, then it's not connected to anything. It's connected to whether sixty managers are right often enough on the five, six, seven thousand aggregate consequential decisions they make every year." The CIO squinted at his PowerPoint. He tried to revive his celebration of being on the same side as Karen Kahn. "It's connected to your ability to avoid being overly fidgety on asset allocation but *also* not overly rigid. It's connected with consistently reading an infinitely influenced market in a way that, like, five people in the history of the world have been able to do. And you have to do all of the above while reporting to a board of very successful people who All Have Opinions and Are Always Right. I mean, those facts are fixed. You don't get to be on the board if you're not successful—way more successful by conventional metrics than us here in the counting house. Okay, maybe you get to be on the board if you have demonstrated a talent to be born to someone successful or a slightly more strategic talent of marrying someone successful."

The CIO could hear Wirbin laying down the phone, pouring more whisky, and then bumping into something. He said "fuck me" quietly before picking up the phone again.

"Anyway, you people gather four times per year to bite your tongues on what the market says I must be paid and find it a complete mystery how a person paid *this* much cannot do his basic job of outperformance. Because, well, I'm not actually investing but just finding other, hopefully better-at-this-game people to do it on our behalf, right? And so there are inevitably the sidebars, the shifts, the interference leading up to the cardinal rule of endowment management: when things go well, it's to the trustees' credit; when things go poorly, it must be the staff. Do you know how many CIOs Stanford has had since I've been here?"

Had Wirbin fallen asleep, whisky spilled on his—"Two?"

"Three. Penn? Three. Cornell? Four. Dartmouth? Three. Harvard?"

"A million."

"Exactly. Harvard has had one million CIOs. They walk down Boylston Street and give every Sean, Patrick, and Maureen a chance to roll the dice for ten minutes."

"Are you quitting on us, man?"

"That turnover isn't because CIOs *quit*. It's because of the corrosion of trust from conversations like this when everyone, no matter how friendly they act when joking about not wearing pants, judges from numbers up. For what job is better than this one when it goes well? Professors are curing diseases. Young Yeboahs are getting free tickets to the meritocracy. Rich kids are getting gluten- and/or cruelty-free dining halls. America, in all its privilege-y awfulness and privileged wonderfulness, is never purer or better than on a college campus. I was talking about this with Emily, or trying to. This *is* an honorable profession if anything is in the world of finance. But I desperately want my daughter to be—to be on Earth. Now, that's a whole knot of issues I may not want to pull on. Maybe it's Jewish guilt, at what I make, at being twelfth this year, at—" Could he get into it, about his father, with Wirbin? "But whatever the reason, I need *my* numbers to allow me to secretly swagger around campus like I used to. I was so proud that no one could detect my 'I paid for this shit' attitude, which was the most James Bond way to have an 'I paid for this shit' attitude."

"Jesus, dude. James Bond?"

"Just listen. I believe totally in outperformance as a good and noble use of my time on earth. Despite my self-image as a loner, I am also an irredeemable institutionalist. But I'm not exaggerating when I say I cannot spend my time on earth generating market returns after a strong head start. None of us *want* that. None of us can live with that. I... I... I...?"

"What?"

"I don't know. I don't even know what I was going to say." He looked at his PowerPoint again.

Could he explain Kahnian simplicity, his hunger for it, to Wirbin? Did it even make sense? Was it her simplicity he admired, or just the fact that she wins? And maybe the CIO's own ovals and trapezoids and maybe-there-a-square were thus just patterns in the sand, ready to get washed away by the market? "I am not too proud, for the record. I'm open to tapping whatever ideas we can tap."

"You're on this Michael Hermann thing, too? Is this what this call is about?"

The CIO looked at the ceiling. Then: "You called me."

"Got it, man. I'm the one holding the endowment back by calling you because Michael Fucking Hermann is going to give us all the answers."

"I've never met Michael Hermann," the CIO said as he checked his words for any hinting—testing—about Hermann.

"Well, I knew Michael Hermann before he had 8 billion dollars"—it was higher, reportedly—"and was the hundredth-richest man on earth. Thirty-five years ago, he was just the kid most likely to get his teeth kicked in by pretty much everyone who knew him. Because the fucker will stare at you with this sinister grin as if he just ate your brain and is registering how stupid it tastes. I've tried over the years to give him a fucking chance. I'm hoping that at some point he will find a woman or man or beagle or sex robot to love and make him a human being. But until then, you people are *pretending*: pretending that it's going to happen, pretending that he has some 'secret' he's going to share with you. Here's what you should pretend: pretend that he went to Yale and is an asshole to *them*. Which is probably what he thinks happened."

The CIO could hear Wirbin struggling to stand up. He grunted and started pacing, his footfalls barely audible on expensive Chinese carpet.

"Let me tell you a story about your hero Michael Hermann. In late 2010, we're doing our biggest campaign ever. And Hermann's smug thin face and creepy-ass eyebrows were still out there as one of the 'Heroes of the Crisis.' As if being right on the timing of a market crash meant that he was Robin Fucking Hood. Yeah, right. I'll give the fucker credit, though. At least he's not a one-hit wonder like Paulson or Phil Fucking Falcone. But anyway, I suck it up and call Hermann in his bat cave in Lake Forest. I am my most winning self. Humble. Congratulatory without being fake. Friendly without trying to snow him that we've *ever* been friends. But I know the rules, and so my nose is so far up his ass it's coming out of his mouth. I explain how important the campaign is, explain that this is the time to put the school in a different category of competitiveness and sustainability. And I ask him for 50 million bucks.

"Do I really think's he going to go from zero—and that's not an exaggeration, the fucker has not given us a single fucking nickel since he graduated—to 50 million bucks after one phone call? I don't know, but he was already then worth, what, 4 billion, 5 billion, so what the fuck does it *matter*? And he says, without pausing to even pretend to think about it, 'I'm not going to do that,' as if I asked him to hand over the cup of coffee he was drinking because I could really use some caffeine. I try to give him the benefit of the doubt. I ask him, 'How much do you want to do?' And he says, 'I am not going to give you anything,' this time as if I'm asking for money to buy crack. Like I would thank him years from now for that stern 'no' back then, when my life was falling apart.

"Well, I lose it. I said, 'Okay, fucknuts, I'm not going to argue with you. I've got a fucking life. I also have to call a list of donors who aren't certifiable sociopaths. But out of curiosity, what is the reason for this? Something political? Some hard-on you get from getting your revenge for how you *think* you were treated thirty years ago? Or have we offended your asshole ego by already not unveiling the Hermann School of Finance, given your amazing generosity to date? I mean, what the fuck is it?' And he said, 'I find it distracting.' *I find it distracting*. Like he's Bartleby the fucking Scrivener."

The CIO laughed.

"Yeah, I went to college, if you didn't fucking notice from this relationship of ours. Anyway, when the Legend of Stingy Billionaire Recluse Michael Hermann comes up at Goldman or at some random-ass dinner party, I don't even bring this story up 'cause it enrages me so much. I just wait for the conversation to pass. Occasionally, someone will do the math and ask me if I overlapped with him at school. I say I barely remember him. I so fucking wish that was the case. But for reasons I cannot fathom, I've come to really, really like saying 'I find it distracting' as a joke that no one gets but me. The type of joke you fucking like, now that I think about it. When my thirteen-year-old daughter wanted to go to Amanyara in the Turks and Caicos, chaperoned only by her friend's college-age *half*-sister whom I'm 99 percent certain has a coke habit, I said, 'Even if I was dead, I would find a way to say no.' When she started to whine and ask why, I said, 'I find it distracting.' That is not particularly helpful as a parenting strategy, by the way, but fuck it. I do find it distracting. I actually find a lot of shit distracting. But what Michael Hermann finds distracting about telling his accountant to write a check, I still have no fucking clue.

"But you wanna know what I find the *most* distracting? Every two or three years, jerkoffs on the committee start talking behind my back about Michael Hermann. As if he's done *anything*. As if I haven't bled my life dry for this fucking school. Is it because I am the asshole investment banker, and we have to get the 'real' investors involved? Real investors like you? 'I think we are going to do 6 percent,' yeah right, you lying sack of shit. I let that pass because I like you, because I have sympathy for all this performance bullshit, and because I know you people can't help but round your numbers up. But you know what? See how you do without me. See how empty and dirty you feel when the asshole tells you that he finds every last fucking one of you distracting. Or better yet, just fuck off altogether."

And Shanghai went silent for the night.

Office
October 26

"Dear Limited Partner," the email started. The CIO's eyes pinballed around disconnected words, bottom paragraph, middle paragraph, obfuscation, clichés, nonsense. His scratched his nails into his palms. His chest contracted. His vision blurred. He stood up fast and dizzying, shut the door, and took just enough control of his rage-shaking hands to make sure the door was clicked shut.

He read the email from PMD again: "Dear Limited Partner, While this situation was unfortunate and effectively unforeseeable, we believe we applied lessons learned over our history to not expose more investor capital—"

You fucking scumbag, Polansky. You fat fucking scumbag. I should forward this email to every LP in the world and start an investigation into your fucking jet and your cheap watches, to claw back everything—everything—we have ever paid you. You fucking—

You marked the deal *up* the quarter before it went bankrupt?

Effectively unforeseeable? Sixteen percent of the fund, you lying sack of—

The CIO grabbed the edge of the laptop and twisted it as he did too often. This time, he heard a crack. He twisted the laptop further, still trying to read and not read and believe and not believe the lies and blather and consequences on *his* second-quarter performance. Polansky's email was, somehow, everything: the world rebuilt on crowded bets, high-speed trading, SPACs, cross-fund bailouts, reset hurdles, self-reported valuations, Fed-fed bull markets, management fee offsets, new schemes, endless schemes, fake edges, criminal edges, Valeant, Theranos, IMDB.

I can't have this happen now. I will not have his happen now.

The CIO twisted the laptop more, kicked his leg as if to fling off shackles, and lifted the computer over his head. He should throw everything in it out of the window and onto campus, fertilizing the pursuit of human thought and human character with this fucking shit.

He closed his eyes. He felt his life throbbing, face reddening, sweat starting. He shouted as loudly as he could, as quietly as he could, through clenched teeth.

I cannot be responsible for all the problems of the world.

He opened his eyes, blinded, and twisted harder at the laptop's screen, his fingers shaking. The casing's crack widened.

Just shout it: I cannot be responsible for all the problems of the world.

Are you *not* shouting now, the CIO asked himself, because you're not him? Because not being him is your life's only victory—with the vanquished a bitter, undisciplined, humorless loser who should have died first?

Does that matter anymore?

Is that even fucking true?

The CIO threw the useless laptop on the floor. It thunked louder than he expected it would. He tried to somehow silently stomp it, Joe Pesci style, you lying sack of shit.

He ground it instead under his foot. He gripped his hands as hard as he could, through the pain, trying to make them into mallets.

He stopped. Lisa was coming closer to his office. He was on the floor now, on all fours, picking up and not picking up the busted computer. Splinters of age shot through his bony knees.

I cannot be responsible for all the problems of the world.

Lisa was walking away. With each of her receding steps, the CIO felt the injustice grow in his throat, in his hands.

He twisted the screen off. He took the remnant keyboard and hit it as hard he could on the ground, to fuck it for the pain the ground was causing to his knees, to his hope, to his Karen Kahn shapes, his Karen Kahn escape. He couldn't see. He needed this rage to end. He needed this laptop to be dust.

I need everyone to stop disappointing me.

The laptop couldn't be slammed again on the ground like he needed to. He couldn't let them hear him. They had probably already heard him.

Well if you have, take this as a lesson and get out. Get out before you recommend investing again with Mark Polansky. With anyone.

When, God, is it *my* turn to get the infallible GPs?

Another disallowed scream traveled through his fingers. He clawed feverishly at the busted laptop trying to pick off letters, pulling on edges, bringing intensity under his fingernails, into his knees, inside his body to shut people up.

I cannot be responsible for all the problems in the world.

The CIO exhaled, now on all fours. He would have to think of an excuse.

When was the last time he was this angry? When Peter, his console privileges taken away for a month, yelled at him, "Who are you? All you do is push around papers."

Jane had told the CIO that he—the CIO—was going to therapy if he ever got that angry in front of them again. The CIO begged Jane to understand that we can't *only* validate Peter's feelings.

"I understand," she said, "but that's not what we're talking about right now."

All he had asked his son was, "Do you have any idea what sort of path you are on?"

He had asked it with the purest of intentions: Who do you think is going to give you more second or *tenth* chances than the ones you've already had because you're a rich white American kid?

He hadn't even said the truth.

The truth: You cannot imagine how much I want to punch you in the teeth. The truth: We were one generation of *not* being losers before you became yet more proof of reversion to the mean. The truth: I worry all the time that you are the sum of my bad choices, to fund the Brian Parks, to admire the Brian Parks, to push my hands as hard as I can into this pile of parts that was once a laptop in order to erase all the inputs and outputs that came through this busted window into—

The CIO pushed his thumb into the screen, watching the thumbprint spread. He wondered what the screen tasted like. He slid it towards the crashed-open laptop base as if the computer could heal itself.

And then he flattened himself hard on the floor, his face near the broken keys, blurry and too close. His chest was knocking into the wood. Was he going to cry? Could he cry? Could he sharpen this laptop shard and shove it into this throat, to speak no more?

All he was asking them to do was make money for a good school, to somehow correct the central injustice of America today of the Mark Polanskys *temporarily* performing but still able to conjure wealth to fly in private jets over kids in neighborhoods doomed by opioids and gangs and trauma and dreadful schools.

How can a nation recover if a person like Emily believes that *dulce et decorum est* rich like Reese Weatherspoon?

And who the fuck was he to tell the world what it is? I can see it only because I have justified half of my fucking life deciding that if you are a good investor, you are a good investor. So what is the opposite? Am *I* the centrifuge that is the financialization of the American economy, the American soul? Am I the mutually assured silence—the protection racket—for white and Asian guys good at math?

The Great Big I-Won't-Look-at-Yours-if-You-Don't-Look-at-Mine?

At least his father, the downsized employee of an American manufacturer, *made* something.

Two nights ago, the CIO had dreamed of Michael Hermann.

Now, the CIO turned his gaze skyward in his office, half expecting to see Hermann reaching out to God on the Sistine Chapel of his ceiling.

Fuck, that hurt.

The dust, light-raised, tickled his nose. He was tempted to pee right into the floor, the culmination of his filth.

He blew an R three inches. He tried to blow the E farther.

He folded his bent legs into his chest and hugged his kneecaps as tight as he could. He held tighter, to compress a fetus into a ball, into one dimension. This was hurting, too. But he hugged even tighter, squeezing the air out his belly, sparking a cramp in his thigh, twisting his neck to complaint. He wanted more pain. He wanted to make himself cry. He wanted to empty himself of air.

Are paper-pushing losers responsible for all the problems of the world?

The CIO un-balled himself. He was hyperventilating, dizzy with vertigo. He had no idea how long he had been like that.

He got back onto hands and knees, still huffing, his body shaking. He crushed his right hand into a pile of letters, trying to draw blood.

He suddenly thought about the metaphor of the age, or just of his father. (He was too shaky to separate which was which.) They—our enemies, the riggers, the elite, the UnAmericans—are in the cockpit. *We* must storm it to save the nation.

But what if they aren't in the cockpit but in the passenger seats of the private jet, discussing watches, lusting for others' wives, cropping vacation photos for Instagram, making Excel prove what they want it to conclude? Isn't the task, then, Emily, to starve capital to the fakers in the passenger seats? Or is it *unparticipating*: revealing the fakers in the passenger seats? Isn't that a worthy enough use of a life—the one-time parachute we get for our soul?

Or are those two different tasks?

And you are never told which parachute works.

Trustee (call)
Office
November 2 (unscheduled)

The autumn foliage had peaked, but not the puffer coats. Gazing out the window, the CIO could learn from the world outside, from that campus that was more of the endowment than the endowment, from that Norway spruce that needed no returns to grow and change and grow again.

I went to the woods because I wished to live deliberately.

He shifted back to his screen. The market had fallen 2.6 percent at the open that morning. It had recovered to down only 1 percent. But there were another three hours before the close—three hours in which the market did nothing, three hours in which the traders (or the algorithms) took off for long lunches or to tune the machines—before the market's second chance to grab you by your throat as you were thinking about the day's escape.

The CIO was ignoring it all.

He didn't like his new computer, thinner, with different ribbons. He didn't like it because the lie to campus IT still embarrassed him. He also didn't like the guy who had destroyed the old one. It was his father, his son, junior varsity Wirbin rage to avoid dealing with the problems of the world. Hard, absurd work, Peter, is the way to deal with the problems of the world.

But his computer had PowerPoint, and that's all he (and endowment management itself) needed now. He had three sherbet ovals and three trapezoids. They did not read Karen-Kahn simple but Intro-to-Finance banal. Where was the line between the two? Or was there no line? Maybe simple was banality gilded by success. For a week, the CIO had ignored the requests from the team to put yet one more GP—"this is sort of interesting," they'd say—on the assembly line to be analyzed. He had not even made any manager decisions. Since switching their Asian long equity exposure to Ledo Road, reupping with VBV, and committing to the oil and gas minerals fund, they had done nothing. Emily was smart enough to not bring up the cannabist again. Karen Kahn and Miller Lamb did not require action. He and Calvin both ignored the mounting emails from Mount Mitchell asking whether they needed any more information for their "diligence." When Calvin asked about whether they should dig into the MIT-anchored hedge fund trading Hungarian McNuggets, the CIO told him that investing was not reacting. Maybe Calvin had believed him.

He needed more shapes. These trapezoids were embarrassing.

Portfolio theory? All passive? Best athlete? Classic Swensen?

What was his *strategy*? To diagnose and not cure? To believe in a lonely fight? For an answer to come in the trees? The trees themselves upending the conventional truths?

He tried to shift his chair back. His office seemed to be getting smaller; the old clutter misled him into imagining there was space to be liberated.

He didn't think about what we has doing as he was doing it. "Is Mr. Trotter there, please?"

Marvin picked up the phone two minutes later. "Whine, whine, whine."

"Sorry?"

Marvin said again in his Buffalo accent: "Wine, wine, wine. Impenetrably fragmented."

Ah: wine. "Sorry for interrupting you."

"Glad to find an excuse to escape that meeting."

"They still ask you to attend meetings?" Marvin was eighty-one.

"More like they tolerate me as a social service."

The CIO laughed in a warm blanket of a Trotterism. God, to have your wealth—not your mouth—prove that you knew what was noise...

Marvin didn't say anything else.

"What was the meeting about?"

"Inventory and margins. Don't even need to know the question. But three hundred SKUs in one category. We deserve the dead stock."

At a routine dinner before a board meeting, the CIO would have pressed. He found—they all found—Marvin's accomplishments, twinkling calm, and 2 billion dollars endlessly probe-worthy. Its inexplicability, on this gentle grocer, made it even more insistent to understand it. But now the CIO didn't feel like learning what dead stock was. It was exhausting to think about someone who knew more about how the world worked.

"I, um, I wanted to let you know the market hasn't been helpful."

Marvin didn't speak.

"With a crash, at least we know where we stand. The question then is just the shape and pace of the recovery. But this quarter has been about as sloppy as I can remember."

"Lots of quarters in life."

Is that a joke or just folksy reassurance, the CIO wondered as he stared at his PowerPoint. He needed someone to see *through* the six shapes and bring them down to three instead of where they seem to be heading: a spill of clichés and truths that needed to climb back to ten, eleven to be comprehensive. "Do you have any, you know—" The CIO couldn't get himself to finish the question.

"Lots of quarters in life."

The CIO didn't know if Marvin knew he was repeating himself. Was he distracted? Was the CIO boring him? Or was this just the caution in advance of Alzheimer's?

The CIO lowered his volume and said, "I heard from"—this was right—"President Corso, who told me that you suggested something about Michael Hermann."

"Suggested?"

Silence.

"Sorry. I didn't mean to."

"I talked to Michael. I found it interesting."

"On the endowment?"

Marvin chuckled. "I'm not sure Michael cares in that direction."

Yes, Trotter was the fifth person to sign the Giving Pledge, but the CIO still needed to force Trotter to be seared by the heat of *his* 300-million-dollar donation, 5 percent of the endowment, incinerated by the market this quarter alone. He wanted to get a rise. He wanted help.

"I think Ben thinks the opposite," the CIO said, eventually.

"What now?"

"Ben thinks Michael Hermann is looking for revenge against the school or something."

"I'm not sure what Ben thinks."

The CIO was silent. He scratched his hand where there was still, he was certain, a faint imprint of the keyboard keys he had tried to grind into the floor. Then he asked, "What do you think I should do?"

Marvin was silent. The CIO wondered how he could clarify the question. He wondered if Marvin was this way twenty-five years ago.

Finally, Marvin answered, "Do you know what Eisenhower said?"

The CIO didn't answer that he didn't know a single thing Eisenhower had said. This fact was not meant to be unpatriotic. The CIO only mumbled, "I'm not sure...."

"If you can't solve a problem, enlarge it."

Investment team
Office
November 4

Emily and the two analysts were waiting for him to speak, and maybe to act.

"How do you want to do this?" the CIO finally asked.

"I would have preferred to do this by email," Emily said.

To me? To Lodgepole? That the CIO didn't know meant that this tone of hers was new.

Because of the numbers? Because of what she had heard? "They know we're not going to re-up?"

"I would say that I was clear. I told their IR guy that the meeting would be a 'challenging' use of their time, considering Fund II and III. But he is so effing upbeat. He said that he and Kevin Doherty would love to stop by, as they'll be in the neighborhood anyway."

"That must be some neighborhood." The CIO placed his hand on his chin and willed it to not rub his eyes. He looked above the three people in his office and studied where the ceiling met the wall.

The trapezoids and ovals and Karenkahnian simplicity were still not working.

The destruction of the computer was still not working.

Emily glanced at the analysts as the CIO continued to say nothing. What else had the CIO not asked about her? Was *she* having a full life right now?

"I would prefer," she said, "for us to acknowledge that it is my responsibility to do this, but..."

"But?"

"I know what will happen. Doherty will immediately look to you because I'm a female POC and you're the boss."

"Then I can do it."

"I would not say that I am comfortable with that."

"We could do it together. Countdown one-two-three, 'bye-bye'?"

"I would not say that I am comfortable with that either."

"Okay, Emily. I—" Why was this so difficult? Why was he scared of everyone now? "Please just tell me what you'd like to do in a non-conditional tense."

Both analysts were watching them, chins alertly up, deer at a roadside. He didn't know if they knew whose side to be on. He wanted to shout that there were no sides to be on.

"I would like to have the data speak for itself. Fund II is now locked in at a 1.02x ROI, Fund III will be lucky to return capital. They have a 28-percent loss ratio, which blows up the risk rating, and they have no companies anywhere close to monetization. And Fund IV is effing random. They have, let's see, a tackle company—"

"Football tackles?"

"Fishing tackle."

"Do people in the fishing business talk about moats?" the CIO asked, almost sincere. One of the analysts, at least, was smiling. "Or is that untechnical, from a body-of-water perspective?"

Emily went on, "They also invested in an urgent care chain in Oregon."

"Maybe it's a 'synergistic' roll-up. Portland Hooks and Retinas?"

"I would say it's incredible how pathetic they have become. You push them on their system and inputs, and... nothing. I don't know why they are in business."

"I think that may be a little..." He had once tried to implant a morality: performance failures as a subset of the human comedy.

Then he'd tried to smash that morality as a virus in his laptop.

Emily leaned forward. She was wearing her hair in tight braids today. He took it as preparation to shame him for any excuse he could make. It could have also just been a hairstyle. Her authority did not allow him to avoid eye contact as she said, "I would say it's better if we talk alone?"

The CIO needed Wirbin here. (Wirbin had still not called.) Or he at least needed to stand up. He was going to stand up. He could stand up and turn around to show the analysts the campus, what they were dealing with, where they could all run. But he didn't move or talk as they haltingly left.

The CIO: "I gather you didn't want others to hear you praising me for my old and improved behavior?"

"I don't think it's appropriate to joke about this."

"I am not sure what you want anymore. You talked to me about respecting your professional reputation. You pointed out that me walking out of meetings was not helpful in that department. Nor was lecturing undifferentiated GPs on their unstrategy. I've tried to stop."

"What were you doing in your office last week? Were you destroying something?"

He needed to keep his body still, to allow himself to be crushed into the invisible. For all he wanted was to push his head between his legs and rub his hands hard over every part of his face. "Is this your job now?" he said, almost winded by the effort. "To police my behavior?"

She didn't respond.

"What would I have been destroying? Do you think I have secret evidence of something?"

Nothing.

"And what would I have evidence of? *Better* performance? Like I didn't want to shame Duke or MIT or little Reed College by being too good?" The CIO looked at his lap, not making eye contact, enlarging the problem. He was desperate to tell her as much as he could about his father's stock trading, his anger, his shitty career. Those facts were not generational adversity, but the CIO's life was the only one he could change. And yet, he couldn't risk her telling him why she didn't want to hear about any of it. So, wincing, he looked up and at Emily. "Please, just tell me what you want. Is it more money? A better title? More responsibility? I'm happy to talk about it. We need you here."

"I would say that we should talk about all those issues at the appropriate time. But right now, I just want to do my job."

"And I'm stopping you?"

"I would ask what you call being the most checked out that I've ever seen you? Destroying university property? Refusing to advance manager recs?"

"Manager recs like PMD and Lodgepole?"

She stared at him.

"I am not blaming you for those—"

"Not blaming me basically invalidates my work. Like, what am I here for then?"

The CIO swiveled slightly in his chair. He was starving to get back to his accusing new computer and finish his shapes. "I'm not blaming you because—I mean, don't you ever just want to burn the whole thing down?"

Please, he thought, don't take that racially.

Emily picked some lint off her blouse. "Last year," she said, now looking at him, "we were in Boston doing diligence on Yockey Westhelle. We met one-on-one with everyone from the directors up. I would have thought they would have briefed the team on what type of questions they were likely to get, as they were raising only 400 million dollars. The second guy I met with had been there for eight years after two years at Evercore. Economics major from Dartmouth. Hunter McGee III. Edgar and I laughed about how his name was so effing perfect: Bland Privilege the Third. I asked him if he thought the generalist model or specialist model worked better in PE. *You* taught me to ask real questions and not waste time judging how well a mid-level guy can recite bullet points from a pitch deck."

"I did?"

Emily shook her head, amazed (but maybe kindly). "Hunter McGee III was so effing proud of his deep voice that projected 'I am a winner.' He kept on making the most obvious points to highlight the wisdom of Yockey's generalist model. 'The ability to move tactically across sectors,' that kind of stuff. I would say I was as neutral as I could have been when I asked him to describe *any* tradeoffs. Talk like an investor, I wanted to say. Or at least talk like a *person*. But I would say that he didn't even stop for a second before giving the most smug answer: 'From the coal face, it's hard to see any material ones.' He proceeded to give us the most effing elementary description of investment underwriting, as if I were in high school. He shifted between addressing Edgar and me. But I would say he definitely lingered just a bit more on the most basic points with me. To this day, I regret not asking, 'Are you talking down to me because I'm Black, a woman, or an LP?'"

The CIO realized that he was holding his breath.

"So do I ever want to burn down why Hunter McGee III was unembarrassed to treat me like that?"

The CIO pushed his face forward, to receive the answer, for all of the winners.

"That's nihilism."

"And?"

"I don't do nihilism."

Lower-middle market private equity firm
Conference room
November 12

The CIO sighed as he watched his team and Lodgepole's IR guy leave the conference room. Effing upbeat as advertised, the IR guy packed up the Fund IV pitchbooks and his iPad as if he had just been told he had been given a 40-million-dollar commitment. Emily looked as if Hunter McGee III had just given her a bucket and a mop.

"I hope this is okay," Kevin Doherty said when he and the CIO were alone.

"Clearly, you're not up to date on microaggressions."

"Sorry?" Doherty's blond hair was graying but not enough to make him look credibly mature. Maybe it was because his hard bent nose, seemingly from some childhood sports injury, begged you to reach across the table to straighten it. He picked at his fingernails. "I just wanted to make sure that there is nothing you wanted, you know, to tell me directly."

The CIO had been married too long to remember how breakups work, emotionally. "I can't think of anything."

They sat for ten infinite seconds.

And then Doherty tried: "This doesn't have anything to do with something you heard about Gilp?"

Mike Gilpin was Doherty's partner. The CIO leaned forward. "What would I have heard?"

"That he's thinking of running for Congress."

On what platform, the CIO wondered? Poor investment returns? Private equity lives matter? But he said, "I'm not sure why you couldn't ask that in front of my team, sparing me apologizing on behalf of White Men Everywhere and you specifically. For the record, when a GP asks us to cover the ears of the children, it's usually about a coming story in the *New York Post* or someplace like that about a married senior partner using generationally inappropriate drugs with a young unmarried person, sometimes of a surprising gender but seemingly always in Miami. I once had a manager stop by a week after the *Post* reported that *he* was divorcing his wife for cheating on him with her life coach. The guy never mentioned it. The most interesting fact of that story was that the coach charged $12,000 per month. It was never clear if that would have been more or less without the sex."

The CIO was exhausted by the act. Doherty didn't even smile. For some reason, this made the CIO feel slightly better about how wryly he could drown.

"Okay" is all Doherty said in a high voice, Midwestern, but closer to Kermit the Frog than ideal. "I guess you got everything figured out."

Emily had given Doherty the facts. The CIO hadn't even needed to finish with pablum about appreciating them coming in.

He said now, "While we lean hard on a theory that it is good for our managers to be actively involved in managing our money, the decision is about the experience across the funds."

Doherty looked around at the endowment's scratched up, suffocating, college-issue conference room. He pushed back his seat, put his hands on the armrests like a paraplegic gathering strength, and said, "Thanks for your time."

What was his relationship to these guys? He met them for ninety minutes each year for five, ten years. Were they acquaintances? Business partners? Fee-paying schnooks and fee-receiving crooks? Everything all at once? Was he supposed to hug Doherty as Doherty crawled into his next life as a zombie fund (and how wretched would he be about fees)? Was he supposed to ask Doherty if he planned on becoming an adjunct at some regional business school? An "adviser" at a more successful buddy's shop? A freelance banker emailing teasers from a decades-old Yahoo account?

Doherty seemed frozen. Maybe he couldn't survive the walk of shame back to his cruise director in the lobby.

The CIO asked, "Is there anything else?"

"Well, one thing I'm *not* going to miss is LP meetings"—why are you telling me this, the CIO thought—"LPs pretending that they are listening to how we've evolved, LPs pretending that they are being, um, compassionate or something when they tell me they're not investing with us. I am like, 'Yeah, that totally makes sense. Why would I *want* to support my kids anymore? Thank *you*.' You know what I don't understand? Why more people don't act like you and just get to the point. Are people that dense that they don't know that my heart is, you know, beating out of my chest because my livelihood depends on whether they are going to make a commitment to our fund? It's like my entire life has come down to one thing: waiting for people to email me back. Maybe that's what everyone's life is nowadays."

The CIO needed to check his phone. Wirbin had still not called.

Doherty grabbed the end of his busted nose. "Even when things were going better, road shows sucked. The good news is that I'll never again have to hear Gilp tell an LP about meeting a CEO when he was 'literally' a truck driver. It got to the point where I wanted to literally blow my brains out. I'm not sure where I am going with this. Oh yeah, I mean with you—I don't need to kiss your ass."

The CIO stared back through tired eyes.

"At least we can talk like, you know, this. Like, uh, human beings."

"I've always been a very human being."

Doherty almost smiled. "Gilp and I liked coming here. We liked your whole quirky professor thing. You are definitely one of the smartest LPs out there. Granted, how we decided if LPs were smart was whether they invested with us. The crazy thing is that I haven't changed my mind on that. Anyway, um, where was I? Oh, yeah: I don't know if you've ever sat on this side of the table. But, like, LP meetings basically come—came—in four or five flavors. You have the grillers, who want to know every portfolio company's margins, market share to the second decimal place, CEO's age, the color of his wife's pubic hair. They scribble into notebooks or type constantly into iPads like they are going to have to show notes at the final exam. The weird thing is that some guys bring in, um, hardcover notebooks with silk bookmarks and then a *woman* will bring in some shitty spiral notebook that she must have swiped from her kids. A thousand years from now, people are going to be like, why did someone take notes on a portfolio company CEO's wife's pubic hair?"

"I got it on the—"

"Sorry, I don't know where I'm going with this. Oh, yeah: the grillers, though, are slightly better than, um, the testers, who do the same stenographing or whatever you call it but also throw questions *at* you." Doherty made the metaphor overly complete with arm gestures. "What's the EBIT versus EBITDA? What's their Medicaid billing protocol? After fifteen years, I still don't know the right answer when they ask us about depreciation schedules. Should I round up? Round down? Make up an answer? I'd ask, um, you, has any LP ever made a decision from those kinds of questions? It didn't seem like that to us. It seemed like LPs had already rejected us before the meeting. Because they would have given Jason excuses that didn't make any sense, like, 'You guys seem to shun asset-light businesses,' or reasons they would have had even before they opened the pitch. That's at least when they gave Jason reasons. Now they don't even respond.

"Where was I going... Oh, yeah, on the complete opposite side of the street from the other flavors, you have the statues. I can never tell if they are strategic or just, you know, culturally that way. Because of our numbers, some of those types now look at us like we're auto mechanics, as if the only question is exactly how we are going to rip them off. But you know what? The last kind of meeting, where everyone is buddy-buddy"—Doherty flapped his hand between the CIO and himself—"which I thought I really liked, was actually the worst. In those meetings, it'd be like 'we' are the good guys, the smart money, executing our awesome strategy together. Those LPs would just nod their head and say yep, yep, yep, yep." High-pitched Doherty sounded like a dog, maybe not unintentionally. "But I've learned that those people are probably just nice to everyone. And, if they actually invest with you, they are the *least* likely to support you through bad times."

The CIO scratched hard on his wrist. He wanted to crawl under the table and let sleep take him for a hundred years. Where would Corso and Marvin and Wirbin be when they measured his trapezoid solutions, his fraudulence, his distance from investing? What was Wirbin trying to accomplish by never calling him again?

If I had a wartime consigliere, a Sicilian, I wouldn't be in this shape.

Who do I have? A thin-skinned banker and a grocery store billionaire who may be in mental decline.

"I, uh, get it," Doherty continued. "Everyone wants to convince themselves of the same thing: that they have put money into a machine. But for fifteen years, I've wanted to scream that you people don't understand how improvised this business is. Maybe it's our fault, on this side of the table: we, this whole industry, created this, uh, myth that we can be money machines. Proprietary deal flow. Value-adding system. Our 'processes,' which are what? Diligence checklists, because we all read the same book by that Indian doctor guy. But what do we do? We find the best deals we can, knowing it doesn't matter if the deal came from an investment bank or a friend of a friend, knowing that there are—like, what?—five hundred other firms wanting the same thing: sustainable competitive advantages, recurring revenue, low customer acquisition costs, and recession-proof variable costs that provide operating leverage in a bull market. We want CEOs that are like Steve Jobs but, you know, somehow ended up running companies that make fishing lures. And we only want to pay eight times EBITDA so we can sneak out a little arbitrage at exit.

"And what do we *do*? We write memos and hire consultants or call randos through GLG. We risk the company's forecasts by a lot, or however much we need to say we're risking them but still produce a decent return. Sometimes we don't have to wait long to see if we messed up. But basically, we wait to see how close we got to what we wanted and try our best to right the ship when it's not happening." Doherty squeezed the end of his nose and ran his hand through his blond-gray hair. "Or, you tell me: maybe people who looked at a guy from Michigan State and another guy with a 3.1 GPA from Cornell and said 'are you kidding me' were right? Do Vista and General Atlantic and Berkshire have a money machine?"

The CIO wouldn't tell him. He couldn't tell him. He was using his brain's last energy to simultaneously calculate and not calculate what would have happened, for the school, for the CIO's numbers, had he invested with GA, Berkshire, or even a second-quartile VC fund at the start of the boom instead of with Lodgepole.

"To keep kinda sane," Doherty continued, "a person in this business has to accept that other guys will end up richer and more successful. I *was* pretty good at that, but now when I hear about someone posting a 10x deal in three years, I am sick to my stomach. It's like a priest getting proof that there is no God. It's like God telling the priest that there is no God. But I, but I... I just assumed that everyone was bluffing—that life is bluffing—and that the only question is how much."

What was his relationship to these guys? What were these guys? He thought he had located Doherty's personality. His job was to locate Doherty's personality. He had attributed persistent hunger—and unglamorous, looked-over value—to Michigan State, Red America, and the working-class bent nose. And the product of that function: real economic damage to the school.

"Were we really any worse than everyone else?" Doherty didn't pause for the answer. "We tried hard. If this business is 40 percent timing, 40 percent luck, and 20 percent skill, why not us? Gilp really *wants* a career in public service. I coach soccer in Bridgeport. For, like, poor, um, African-American kids. We are not trying to strip businesses or fire people. We aren't competing on how little diligence we do. We are not putting in crazy assumptions. We aren't inflicting bullshit fees on companies. We never tried to sell a GP stake to a group like Alderine. We're just trying to help companies grow and make money for them, for you, for us along the way. And we put up with a lot to get there: the assholes, the endless negotiations by lawyers over edge-case nonsense, the random shit that can happen to any company any day.

"When I told my brother—he still lives in Grand Rapids—that you gave us tens of millions of dollars and Brown and Johns Hopkins did too, he couldn't believe that could happen. I bet in a few years that I'm not going to be able to believe that that happened either. And you guys weren't stupid for doing it. Gilp *was* good at investing. I wasn't horrible—look at Fund I—even if I shifted too much of my focus to administrative bullshit. So what happened? Why couldn't we build the machine that people wanted us to build? Private equity is the king of Wall Street. Kids that went to places like here, that I didn't even dream of applying to, angle for the chance to run Excel models for guys like us. Crazy, right? I just—I just want someone, once, to know how it *feels* to fail, to be looking at the speedometer to see if you've reached escape velocity only to realize you're not going to make it."

The CIO needed him to stop, to disappear, to die. The CIO would give him a commitment just to leave, so that the CIO could be alone in his office to stand up over everything, to stand on his desk, to throw something again, against the window, for escape.

But Doherty was still talking: "I'm not sure why I'm telling you this, but do you know how I spend my nights? My ex-wife and kids are in what was once *my* house, sleeping under child support math calculated off such different Lodgepole management fee expectations that they will not be able to process what's going to happen. And every single night, I'm in a condo doing the math of the alternate universe, not about deals that returned 1.5x instead of 1.8. I'm talking about life-changing stuff that was in our grasp. There were five fund-making deals that we could have done and skipped for stupid reasons. There were six shit deals we shouldn't have done. And there were four we sold way, way too early. That's fifteen decisions over a decade, mainly in Funds II and III, that we were close on. All we had to do was say yes, no, yes, no fifteen times. That takes like a minute, right? To do that? Had we done it, people would literally think I'm a genius. And now I don't even know where I'm going. Or going with this." Doherty laughed. "And Jason probably thinks I've saved the firm."

Doherty looked at the closed door. Then looked down at his shoes, as he picked at his fingernails. He started talking again. This was never going to end. "I now get why I needed your people to leave. It's their *age*. The hardest thing about these LP meetings is them—all the junior LPs. A lot of these girls are really attractive, and—where was I? Oh, yeah: I can take from *you* whatever contempt you have for us. You paid for it. But I can't take it from some girl two years out of Harvard who can't imagine how much we want to succeed. Investing is really fucking hard, much harder than asking questions about investing. It's the difference between fishing and throwing a fish in the water. But these Harvard girls look at us as tired, failed, asshole men. On the phone they have sleepy voices, like I'm interrupting their nap." He made his high voice even higher. "'Yeah... yeah... okay... that's interesting.'" Doherty stopped. He looked around the room as if for the first time aware of where he was. He grabbed harder on the armrests. "This may be the last LP meeting of my life. So I guess, maybe unconsciously or whatever, I couldn't have this one be with people who think investing is running a highlighter through *Pioneering Portfolio Management*. I get it. The numbers suck. There is no alternate universe. But just once I wish someone looked me in the eye and said, 'I know you tried your best. I know you sacrificed a lot.' I mean, where did we get this power to make hundreds of millions of dollars grow or disappear? Why do we even do it?"

Doherty pushed the heel of his hand up into his cheek, under the hard bend of his nose. He looked at the CIO.

Was the CIO supposed to answer?

But the CIO couldn't, for Doherty. He was welding shut his mind, to not think about anything anymore. He had tried every angle on human disappointment: his father's, Marvin's, Wirbin's, his own. They all exhausted him.

He would never see Doherty again, so he allowed his left hand to come to his face and rub hard and circular over his high forehead and eyes as if scratching for fleas.

University President (call)
Office
November 18 (unscheduled)

"I called twice," Corso said.

The CIO was silent. What lie could he offer if he was finished with lies?

"I wanted to talk about the Larry Galanos meeting. But in the meantime, Ted has been in my office with some frightening numbers."

The CIO didn't speak.

"Which of the two do you want to talk about first?"

The CIO looked around his office for an excuse, preferably death. The few remaining devices for possible self-maiming were eight finance books that had survived his and Lisa's culling. At least they would have a use, in the final analysis. But he couldn't figure out the mechanics. No wonder people loved guns.

"Are you there?" she asked.

"Yes, sorry. Strawberry or chocolate? I just can't choose."

"Well, personally, I have never been a fan of chocolate ice cream."

"I guess start with Professor Ponytail."

"You'll be delighted to know he came to the meeting in a kind of man bun."

She was too soft on the CIO. He wanted this to be difficult.

"A yoga instructor man bun?"

"More like a Continental Congress man bun."

"Does academic freedom have no limits? I thought tenure could be revoked for gropers, Klansmen, and man buns."

Corso laughed, unhelpfully. The CIO's heart was still beating at double normal volume, triple a healthy pulse. She went on, "Larry and two others from the Faculty Senate were on one side of the table. Ben, Jim, and Connie on the other side. They were just missing little flags to make it look like a tiny peace conference between tiny countries. Larry read an opening statement, dramatically of course, that covered the climate crisis, conscious capitalism, 'Rawlsian theories of justice,' and an analysis of impact investing returns. It wasn't as bad as I would have expected. And the numbers seemed—"

The CIO realized, exhausted, that Wirbin, unprecedented in situations like this after nine years, had not called him to be briefed.

He explained to Corso, "These impact numbers ignore the coincidence of energy price deflation. They are *not* proof that virtuous investing always succeeds."

He could almost hear her smiling patiently. "As soon as Larry finished his opening statement, Connie started to speak. Then Ben interrupted her, asking Larry what he thought about Boycott, Divestment, and Sanctions. Larry priggishly answered that the Faculty Senate's remit to the 'special committee' had nothing to do with BDS. But Ben kept on pushing him on what *he* thought. Larry said it was not appropriate for him to express his personal opinions. And then Ben said, 'Listen, Thomas Jefferson, your declaration was too good to *not* involve personal opinions, so I just want to know what you think.' Larry put prayer hands to his face to stop from smiling. And he actually apologized for not being able to opine.

"Ben then told him that the reason he is asking about BDS is to establish how 'we are mixing personal opinions with the sacred duty of the endowment.' I thought the faculty would roll their eyes at that, but everyone went silent. And Ben proceeded to reel off facts and figures about how the school would basically have no ability to be 'a place of opportunity and inclusion' without the endowment. Did you give him that?"

"No. Maybe Goldman Sachs has some group..."

"Amazing. Anyway, Larry said something like, 'I am—we are—here to save the university. It is not a "political opinion" to recognize the imperatives of the climate crisis. *Our* plan is the financially prudent one. By total divestment of stranded assets and by an impact allocation, we will enhance the endowment's returns.'"

I give up, the CIO thought.

"Then it became *High Endowment Noon* with them staring at each other and then talking over each other. I told Jana that it was American male ego at its apotheosis: the self-righteous academic left versus the self-important Wall Street rich. Ben somehow puffed himself up so you forgot how short he is. He said, 'I'll bet you a thousand bucks that I'm right.' And Larry said, 'You're not going to bully me with your wealth.' And Ben said, 'Okay, a one-way bet, Larry. If you're right, I'll donate $50,000 to Ethical Biology'—Larry corrected him—'*and* I'll bring your plan to the trustees for a clean vote. Up or down. And if I'm right, just a personal promise. Give it a rest. No more agitation of the faculty or the students. You and I will pick who does the analysis to make sure it's unbiased.'"

"I don't like where this is heading."

"Yessir. It seems that you are to lead a search for a third party to conduct the analysis."

"What would that even mean? How do you parse deflation from stranded-ness from sector cyclicality? There are a thousand variables it's impossible to control for."

"I thought it was clear that Larry's numbers were ignoring

something?"

"They do. They must. But why is 5 percent of the endowment allowed to cause 90 percent of our headaches? I don't have time for this. It doesn't make sense to have time for this. Do you know how hard we're swimming to keep our heads above water? Do you think paying a consultant to invent math to confirm the obvious is going to help with that? Unless something radically changes, this is going to be the worst year, the worst *three* years, of relative performance of my life, and I'm trying to find a way to turn that around—"

"Ted said that if the endowment contribution is down this year, we could cut the lesser sports or just do what we don't want to do around enrollment management."

The CIO closed his eyes. He tried to picture what seemed impossible: Corso's arm shaking in fury at him, her runner's watch beeping in alarm, one part of her unpoised. He opened his eyes to squint at the bookshelf, willing the books to fall on him from across the room. "Great," he said, "we'll have a sit-in by squash players. 'No racquets, no peace.' Or we can just make our mission complete: turning the One Percent into the 0.1 Percent, one kid at a time. For the record, we—you—ought to think about the payout formula rather than Ted's linear cut. If our assets are down 5 or 6 percent and we're paying out 4.6 percent, that's a fast slide to zero."

"Is there anything you can do?"

"I'm trying everything I can think of. I called Karen Kahn and asked her for advice."

"Who's Karen Kahn?"

"The rarest of breeds: the talented and demonstrably consistent hedge fund manager."

"And what advice did you get from that talented, consistent, and presumably female hedge fund manager?"

"We—just *one* of her investors—have compensated her firm with"—the CIO scratched out the numbers on a pad to depress him—"3 or 4 million dollars in fees and carry *every year* for almost fifteen years. And what advice does 50 million dollars get you in America today? Well, apparently none. It was like I was a high school reporter at a Department of Defense press conference asking for the nuclear codes."

"That's a very specific metaphor."

"It was like I was a pimply, scoliotic high school reporter at a Department of Defense press conference..."

"Scoliotic?" Corso's laughter hugged without justice.

I don't do nihilism. I do mild irony. Maybe that was the original sin. "None of this is funny, Meg."

"Listen, I know nothing about Wall Street. I know the numbers Ted sent me are scary, but I also know that you are also demonstrably talented, according to *The New York Times,* no less. And I know that the endowment is 6 billion dollars now versus 3 billion dollars when you got here."

The CIO looked out at campus, at the trees that had given up their leaves. He exhaled as if he could put in words what those trees could do.

"Money grows," he said. "That may be its most salient feature. So complimenting me on it growing is like saying, 'We know Little Otis still can't read, can't add, still bites his teachers on their faces, but look how much taller he is than last year.'"

"I think that's how they do it in Finland."

"Seriously, I can't take kindness on top of this."

Corso seemed to be drinking something. Probably very organic and authentic tea. He thought he heard a mug being placed down as she said, "Okay. Tell me what we're trying to do?"

The CIO looked at the campus again. The air bit, just above freezing. The stonework matched the sky. The grass had dried to a yellowish gray. Explain investing? Explain life, from its first spark.... Had Jane ever asked this? Or had she simply absorbed investing before she became terminally bored?

The CIO asked, "Like what actually goes on inside the counting house?"

"How very Victorian of you."

"*Hasta la Victorian siempre.*" Was he flirting with her? Was this how he ended? "Okay.... Let me... Well, the university has assets—assets of all kinds. The buildings we're in are assets. This perennially disappointing chair is an asset. Our reputation is an asset. The systems and processes we have to educate students are an asset. As are, most fungible, our financial assets. Now, in the classic explanation, these financial assets are the storehouse of our labor, the apples we picked and didn't need this year. But obviously, in our case, these financial assets are subsidizing an anti-profit enterprise. So these assets are, I guess, the storehouse of other people's labor, who then gave it to us to get tingles imagining future generations studying in Dead Rich Guy Hall while mournfully reflecting upon Dead Rich Guy's singular life."

Corso laughed, seemingly with a mouthful of tea.

"All these assets have a productive use in this world. It's a shame to have *any* asset underused, to let the apples rot in the orchard rather than selling them to people who want to make applesauce. Us, too, across all our apples. We maximize enrollment. We rent out Dead Rich Guy Hall to a concert promoter to bring in a band or a laptop or whatever kids listen to nowadays. And so *my* fundamental job is to not let our financial assets sit idle, make sure we get the best deal for the use of them from investment firms that want to rent our capital from us. The best deal, by the way, is not just the highest possible returns, because that *should* mean taking on the most risk. Like, if you rented out an apartment above your garage to a hit man on the lam, he'd probably pay you above market rent. But you might want to rent your apartment for less money to a monk who will contemplate eternity all day."

The CIO paused to wonder what he was spewing. "It's the same here. The best deal means that we are getting better-than-market returns by taking on lower-than-market risk—where there is a disconnect from a usual relationship between risk and reward. And that's what people talk about when they say our 'cost' of capital—what we are looking for others to pay *us* to make applesauce from our assets. We have, in aggregate, a pretty high cost of capital: we want 9 percent annual return blending different risks across different strategies. We have no guarantees that the risks we take in any of these strategies will be worth it. But our other option is to accept a 'risk-free' rate of returns, which is what the safest bonds will offer, which is like 2 percent if you are honest. Are you still there?"

"Yes. I find myself jotting down some of these phrases."

"Well, that's not a good idea. So, what do the investment firms do with our capital? What's the applesauce factory? Well, sometimes they are just re-renting their capital, which they pool from us and others, to—let's see, join us for a tour of visitors this year—invest in companies to make machines that very slowly boil chickens, build the distribution centers from which to ship the slow boilers, buy out fish-hook manufacturers. This is the purest of form of what we do. But sometimes the renters of our financial assets just buy stocks in China, assuming they'll go up, or—this is the stuff Karen Kahn does—derivatives related to Turkish debt fatally loved by the Japanese. Those investors are, in effect, making sure that the market is liquid and efficient. Or they are just good gamblers at a casino."

Corso didn't say anything. The CIO looked at his credenza, cleared of noise but now conspicuous for its scratched cherrywood veneer. He looked at his new computer and wanted to smash this one too. Because all of it was true. And because all of it was false.

"That's it. You can now print yourself an MBA in the secret diploma machine in your closet."

"I'm printing two of them right now. This—no offense—seems incredibly straightforward. So why is Wall Street always allowed to, you know, win?"

"Well, we aren't talking about apples, at least outside the Matt Damon way of 'how do you like them apples.'"

"Huh?"

"That didn't exactly work." He was glad he had tried. "But what would Ben say?" The CIO winced at the missing side of his triangle with Corso and Wirbin—at so much missing the missing side. "'I haven't got a fucking clue in fucksville.' I very much wish investing was a lower-volume enterprise. There *were* periods in American history when there was less money to invest and finance was a less conspicuous winner as a result. But the quantum of capital today is mind-blowing. *That* difference is maybe why the people feel different than when I started in the nineties. We deal with some of the most successful people in the world. The money, they will tell you, 'doesn't really matter' even if everyone is scheming and clawing for a larger piece of the pie. And the worst thing the money does is convince these people that they could have chosen *any* career and been equally successful at that too—and indeed can do everything better than everyone who is currently doing it, from cleaning the bathroom to running the country. I'm sure J.P. Morgan or Jay Gould felt the same way, but there are co-op buildings in Manhattan in which every apartment is occupied by a J.P. Morgan. In which even the dog is a J.P. Morgan. Karen Kahn reminded me what these people are like, with her iced-vein replies: 'Do people really outperform or do they take on more risk?' Well, what did I expect when I called her? To change two words in one trapezoid, and turn conventional wisdom into a philosophy?

That's really it, that no one else has figured it out, that there are no costs to this, this... futzing. And she reminded me—well, I was actually reminded of that by the *least* rare of breeds, an inconsistent private equity manager. He said it's *easy* to ask questions, like throwing a fish into the water versus catching a fish."

"I'm not sure—"

"I'll have to work on that one. I'll add apples to it, or use a Boston accent. Or describe the fish as scoliotic. But what I call it doesn't matter. My job seems to be, day after day, to throw fish into the water."

"Marvin still thinks you should call Michael Hermann."

That's because, the CIO thought, old people repeat themselves.

Investment team
Conference room
December 1

The conference room was jammed with nine people, armrests knocking into armrests. At least the new intern was away, in class. The CIO had to get back to his shapes, to the plan—any plan—to do something different. Jane had told him last night that he couldn't come to their bed if he was going to work on his laptop for another night before bedtime. It was ruining his sleep. It was ruining her sleep.

Life is not just about the conditions for sleep.

Do you think you are going to think clearly if you don't get a good night of sleep?

I am not Peter. This is my *job.*

He had slept in the living room. He had only so much time.

At the meeting, Calvin asked, "Why are we even doing asset allocation?"

The CIO wasn't sure if more sarcasm had snaked into Calvin's voice since yesterday.

"What is that supposed to mean?" Emily asked.

"Seth Alexander stopped doing asset allocations years ago," Calvin answered. "MIT just picks the best athletes, with equity beta and illiquidity targets."

"Well, Penn is still doing asset allocation," Emily said. "Stanford is. Yale is. Bowdoin is, and Paula Volent has the best three-year numbers."

The CIO interrupted. “Do we think our asset allocation should be set by what David Swensen and Some People Who Used to Work for David Swensen do? As this Lincoln-Douglas Debate illuminates, David Swensen and Some People Who Used to Work for David Swensen don’t even agree with each other. Well, I suppose David Swensen agrees with David Swensen.”

The CIO, wondering if he agreed with himself, needed to stand up again. So he tried to steer this meeting to its quickest end: “How far are we from target allocations again?”

The director of investment operations recited, “The target allocations are 35 percent in public equity, 25 percent in private equity and venture, 20 percent in absolute return, 7.5 percent in real estate, 7.5 percent in natural resources, and 5 percent in fixed income and cash.”

Calvin rolled his eyes; everyone knew the allocation. It was Mies van der Rohe: clean and true.

“As of September 30th, we were underweight public equity and absolute return by about 3 percent each. As of today, more?”

“You don’t have to put up your hand,” the CIO said to the youngest analyst.

“Apologies. Habit. Are you going to recommend a change to the asset allocation or are we going to tactically rebalance?”

He wanted all of them to thrive in this world, but not if talking like this, this soon, was the bill. “We didn’t rebalance to get here,” he said. “Stocks fell. Private equity guys are showing incredible intestinal fortitude in not writing down their investments to such noisy things as actual value.” His team was staring at him. He knew they wanted him to be normal again, or whatever normal he used to be. “Landing on an asset allocation in this market is like spinning out on ice in your car and not knowing which way to turn the steering wheel.”

The analyst asked, “Which way are you supposed to turn the

wheel?"

"Well, I've never actually spun out on ice in my car, so I have no idea."

Josh looked at his phone. "Google says it's better to turn the spinning wheel in the direction you're spinning."

"Well, then let's spin the steering wheel." The CIO spun his hands in comical clumsiness.

The rainbow of faces seemed more confused. His own face felt pre-vomitous.

"Who wants more apex predators? That's hedge funds, people. Anyone? Paying two and twenty for 'reduced risk,' disproportionate opinions on Tesla, and alpha that rotates between managers chaotically? Is this a financial objection? A *cultural* one? But, moving on, real estate? Real Eeee State? Bueller? Bueller? Well, it *is* late cycle. But let's get some contrarians out there.... Natural! Resources!"

The faces at last smiled.

"Emily seems to actually want to chop off her arm to prove how unraised it is. Private equity and venture."

Three hands went up but not Emily's. He cared only about Emily's.

"Some support for the illiquideers. The rest of you, I guess, got Lodgepoled. U.S. public equity? No one. Wow. The MAGA types are noting your non-support in the brims of their red hats. But, I get it: sure, the S&P 500 tripled in a decade, and we were idiots for not having more of that beta, but it's been pretty naughty lately. Um, international equity? Two votes"—including Calvin—"for seven billion non-Americans and the stocks that track them. Fixed income? The youngest among us may not even know what fixed income is, the cassette tape of endowment finance. The managers do tend to lack inputs and hunger. And last and actually least: cash. Who wants more cash? The green stuff that folds up and smells like cocaine and pockets? We'd never have a down year...."

Emily's glare had not unglued from the allocation printout. The CIO paused, almost winded. He wanted to ask her if this was nihilism or irony. He ached for it to be neither. But maybe what the last few years' performance had finally proved is that the world is ruled by momentum.

He brought a pad of paper closer to him and took a pencil out of a bin. "That was fun. Let's see, out of seven voters and eight categories, we got a response rate of five votes. That's 8.9 percent? We will have to work on our democratic participation. But we have three votes for PE and venture and—carry the two, move the hundred—two for international equity. So, I guess the new asset allocation is 60 percent private equity and venture and 40 percent international public equity."

The youngest analyst raised her hand again.

"Alas, the voting is over."

"I just had a question."

"Again, there is no need to put up your hand if you have a question."

"I know you're joking, but I just don't know how *much* you're joking."

The CIO looked at her, almost in thanks. Then he looked at—watched—Emily. He would not take his eyes off of her until her eyes met his, until she accepted that this was leading to some kind of breakthrough. "The question on the floor is how *much* am I joking? Hmmm. Well, if you look at our ten-year numbers, and we sweep the big underallocation to U.S. equities under the rug, private equity/VC and international equity are probably our best asset classes. Which is why they got the votes, I suspect. Why fight the human inability to resist backcasting forecasting? I, uh, too share all the human inabilities. And it's not a *crazy* asset allocation. Do I need to own real estate ever again? Do I need inflation protection if there hasn't been inflation in two decades, thank you, Chinese workers and mass global migration?"

Emily had bent her neck in as if to stare into herself.

"Sixty percent private equity and venture, 40 percent international equity? I mean, why not? Sixty percent should generally be no worse than equity beta with the right managers and will have low quarter-to-quarter volatility, however self-policed. And 40 percent Vanguard Total World Total Orwell Index or just rotating bets on high-volatility countries. Karen Kahn would have something to say about... Anyway, sixty/forty. The *New* Sixty/Forty."

Josh sort of smiled. Didn't the rest of them get it?

"It'd be a good way to get our name in the paper again. I can see it now. 'Through a proprietary process formed by the wisdom of the crowds, aka the occasional hand-raising of a begrudging investment team, America's twentieth-largest college endowment is paving a new direction in asset allocation.' We need a name, though. I'm not going to NMS without a cool name. Illiquid International? Sounds like a narco front or an anti-diarrhea spa camp. Private and—hmmm. Private and progressive? No. Private and pistachio eaters? I guess everyone eats pistachios, and we don't want to be overweight Iran and other pistachio-forward nations."

Josh said, "Private and Pangeo."

"Charlie, my boy! You won! The chocolate. The factory. The Oompa Loompas."

Emily stood up and left. She did not try to be inconspicuous. Except for those of grinning Calvin, the eyes of everyone else hummed with a triple compulsion to be directed at her, the CIO, and each other. Only Josh, his younger self, looked at the CIO first, unashamed but unreadable. The CIO smiled at the remaining kids, sharing a wonder about what that could have been about.

Office
December 3

Dear Trustees and President Corso, the CIO typed.

It has been my privilege to serve the university, but I hereby resign effective June 30. This date will provide the Investment Committee seven months to find a suitable replacement before the end of the fiscal year. It has been a great honor to build a modern endowment for the school and help guide this institution to greater financial health and competitiveness for the "best" and "brightest."

He deleted the last three words.

"the best and brightest"

Delete.

an increasingly selective student body and faculty. While the last two and a half years' performance has not met my goals, even with it, the endowment has generated nearly 500 million dollars net more than the benchmarks over my tenure. And while this is less than we would have generated through a sixty/forty stock-bond passive portfolio, I continue to believe (kind of)—

Delete.

that your endowment will show greater resilience in times of acute financial stress, such that the benchmarks remain the appropriate way to measure the risks we choose to take.

Delete.

Dear Trustees and President Corso,

I hereby resign. I should have resigned the day I started losing my mind, which may have been the day I lied to Trustee Wirbin.

Yes, lie is a strong word for hyping my performance from shitty to merely bad. But my job is to read through and be better than hype. That is the Wall Street definition of honesty

Delete.

Dear Trustees and President Corso,

I resign. Because I'm tired. Because even when I beat our benchmarks for six of my first seven years here, sometimes by a lot, I lived in fear that I was making it up as I went along. And now, we've come nowhere close to the benchmarks for two fiscal years. And in the recent sloppy market, our performance is basically the same as sixty-forty, calling into question the bear market resilience of

Delete.

Dear Trustees and President Corso,

All of you have on occasion praised my sense of humor. Except for Trustee Connie Feldman, who, I suspect, thinks I'm a class A weirdo for my Costco pants and compulsive need to joke. I always thought Jews automatically found Jews funny, as the main (and frankly only) qualification for being Jewish nowadays. I guess some still have God, and taste.

Delete.

qualification for being Jewish nowadays, other than guilt. I have enormous guilt, which may make me enormously Jewish. Or maybe just enormously guilty. My father never felt Jewish guilt. Nothing was ever his fault. I sometimes think he had Jewish rage, but I'm not sure if that's a thing or

Delete.

You have on occasion praised my sense of humor. And I have shown myself to be down with sick, cynical, and usually high-rate Wall Street humor, although I'm definitely not privy to the subcategory that involves technical descriptions of the female anatomy and/or penile shortcomings. Which may be 92 percent of the good stuff.

Delete.

You've praised my sense of humor. Why do I bring that up? Because I've always suspected that my investment talents (or, more to the point, manager-selection and allocation talents) were due to a point of view. When I've talked to you about hunger, inputs, and system, those were tactics born to a strategy born of a point of view that accepted the absurdity in the human condition but did not lose faith because of the absurdity. If we are just assemblages of proteins and chemical reactions that have no privileged place in the cosmos, how do we bear being alive? Great question! And what the fuck does that have to do with how this particular Chief Investment Protein Assemblage invests? Well, stay with me: People with no humor, I believe (or believed), can't both 1) see through the colossal bullshit that is Wall Street, its middle manager decamillionaires, and its allocation-of-capital faux-purpose, and 2) still enjoy finding the acrobats who can outperform preferably if not exclusively by allocating capital to productive ends. What is a contrarian other than the guy who uses the conventional wisdom to set up the joke?

Delete.

Dear Trustees and President Corso,

If you hear a complaint about me from Emily Baptiste, understand that I resigned before Ms. Baptiste's complaints could lead to an investigation. I am genuinely interested in what her complaints are, though. That, despite being warned, I undermined her professional reputation by insufficient respect to visiting GPs? That I did nihilism? That I stepped off the deck, forcing her to mutiny the Bounty as it was heading towards the shoals? But I was in the chart room

Delete.

Her complaint could be that I made a performative reference

to a movie that most young people have not seen or, if they have seen it, saw it as a Johnny Depp remake instead of the Gene Wilder original (with the caveat that I never saw the Depp remake and can't imagine a worse idea than

Delete.

reference to a generationally specific, very white cinematic experience. Or, here is what every white boss fears: that I'm a racist both for advocating the enslavement of Oompa Loompas and for leaving them to Josh Kaufman

Delete.

whether it's that I lost control of the ship or made a reference to a somewhat dated (if still enjoyable, I think) movie or am a racist for privileging another straight white male because of the so-called "airport test," a narrow sense of what talent looks like, et cetera. But to the extent you care about what this resignee—resignor?—thinks, I would recommend Ms. Baptiste as the interim CIO and potentially my full-time successor. Yes, Ms. Baptiste may have been overly formal in her past interactions with you. And yes, she seems to get lost in the analysis of certain opportunities and does not give enough people the benefit of the doubt. Nevertheless, she has a fine mind, a daunting work ethic, a purposefulness to the job that I have lost, a rooted point of view, a bias for contrarianism, a few documented occasions of Actual Investment Enthusiasm, and an integrity and fairness that I believe you will increasingly see as nonnegotiable. Also, no nihilism. Also, no sense of humor, as she does not believe in humor as a competitive advantage or a necessary human trait, which in hindsight might be a good way to behave. She'll probably also fire Calvin Hu. I probably should have done that a year ago, had I been able to stomach a few moments of interpersonal discomfort and not continued to pretend that I had pulled off the HR steal of a lifetime because Calvin graduated from Stanford. The crazy thing is that while I know Calvin is annoying, I can't prove if he's bad at his job. I like this Australian he brought

Delete.

Dear Trustees and President Corso,

I have been working on a new asset allocation, and I thought it would be easier to explain it in an email in advance of the board meeting. Following the lead of Karen Kahn, the most successful GP relationship in my tenure (and, okay, before it), I've been trying to distill our investment strategy to the simplest possible principles. Full disclosure: Ms. Kahn has not endorsed these goals or even this project. Frankly, when I tried to discuss it with her, she was kind of a fucking

Delete.

This distillation project is different from the various tactical heuristics I've discussed over the years. The purpose of this exercise is to analyze pathways of performance. The attached schematic organizes eight concepts: Structurally Inefficient Markets, Fundamental Profit Growth, Earned Illiquidity, Necessary Liquidity, Access Talent, Minimize Fee Drag, Conviction in Projections, and Modesty before Efficiency. The fact that some are verbs is annoying. However, that awkwardness feels right until I get the concepts to

Delete.

The purpose of this exercise is to follow the philosopher Isaiah Berlin. I hereby cut and paste from a file: "Of course social or political collisions will take place; the mere conflict of positive values alone makes this unavoidable. Yet they can, I believe, be minimized by promoting and preserving an uneasy equilibrium, which is constantly threatened and in constant need of repair—that alone, I repeat, is the precondition for decent societies and morally acceptable behaviour, otherwise we are bound to lose our way."

Delete.

follow what the philosopher Isaiah Berlin said about preserving an "uneasy equilibrium" among positive values that, by their nature, conflict. In our context, this means an equilibrium that captures both inefficiency (sometimes known as value) and fundamental economic/sector growth. Those are both "goods" to be weighed and balanced, as is the desire for talented managers and a recognition of the fee drag of using talented managers and the need to lock up capital to benefit from private strategies and the need to not expose yourself to the dangers of too much illiquidity. On top of that all is balancing the Bogleish attitude of being very modest, and passive, in the face of efficient markets with the need for some conviction to achieve outperformance. Balancing these eight concepts is the fundamental mission of any

Delete.

Balancing these shapes is what I have no fucking clue how to do. I've sat here for two months staring at a computer, causing Emily Baptiste's blood to boil, causing my wife to be on the edge of whatever she's on the edge of. Maybe I should have brought Emily into the project to quantitatively steer the portfolio to an uneasy equilibrium. For, instead of an Archimedes moment, all I've achieved is letting the endowment slip into a bathtub of mediocrity and a near double-digit decline starting last October. Is the problem that I lack a Theory of Everything? Is it that I'm just a second-rate investor, who never generated outperformance when he was on the front lines but has still convinced himself that deep, deep down he still has an edge? Is there any evidence that I'm not totally replaceable and second

Delete.

Dear Trustees and President Corso,

I'm not a magic man. The idea that you can throw money at the problem that the richest and most powerful institutions are also trying to solve

Delete.

I'm not a magic man. I'm not even sure I'm a human being if my ego, my life, my purpose is determined by whether a bunch of other people's investments to which I allocate other people's money can outperform. If the world wanted to outperform, it would take the best and the brightest and make them bricklayers and let the bricklayers allocate assets. Then we'd have some in-performance. Then we'd be doing well by doing good

Delete.

Dear Trustees and President Corso,

I believe—believed—that a sign of character is a contrarianism about everything, including the liberal consensus. But maybe the contrarianism has gotten stuck as my only point of view. Maybe I get frustrated by Larry Galanos because I want the freedom to be Larry Galanos and not accept the world as it is. For what is this endowment for? For the self-preservation and self-glorification of a world-class university that the country has dozens of others of? Can we not be more? Can we

Dear Trustees and President Corso,

To make it clear as I resign, or get fired, or shoot myself in the face, I always cared. I still care. I can pretend to be more cynical about it than I am, to make me hip to the game. But I believe all of Ben Wirbin's points even if he refuses

Delete.

I believe in Ben Wirbin's conviction: this endowment is more than just a pool of money. I believe that making good things happen can be a sacred duty. I believe that the university—"our" university, the university is general—is one of America's greatest treasures. Even accounting for everything negative on the ledger (the costs to families, the administrative superstructure, the intellectual deadwood, the advantaged access for the legacied and the rich), it remains unmatched in advancing equality, knowledge, and individual students to be better than they would otherwise be. Yes, I have one of two children bound for responsible citizenry, a happy marriage with enough years of accumulated strength to (I pray) resist my recent attempts to destroy it, and employees who (I hope) will remember me fondly as a man esoteric in references and a bit nutty at the end but also a compassionate, instructive, trusting boss who wanted them all to succeed in honorable professions. All this would still be true regardless of whether I'm up 3.8 percent or 9 percent—or down—in a year. But still: the half a billion dollars in outperformance, however it falls this year, is the only thing I have ever done that has undeniably served humankind. How did that happen? Everyone can despair by pulling on the string of events that is a life, and this economy, and our culture. But I do not remember, really, what I thought I was before I became a CIO. So what must I do to prove what I believe?

Delete.

The CIO picked up the phone. "May I please speak to Mr. Trotter?"

Trustee (call)
Office
December 12 (unscheduled)

“So how is this that Ben did not tell you what happened?” Ghosh asked.

The CIO didn’t know how he could begin to explain this to yet another male Immediate Expert on All.

“Whilst people kept on calling it the ‘executive session,’ there was very very little reason for it to be an executive session. You could have been there.”

The CIO kept silent.

“Everyone was looking at Marvin”—almost *Marwin*—“because there was a sense he was to say something. I guess Meg Corso knew. But the conversation reached an awkward moment. We were posting our eyes to Marvin and occasionally to Ben, who was not talking as himself if you see what I mean. And then, well, Marvin said, ‘I think we should be interested in hearing Michael Hermann’s perspective.’”

The CIO held his breath. He had barely survived Wirbin’s look during the earlier part of the meeting.

“We all switched our eyes to Ben, like at a tennis match. Ben stood up and said, ‘Got it. It’s been real.’ And then it changed to a pandemonium. Jim, Blake, and Connie at the same time said, ‘Ben, sit down.’ And Ben said something like, ‘I made clear my opinion on the matter. I believe Meg has my irrevocable’”— *irrewocable*—“‘opinion on the matter. You all know what I think about this school, but I must be a man of my word or I am nothing.' Jim tried to start to talk, and Ben said, 'No, Pascky,' as if Jim was his son-or-daughter. And I speak up, because this endowment really has very very bad processes for productive discussion. 'I don't understand,' I say, 'what is the harm of talking?' And Ben answered, 'I find it distracting.'"

"Oh, fuck."

"You know what this means?"

"Hermann said that to him once."

"Ah well. None of us understood, and we ask him why he finds it distracting, and he says again, 'I find it distracting.' We all don't know is this truly about Michael Hermann? And Ben was not giving us any clue as to what we should plead about. I think this must be something they teach at Goldman Sachs. Because we were losing very, very much, and we did not even know what we were playing. Then Connie asked Marvin, 'How important is this?' And Marvin said, 'You don't know until you know,' which caused Connie's mouth to be wide open. And what *are* the Robert's Rules, right? No one on that committee knows. Do we ask Ben to leave the room? Do we try to persuade him? Ted finally said that Marvin's request does not need a vote. It is not—right?—a policy change. So we can leave it to Ben and Marvin to decide the best course of action. I thought this is a bad idea."

"So you don't know..."

"No. That is why I called you. Have you not spoken to Ben at all?"

Quantitative hedge fund
Conference room
December 15

"Most quantitative strategies," the non-Dutch one explained, "are self-segregated into being oriented towards stocks *or* flows."

"Most?" the Dutch one interrupted him.

"Okay: all. I said 'most' to be conservative." The Dutch one looked at Calvin and rolled his eyes. "You have two flow types of quantitative strategies. First, you have guys who look at trading patterns—"

"Ha! The voodoo." The Dutch one dutched the phrase into *da vuhdo.*

"Thank you for that. Incredibly helpful. So you have guys obsessed with trading patterns in a war of computing power against randomness. They hope that enough power gives them enough attempts to be 53 percent right. And then you have guys looking for real signals in the market of how one flow interacts with another. They use *okay* data science, lot of analogies to fluid mechanics, but still just flow stuff—momentum patterns. These guys, and there are so, so many of them, have put all their eggs into AI. Artificial intelligence," he clarified, looking at Calvin, then their analyst, and then at the CIO. "Which is a fantasy: push a button—*buy* a button—and let a machine figure out how to figure out how data moves. And over here, you have the stocks crowd—"

The Dutch one tried to interrupt, but the other one gave no opening. (And what was he? Arab? Moroccan Jew? Business cards to Vest People were Bronze Age tools.) The Dutch one then smiled a wild programmer smile and mouthed "touchy" to Calvin. Did Calvin bring them in as another provocation? Spelling out AI? The CIO may not own a supercomputer, but he was not an infirm idiot. In fact, he had already written into PowerPointy shapes exactly what they were explaining: structurally inefficient markets, earned illiquidity, necessary liquidity. But he had done it as an investor, not a programmer casting about for gimmicks.

And here we are: down 6 percent.

The other one continued: "The stocks-obsessed guys are focused on the mispricing of assets. They try to apply data science to pricing models across assets and securities with some depth of iterativeness, complexity, and back-testing. You have short-, medium-, and long-term strategies, which adds some complexity. It's all very logical, if a bit undergrad. The problem—"

"Da problem Walid is trying to explain"—the Dutch one claimed the floor—"is dat asset mispricing can't autocorrect on any fixed timeline, no? Even with a predictable catalytic event. And asset pricing is incredibly dynamic and changes Heisenbergly *during* a catalytic event."

"I would say 'dynamic.' By definition, it's credibly dynamic."

"Oh... kay."

Calvin turned to the CIO. "Don't worry. This is just their act. They actually work really well together."

Both quants looked ahead, neither endorsing nor denying this claim. Ethnically mismatched, they were akin in too much hair, too little body fat, too few years to be this rich.

The CIO sighed, hopefully not aloud. It had been fourteen days of pained coexistence with Emily since she walked out of this room, three nights of being tongue-stapled in front of Jane when she asked why he wasn't going to bed, three nights of checking his email at 2:00 a.m. from the couch for anything from Wirbin.

"Da basic point Walid is trying to make is that you have people stuck in der separate vision of da world: stocks or flow. Everyone acknowledges both stocks and flows are part of investing, but dere are, in da code, intrinsic, implicit patterns of analysis dat are hard to unravel." The non-Dutch one tried to interrupt, but the Dutch one said louder, "All this leads to very median returns, no? So what we have done is created systems dat not only independently conduct parallel strategies with stocks and flow orientation, to anticipate market consensus of da other strategies, but have a proprietary level of integrativeness."

"I don't think that's actually a word."

"No? Ha! I'm Dutch."

"What Johannes is trying to say is that a successful system must work in four dimensions. We must have an understanding of conventional stocks and flow architecture of other data science-grounded investors and build effective parallel systems. Many of the strategies out there have the same basic pattern matching and same basic machine logic. And so what patterns *they* identify and what *they* arb away are a foundational part of our strategy. And then"—he held his hands up—"we have built our proprietary interaction between the independent stock and flow systems to set forth inefficiencies and time-predicated dynamisms that each independent system misses."

Vertigo grabbed the CIO. There has to be reality—the allocation of capital, the efficiency the markets, his eight shapes, the productive applesauce from the university's apples—or the CIO was struggling for nothing on top of struggling with nothing.

Please, Emily, I need to talk to you.

The analyst was chipperly clacking away on his Surface as if he already knew where to situate these guys' edge. But was this investing? May the best computer win?

"Did you say something?" the non-Dutch one asked.

Calvin turned to him. *Had* he said something?

He managed now to say, "And this works?"

Calvin, now apparently A.dV's head of investor relations, said, "Their returns are *sick*. Year in, year out, absolutely *sick*."

"Maybe I missed this, but what do you trade?"

The geniuses didn't seem to understand the question.

"Tesla shares? Bitcoin? Guilders?"

"Ha! Guilders exist no more."

"Okay, then. Orange juice futures like Winthorpe and Billy Ray? I mean, what?"

The non-Dutch one said, "We don't talk about that."

The CIO looked weakly at the analyst to study his reaction to this and then turned back to the quants. "You don't talk about that?"

The Dutch one answered, "We can't talk about it. We are happy to share da process and da intellectual architecture, but actual tactics is IP."

Calvin added, "If other people got their hands on what they were doing, it'd be like finding the recipe for Coke."

"Fear not," the CIO said. "If I got my hands on what they are doing *and* the recipe for Coke, I would not make a single competing soft drink rooted in time-predicted dynamisms. I am just curious if *you* guys know what's in your book, or is that a complete black box even to you?"

"We are not really able to go into that—" the non-Dutch one started.

"Me, I don't mind, no?" the Dutch one interrupted. "But Walid is a bit Edward Snowden."

"So other endowments are comfortable not knowing what you, as compared to your computers, actually know? With the risk every day that a *Wall Street Journal* article will come out about how you lost their money day-trading CBD oil or Iranian rials?"

"Princeton and Columbia are both investors," Calvin said.

The CIO asked, "During Narv's time or after Narv?"

"Both," Calvin answered.

Why had the CIO humiliated himself with that question? He should go in his office and hit send.

Emily: here. Ben: here.

Calvin, again: "Walid and Johannes got their PhDs at Columbia before their time at Two Sigma."

"I saw that, Calvin. Thank you."

The Dutch one started again. "So, what we are saying—what we can say—is dat it seems obvious—no?—dat you must apply data science to both stocks and flows. But it requires cutting-edge data science to *integrate* static and dynamic analytical systems. It's like using da same instrument to play a sonata and complete da structural engineering of a skyscraper."

The CIO rubbed his face. He tried to understand what had become of his mind and his skills. He tried to understand if these quants were beyond him, or hucksters, or the lucky survivors. But also: did they really care that much about being rich? Was this all that their PhDs opened them to?

The non-Dutch one looked at his watch and showed a text to the Dutch one. Calvin looked at the CIO as if the CIO was going to approve a hundred-million capital commitment right then.

The Dutch one said, to Calvin, "Well, dat's our story and we're sticking—"

It had been four days of a tight stomach, of every moment away from the phone or email an assault gripping his chest, on what would come next. It had been four days of fear of what he would do to his marriage. "Can I ask you a random question?" the CIO surprised himself by saying aloud.

"Oh, yes. Please do. Dose are da best type of questions."

"What do you think of Michael Hermann?"

The two quants looked at each other again, stifling their laughter.

"Dis Great Man theory of hedge fund alpha by being a 'stock picker' is a bit hocus-pocus, no?" The Dutch one giggled, high-pitched. "I'm King Canute who commands da tides."

The non-Dutch one added, "There are guys who are literally trading on reputations built in more inefficient markets. They have no idea whatsoever how advanced investing has become."

And then Lisa came in and told him that Ben Wirbin was on the phone.

Trustee (call)
Office
December 15 (unscheduled)

"Fuck Marvin. Fuck the loser Trotterheads that have inflated his fucking ego. Fuck his reputation, fuck his produce day-fresh snob shit, and fuck his fucking bread—as if no one had ever baked a good loaf of bread until Marvin Fucking Trotter put a better bakery into a supermarket in Elmira. Fuck that. And fuck Michael Hermann, too. Fuck whatever Bohemian Grove billionaire fuck club these rich assholes hang out at to measure each other's dicks. Now I know why people hate them. It's not the fucking money. It's their arrogance as if no one else has the right to *dislike* them. So fuck both of them. *I* can do whatever I fucking want. I'm sure they'll live happily ever after running the investment committee or whatever their plan is. They can build, right on the quad, two 50-foot statues of their billionaire dicks and another 50-foot statue of an Elmira baguette rising up to fuck the world. Are you going to say anything?"

The CIO's heart had not decelerated since Lisa brought him out of the meeting. "I don't know—"

"Well, Mr. Suddenly Silent, here's what you should know: you're supposed to be in Michael Hermann's office in three days."

"And?"

"Why the fuck am I the one telling you this? It's making the prisoner of war dig the graves."

"But I—"

"Your eloquence is reaching an all-time high. You. Are. Supposed. To. Be. In. Michael. Asshole. Hermann's. Office. In. Three. Days. Got it?"

"Are you going to, you know, be here afterwards?"

"Why don't I quote your fucking idol Marvin Trotter: 'You don't know until you know.'" The CIO knew that Wirbin was smiling when he added, "Riddles ain't just for the rich, bitch."

Michael Hermann
Office of Hermann Capital Management
December 18

The CIO had been in small rooms with Michael Steinhardt, with David Bonderman, with Henry Kravis and John Bogle and Bill Gurley and Howard Marks. He had not been intimidated by intimidating men. It's not personal, Sonny. It's strictly business. But Hermann still hadn't said a word. And the CIO couldn't think of how to start, or even be, as he sat schoolboy on the guest side of Hermann's desk. Or the anti-guest side, as one of the two screens of Hermann's Bloomberg terminal half-blocked the CIO's face.

Four minutes of infinity ago, the CIO had thanked Hermann for his time. Hermann had nodded, acknowledging that words had been spoken. It was unclear if the acknowledgment extended to the fact that a human being had been the one to speak them.

There were no pictures on Hermann's desk, no power wall of photographs of Hermann with presidents, kings, Clooneys. Yes, the woodwork was walnut, not cherry veneer, but Hermann's twelve-person suite was more appropriate for one of suburban Chicago's better-off accountants. The CIO wasn't sure if he felt more disappointed or affirmed by another office below its means.

Hermann was still reading from his monitor. Unable to be silent any longer, the CIO said, "This is a bit awkward, like a blind date arranged by your great-uncle and the guy who sells him meat." No smile. "I'm not sure what Marvin wants...."

Hermann kept on reading. Two minutes later, he asked, "What

do you do?"

The CIO told him that he was the Chief Investment Officer of the university.

Hermann didn't say he knew that. He knew that.

The CIO shifted, to be less screened. "Do you mean what do I actually do all day?"

Nothing.

It was time, as with any GP, to establish some balance of power. "Most of us operate in normal science in the Swensen Era. We have an asset allocation, which isn't terribly interesting. We have a 'risk posture,' which is even less so. We then allocate capital to about sixty managers in our case—more in others—who have convinced us they have some structural advantage to generate above-average returns within their asset class without taking on incommensurate additional risk."

"And you think that makes sense?"

"That's the question, I guess."

The CIO had wanted the decade-old picture of Hermann on the Internet to be wrong, for Hermann to physically justify being a recluse: four hundred immobile pounds or a face like a plate of rigatoni. But Hermann was unchanged from the picture, his skin tone one shade paler pink than the CIO's, his brown, slightly waved hair receding high on his forehead, his eyebrows thick in the center and fading at the end. He wore what even the CIO knew were out-of-style frameless glasses. Maybe they were the only ones that could grip the bridge of his thin, long nose.

Hermann finally spoke as he continued reading from the monitor. "What do you bring to this search for managers with 'some structural advantage?'"

"Some history, a few heuristics"—Hermann's lip turned up as if signaling his physical capability of, if not any interest in, a smirk—"and our own competitive advantage in one regard."

"What's that, 'duration'?"

The CIO smiled, abashed.

"Do you think that is a unique advantage?" The Bloomberg had caught Hermann's attention. He squinted at the nearer screen, then at the screen half in front of the CIO's face. The CIO looked behind him at the still closed door. Was this how Emily felt in his office? At least he was learning that lesson. Hermann finished typing and then, not looking at the CIO, said: "One, every asset allocator claims they have duration. Two, everyone who claims they have duration also has a boss or a board that cares about interim numbers. Three, even if your duration confers some 'structural' advantage, which I doubt, good luck finding asset managers who don't want to get paid faster rather than slower. That's a structural disadvantage more relevant than your advantage." He started typing again, and Hermann mumbled, "Unbelievable," hopefully to himself. He then said, "Are we done? You can tell Marvin Trotter I met with you. And I gave you some advice."

You were right, Ben. I'm sorry, Ben. "And that advice was?"

Hermann was still looking at the screen. "Ask yourself if it's a good idea trying to do something you are incapable of doing."

The CIO scrubbed hard his forehead and eyes with his left hand. It was too obvious for this to be who Hermann was. The CIO should just lift himself up in resigned defeat like Kevin Doherty except, Christ, Hermann's guest chair had no armrests. You weren't supposed to get comfortable, it seemed, as you absorbed the radiation from the backside of his monitor.

Hermann looked at him and then at the monitor as he spoke. "Besides, why does a university have a business model in which its ability to provide educational services depends on generating income from prior donations? What would you conclude if McDonald's strategy was to rely on investment income to subsidize the negative margin of every cheeseburger?" Hermann started typing again.

"I guess I have my report from the mountaintop."

"You people should have had a better strategy."

"Sorry?" It was like the day after a fight with Jane over Peter: every pause a trap door.

Hermann, reading his screen, was typing quickly. His eyes leaped to the other screen—new information. The CIO then understood what Hermann thought he was there for: Wirbin's second attempt. He was sharply insulted to be thought of as development. He was also flattered to be assigned, however wrongly, to Wirbin's team.

He said calmly, "I'm not here for money."

"So if I wrote you the check Ben Wirbin begged me for, you would say no?" Hermann stared at him. The lenses of his glasses were clean, but a curved trapezoid reflection of the Bloomberg screen prevented the CIO from seeing anything in Hermann's eyes.

The CIO said again, for his team, "That's not why I'm here."

"Do you think I believe that?" Hermann started typing again.

The CIO found himself getting up and walking to the closed door. He felt his father, the blindness, a twisted laptop coming. He felt his father, for whom everyone was using more success as more power. He had to get out of there quickly.

Still, hand on the doorknob, he turned when Hermann said, "You want some advice? If you have the duration you claim, go 85 percent equity instead of 60/40. Sixty/forty is folk wisdom because it looks humble. It is not based on any understanding of debt or equity."

The CIO said, "Okay," still standing.

Hermann looked at his Bloomberg, annoyed that a better companion was not winning his time. He shut off the monitor. "I don't have time to listen to any more Marvin Trotter koans. So let's get this over with."

The CIO sat. His heartbeat had still not decelerated. It's not personal, Sonny. It's strictly business. "Blended fixed income generates about 3 percent. Equity returns through the cycle generate, what, 6 or 7 percent. We choose to pay out 4.6 percent—"

"Because you have to?"

The CIO paused. Was that an actual question? "No," he said and waited. "Mandated distributions are only for foundations." Okay then: "An endowment could hoard the money for thirty years and then spend it all on golden lacrosse sticks. But, yes, we have negative gross margins despite charging $70,000 for room, board, and tuition, despite half of the families paying that in cash, and despite others borrowing that to turn their children into social media influencers and investment bankers." The CIO caught himself. He couldn't imagine Hermann having children, but... "And now, thanks to right-wing hatred for post-structuralist humanities professors, the largest endowments have a 1.4 percent tax on their returns. But that's a rounding error next to the biggest issue: we don't deal with a general inflation rate of 1-2 percent but the academic inflation rate of 4 percent. Fattened on government loans and scarcity premiums, productivity gains are not really our thing. So you need an 8-ish percent real return to keep flat."

Hermann's face was a half-moon partially obscured by the terminal screen, just as unreadable.

"I could try to achieve that with asset allocation boldness. George Soros for Dummies. Go long Chinese mid-caps this year. Next year, decide it's going to be a ripe vintage for venture. Call a market turn, and not be early. Or three years early, as the particular case may be. None of this is, theoretically, out of bounds. We just took a vote, and my team voted 60 percent privates and 40 percent international equity. Well, it wasn't really a vote. Hafez al Assad came in third." The CIO stopped. What was he doing?

Blathering so chattiness became infectious?

But the replicant across from him was impervious to infection. He turned on his screen and began reading as if he had just done his good deed for a lifetime.

He was also apparently impervious to thirst. The CIO was desperate for water, and there wasn't a glass for anyone in the room.

The CIO tried to fill the vacuum caused by the needs of the flesh: "For what it's worth, not many CIOs stick his—or her, lots of hers in this line of work—neck out on asset allocation. People are up or down 5 percent on the basic allocations—10 at most—maybe on perceived available manager quality. But even that is aspirational. You can't fine tune the dollars at work in privates, and every day an asset allocation is getting untuned by the market. A popinjay who works for me tells me that the smart money has thrown out asset allocation altogether and just goes with illiquidity and beta targets in a search for the 'best athlete.' I find this confusing. I don't want to field an offense with seven quarterbacks, a right fielder, and a pole vaulter. I've also not yet seen any data that proves this works. *And* I suspect that once these endowments tally up their commitments to pole vaulters and Ultimate Frisbee players, they probably have more or less the same illiquidity, beta, and allocations as everyone else. But the best athlete strategy is indicative of a cultural trend: an 'alts-heavy' allocation to hedge funds and private equity doesn't make you look smart anymore. *Toddlers* know that manager performance distribution within asset classes is so wide that outperformance is about picking the best managers."

"And this is something you can do?"

How could he recreate it, being in the room and judging, as God, which of *them*—Mount Mitchell or the Australian, Miller Lamb or A.dV, Karen Kahn, Brian Park, Scumbag Polansky, Kevin Doherty, a North Meadow of good diplomas and funnels and moats—was provably good? "Who is afraid of the efficient market?" the CIO eventually answered. "Who cares that to believe in the persistence of GP outperformance, you have to ignore a lot of research? Our self-image comes down to this: are we the smart guys who pick the best managers, have access to the best managers, and pass on the overhyped managers? This is an odd thing for a life to be about. But we are trying to pay attention, to *see*. We have invented, or intuited, tools to do this: gossip, narratives, heuristics, etc. I hate gossip out of pride, but some manager selection follows a tight reasoning: I heard Princeton is doing it, and Princeton has its pick of the litter, so who are we to think we're better than the Man with the Golden Name. Even Harvard still has stroke in that regard. Or you can go with narratives: invest with whichever manager's value proposition is the easiest to describe. The memo of least resistance. That's often the newest GPs. But even veteran managers with 'Proven Mediocrity' tattooed on their foreheads are ready to help us Simple LPs construct a narrative about their Discipline and Structural Genius. I've always been a heuristic guy, even if I suspect you don't like the word."

Hermann stared, his glasses reflecting the monitor again.

"I was very proud of one for a while, my signature invention. We are—were—looking for managers with three things: an alchemic system, private inputs, and persistent hunger. This elegantly worked across asset classes. It particularly seemed to help with what is 70 percent of this business: don't do stupid shit. It's not like we expected to get all three all the time. If a manager had an alchemic system based on very private inputs, she tended to get rich and satiated. So it was about balancing goods. I used to tell people to shortcut their thinking by subjectively assigning a one-to-ten score in each of the categories. A woman who briefly worked for me became obsessed with deciding if some GP in some category was a seven or a six. Now, we just say that so-and-so is pretty solid on system but probably not hungry. Or, these guys are persistently hungry, with a decade of stuff to prove, and some system that *seems* new."

"And you believe this works?" Hermann asked as he leaned back in his chair and allowed what seemed like it could have been a smile.

"For seven years, it seemed to work." The CIO didn't like to have to say it. He had soared when he was above it. But now it seemed essential to clear up. "I had exceptionally good numbers. And so I encouraged my underlings to be mum about the cold fusion of endowment management. I was going to gift it upon humanity in my book, *Re-Viewing Portfolio Management*. Re-dash-viewing. A pun only an intragovernmental panel could love."

Hermann was reading something on his monitor. He paused, looked at the CIO, seemingly only to confirm he was still there. Facing the monitor again, he asked, "Do you not think that it would be a good idea to bring data to this task?"

"There is a rebel band that thinks guys like me are antediluvian plodders. Those guys talk about streams of risk and streams of returns, put on portfolio overlays, constantly toggle risks they 'want' to have and spend every second trying to 'isolate alpha.' They love macro calls. They love liquidity. They *love* Ray Dalio. I don't really understand it. I think it's a dangerous game. And I hope to God those two statements have nothing to do with each other. But it seems that these guys want to run multi-strategy hedge funds and graft that desire onto what is supposed to be the prudently managed savings account of a nonprofit institution. So far, none of them have blown up spectacularly. I guess they listen closely enough to Bridgewater. Then again, when we are all hit in the face with our relative numbers each year, those guys are also not consistently doing better."

Hermann turned on his monitor and read something. The CIO

wondered if his own avalanche of words was there to hold himself down, to not rip a monitor out of Hermann's attention and throw it against the wall.

The avalanche continued: "The rest of us have plenty of instrumental data to put into our memos, even if we know the footnote of every pitchbook is the moral of every story: past performance is no guarantee of future results. But we keep ourselves off the streets by slicing and dicing data: individual partner track records, cycle track records, public market equivalents to compare a private equity firm's performance against what would have happened had we just bought stocks. Our memos always attribute success to *something*. But I'm not sure if we write memos to convey information or just to cover our tracks. I'm not sure if GPs themselves know why they outperform. Asking too many questions disturbs the incalculable self-regard that is every investor's greatest formula. But, yes, we stare at data all day long, asking the same questions. Is it the seat or the person? Is it the sector or the strategy? Is it luck, and our selection bias steers us to the luckiest on an inevitable distribution curve of luck? Or maybe I'm just an amateur, and the Swensenian spawn have the answer and are not sharing it with schmucks with lesser pedigrees. They could be smarter, or have built-in advantages. Maybe the real genius GPs want to take *their* money because having a Yale GP sticker on the back of your Model X is the next best thing to having the Yale Dad sticker there—or a way to get one. In this winner-takes-all world, are we the Two Percent being squashed by the One Percent? Then again, Harvard.

"Obviously, some GPs have something: Benchmark, Sequoia, Renaissance, Appaloosa, Two Sigma, Tolemy if you know Karen Kahn. I assume—" the CIO stopped himself from talking about Hermann's numbers. "But there are not enough of them for all the capital we need to invest. And so we all daydream about answering your question by becoming the Billy Beane of Endowment Management. Instead of tracking right-field doubles off Dominican curveballs, we would measure credit strategy performance by Ashkenazi Jews in Midwestern cities with low Sharpe ratios. But as we wait for *that* to happen, we are all fat ass scouts: to find the systematic talents, who have private data or catalytic investment opportunities, who are not just adding competition to an already saturated market, and who are relentlessly disciplined in maintaining their outperformance despite getting rich, we trust our gut, our nose, and some tricks."

"Such as?"

"Check the PGA website for a GP's handicap. Multiple marriages: good or bad? Two demerits for French cuffs. Uptalk by grown men: discuss. Why does anyone live in Florida? It's an important question. I have a college I've never had luck with, and while I'll not blackball someone for just doing undergrad there, life is too short if he went there after Andover. I go back and forth on intellectual breadth: sometimes I think that a GP who name-drops John Updike or the Fifteenth Amendment must understand the world, and thus finance, better. Sometimes I think I should stick with clever guys with fast-twitch minds—my opposite, at least by self-image. Then again, I had an experience with one of those bent-nose guys last month, and I still can't shake it off." The CIO stopped. How could he continue? He continued. "I have a thing about cellphone lock screens."

"Do you think I understand what that means?"

The CIO felt in some groove. Could Hermann's tolerance be an equivalent of respect? "GPs come into our downscale conference room and put their phones face down. They act as if donating bone marrow to your dying child is a less generous act than not reading their phones while asking you for money. They all take one last look to make sure the screen is locked, a bit stunned that this separation is happening. More often than not, the rest of the room can glimpse what is on the screen. And here comes the brilliance: *if* it's a picture of the manager, alone, finishing the San Diego Marathon or reeling in a tarpon, and *if* I find out that that guy has your standard hedge fund four-pack of children, again, life is too short."

Hermann didn't speak.

"For years, I held out hope that the Oleg Test would work. There are, like, three livery car drivers in town, but Oleg gets most GPs coming to us. He was a martial arts instructor in Minsk, so maybe he karate chops the others when a Wall Street baller needs a Suburban. His wife is a nurse at the hospital. About five years ago, I ran into him at a birthday party of a doctor whose wife is friends with my wife. He said to me, 'Oh, Chief Investment Officer, I know about you.' And out of the blue, he asked me what I thought of Seth Klarman, who had come in two months earlier. Oleg then proceeds to tout the upside of a semiconductor stock that I had to pretend to have heard of. But he seems to legitimately read *Institutional Investor* or something because he knows a lot of GP names. I run into him every four or five months.

"Two years ago, I'm buying cherries when he appears next to me at the store and says, 'Oh man, David Rubinstein!' A trustee had asked that I meet with Rubinstein when Carlyle had some short-lived idea to push into E&Fs. I was by then less surprised by Oleg knowing Rubinstein than by the fact that Rubinstein was driven by Oleg. I guess I assumed that Rubinstein had one of those C-4 cargo jets with a town car inside it. Anyway, I make small talk about how Carlyle is not really our speed, and Oleg says, 'Take big man to say no to big man, right?'

"A year ago, an emerging markets credit group comes into the office laughing about Oleg's take on Petrobras's valuation. During their pitch, I can't quite figure out if the GP is a poser. The managing partner used the word 'exceptional' every five minutes, which annoyed me. So—maybe this is when I started losing it—I ask my wife to blah, blah, get Oleg's number. And I call him and ask if anything had come up in the car. Oleg answered, 'Oh, this is real Belarusian stuff.' It was as if I was the KGB—the *B*-KGB. I had been humiliated *before* I called him, from the amateurism. And then to be shot down while being an amateur. I'm not even sure what I thought Oleg would tell me. Were the guys talking to interior designers? Arranging threesomes? Are they jerks? And what would that have answered? Is being a jerk to your one-time driver of a very large Chevrolet a sign of persistent hunger, and we should invest with them because of that? Is it a sign of lack of empathetic judgment that will cause them to miss investment clues? Is there any correlation to performance, to anything whatsoever?"

The CIO stopped.

Finally Hermann asked, "Do you think I have time to unearth the layers of stupidity imposed on me over the last fifteen minutes?" Declarations of stupidity on Wall Street were often declarations of deepest bro love. But then: "How much do you get paid to do this?"

The CIO had nothing left, no reason to not answer. He wanted to answer, too, to find out if Hermann would think it was offensively large, invisibly small, or had meaning in any way. *I don't do nihilism.* "With average 'good' performance relative to our benchmarks, it's been about 1.6 million dollars a year."

The CIO had thought that he had already seen Hermann's eating-your-brain smile. He hadn't. Hermann now seemed to be actually cleaning his teeth of residue.

Hermann then said, "The only problem with the investment management business is the investment management business."

"That means?"

"For 1.6 million dollars per year, you can't figure it out?"

The CIO needed to stand up. He was taller than Hermann, taller than Emily, standing accomplished something. Eleven billion dollars didn't allow you to control who gets to stand.

But the CIO remained seated. Maybe the moral of today's America is 11 billion dollars—almost twice the endowment—allows you to control who gets to stand.

"I'm trying to decide," Hermann went on, "from your phrenology, if LPs have gotten stupider since I last dealt with them."

The CIO, parched, could barely speak. "You don't have any LPs?"

"I have nine legacy individuals whom I allow to remain investors under instructions that if they ever, one, contact me or, two, ask for an allocation for someone else, I will return their money. One and two are redundant, but I like the emphasis. I have one institutional investor who proposed that same arrangement to me and has lived by it. I haven't seen them in a decade."

Over the years, the CIO had disbelieved what he thought was a Paul Bunyan story, alternatively about MSD, the Getty Trust, and the Grand Duke of Luxembourg.

"In 2009, I had three useless people working for me: one to deny new investors, one to stop existing investors from asking for my time, and one to deal with reporting." Hermann turned on his screen and pushed on his glasses to read something more closely. He kept talking. "And then I calculated that when you yourself represent half of your capital base, if an additional 20 percent on your total return, achievable through carried interest, makes you a 21 percent worse investor, that's a loser bet."

"Is that the math?"

"Do you think that is math?"

The CIO understood there was no need, ever, to speak.

"The last decade has confirmed that focus generates more wealth than carry."

The CIO felt himself reverting to a five-year-old. He had no focus nor carry, no means of generating one from the other. He tried to find the words. "I've been trying to think about the business differently."

"That is a good idea."

"I've been pushing on the idea of an uneasy equilibrium."

"'A little dull as a solution, you will say?'"

"What?"

"Also Isaiah Berlin. I assumed you would get that unless you took your Berlin from a philosopher-of-the-day self-improvement calendar or an investing podcast."

"I threw away my philosopher-of-the-day calendar when it quoted Hegel on podcasts."

Hermann didn't speak, but the CIO rested his back, cupped, into the never-to-be-comfortable chair. He had not been intimidated by Bill Gurley or Howard Marks or Henry Kravis. He could do this. "I got my Berlin from reading Berlin. I just didn't recognize that line."

"That line is more appropriate than your application of Berlin to a 'discovery' that investing must balance risk and reward."

And thus endeth two months spent developing eight breakthrough shapes.

Hermann looked at his screen and began typing. Was he trading? Taking notes? Emailing jokes?

What could a Michael Hermann joke possibly be?

"Do you study Berlin?" the CIO asked, almost out of breath.

"I stopped."

"Why is that?"

Hermann shut off the monitor. There was a possibility that he looked at the CIO as more than a background shape. "Again, the biggest problem with the investment management business is the investment management business."

"Which means?"

"You get paid 1.6 million dollars per year to observe investors. Your job, such as it is, is to take your chips to a new table when your 'heuristics' divine something amiss. I'm talking about something different. Take Ken Griffin." Hermann leaned on his desk. "I wouldn't buy a 250-million-dollar apartment in Manhattan less because I would not live in Manhattan if you paid me 250 million dollars, although that is true, but because a 250-million-dollar apartment involves months spent with lawyers, architects, and PR agents to deal with the blowback. How much time was lost to that? Cohen?" Hermann began counting billionaires with his fingers. "I've never admired his strategy of regulatory arbitrage, but it has worked if that is all you can do. But do you think there is any debate of how he should spend his finite time if the choice is trading or selecting picture frames? Singer? How much time does he spend trying to make Republicans like gay people? Look at his dollar-weighted returns. Simons? He has computers to do his work, so I guess he can spend time with his math club. Ackman? Einhorn? They are public figures because they want to be public figures. Are you surprised how this impacts performance?"

Hermann waited.

"There are two clear signs of my peers not focusing on performance," he continued. "One: owning a major league sports team, which combines their need to compete on things that cannot matter and to purchase interesting non-white acquaintances."

The CIO smiled about Brian Park's exercised arms and the Sacramento Kings.

"But the distraction more corrosive than owning a sports team is trying to become a public intellectual. Dalio is smart, Soros is smart enough, so stupidity alone cannot explain why they are spending as much money as necessary to get people to listen to their opinions on the normative human experience. Do you think that is their job? Or is their job turning a dollar into two? That's why I stopped reading Berlin. It was too tempting to communicate how I improved on his ideas. Although, one, I have improved on them. Berlin's ideas about equality are not well-reasoned. And two, I have the means to make that improvement known."

The CIO had rushed through the grip of Chicago winter on his way from airport to car to Hermann's office. But he now needed to be outside, to be punished by that familiar cold, to have a body released from this office, with its tidy stacks and blank walls and first-class Steelcase shelves, its no place and every place.

And yet...

He reached for a Hermannesque phrasing: "Don't you think your peers decided that there is diminishing marginal utility to making more money versus what they could do with the money?"

"What is the utility of owning a basketball team? Increasing the median height of your sycophants? What is the utility of buying a 150-million-dollar painting? I know Cohen enough to bet he gets more joy from a trade that banks him 150 million than from spending that on a piece of colored canvas. So why does he do it? Why do they all do it?"

The CIO didn't speak.

"They are under the impression that being a good investor is not interesting. Being the world's most profligate art collector, on the other hand, is 'interesting.' And easy: what is the barrier to entry to that? But your question does not get to why I object. Why would I care if people can stop being investors? I do not judge Tom Steyer for doing full-time whatever he believes he is doing on his journey of self-exculpation, however unappealing. My contempt is reserved for people pretending they are still committed to investing."

Hermann turned on his screen and started reading. After two minutes, he began talking again. "I make sure that the Bloomberg index and *Forbes* list are accurate. I do not like people making up numbers. But I do not respond to reporters' requests for interviews. If a reporter gets the phone number to this office, my assistants say, 'There is no need for this call.' I am, however, tempted to give an interview to whichever reporter abandons her dream of the Most Mysterious Man on Wall Street stupidity to write a profile of the Most Uninteresting Man on Wall Street. I will sit in the lobby of a Residence Inn and talk about the weather."

The CIO needed to find a fingerhold, to make him—Hermann—articulate winning. It felt close, possible. Through chitchat about snow? "And what would you say if they asked about your work?"

"What do you think I would say if they asked me about my work?"

"I know you are an equity investor. But this black hole you've made is a very black hole."

Hermann pushed himself closer to the desk, turned on the monitor, and began typing again. The CIO wasn't sure if he was messaging his assistants to call security or emailing Carl Icahn that he had someone that was more his style. Hermann's thin nose seemed to be getting thinner as if his concentrating, narrowed eyes could turn his face into angles and planes.

As two turned to three tightening minutes of silence, the CIO realized that Hermann was doing his job, making money, being uninteresting.

Hermann at last stopped typing. He said, "This is why I don't engage with people like you."

The CIO didn't have the energy to sigh.

"It'd be pointless to explain it."

The CIO shook his head and chuckled mildly.

"Did I say something stupid?"

"I am the CIO of a 6-billion-dollar college endowment. I spend my life talking to what should be generational talents of investing.

And while I was recently told by some quants that they *can't* tell me what they do, I've never had anyone imply that I couldn't understand what they do."

"Imagine that: you get flattered by people who want your money."

For some reason, the CIO wasn't bothered by this. "Well, how about the other Most-Mysterious-Man-on-Wall-Street question?"

"And what would that be?"

"What do you do with your money?"

"I find it distracting."

The CIO tried to hide a smile. Snapping his lips over it made it feel like the first real smile of his life. He asked, mainly composed, "You don't think about what to do with"—he paused, but the number had been proclaimed accurate—"11 billion dollars?"

"No."

"Because?"

"Did I not tell you why?"

The CIO was still.

"I find it distracting. Look at Loeb and charter schools. One, his children have no risk of setting foot in a public school except to pad college applications with a passing proximity to poor people. Two, he is obsessed with a technical fix to public education administration that is 5 percent of the problem. But the reason he is an idiot is because every time he thinks about charter schools, he is eroding the talent that makes people listen to him. Private equity is worse. Do those people work at all? Why does Steve Schwarzman drain his energy finding new opportunities to put 'Schwarzman' on buildings?"

"As revenge for having to constantly spell 'Schwarzman'?"

Hermann paused, waiting for the noise of humor to pass out of earshot. "Or your friend David Rubinstein, with his pandas and Magna Cartas. Why is he concerned if Washington, D.C. lacks copies of feudal English political documents or oversized Chinese raccoons?" Hermann turned off his monitor and looked at the CIO. "Do you think I *don't* understand the conventional explanation for this? Philanthropy is today's indulgences. Dollar for dollar, virtue is cheap and easy to buy. Sign the Giving Pledge, and you can have your staff change your Wikipedia page to 'philanthropist and...' That is at most 20 percent of the reason. It is also useless. Does anyone believe that he can adjust his hedonic settings via action?"

The CIO's thirst was rioting. He pulled in his lips to wet them. Eventually he managed to say, "You have to make some arrangement for your money."

"Do you? Most people in the world die intestate."

"You'd want that?"

"Do you think I believe that the optimal stewards of this capital would be the federal government and the fiscal incompetents of the State of Illinois? Then again, avoiding taxes is a stupid distraction. Look at Robertson. Maybe if he spent less time documenting the seconds he was in New Jersey, he'd have more than four."

"So what's going to happen to the money?"

"My niece and nephew have been given interest in HCM from its inception and have become wealthy on a tax-efficient basis. The rest goes to the Uno Anno Tempore Foundation."

At last, love and women and a soul with a hedonic setting moved by something other than correcting the CIO. "Ann Otemporay?"

"Uno *Anno* Tempore. One year long. I assumed you knew Latin, with your name-dropping of ethical philosophers. The foundation will give away its capital in one year and shut down. Does anyone think it is a good idea to set up a permanent institution that employs people like you to invent ways to maximize their necessity and rent?"

"But I don't understand. What will the foundation do?"

"I have no idea."

"You don't think about it?"

"I find it distracting."

"Come on, man, never?"

Hermann looked at the CIO. It felt like the look could have been meant to decompose him. But that would imply that Hermann saw him. Hermann glanced at his screen and said, "I understand that it is easy to think about it. It is even interesting to think about it. But I find it distracting."

"But with all the needs in the world, all the good you can do, you don't think it's worth it to be a *little* bit distracted?"

"What about chickens?"

The CIO examined Hermann's face for a clue. "Huh?"

"Should Uno Anno Tempore give its assets to organizations that advance the well-being of chickens? Debeaking. Overcrowding. Chicken cancers."

The CIO waited for the punchline. Hermann waited for the CIO.

The CIO finally asked, "Are you a vegetarian?"

"Why would I be a vegetarian? Why would anyone be a vegetarian? But why have some animals—dogs, cats, horses, any animal unfit or stupid enough to be endangered—been chosen for philanthropy? Somewhere between housecats and lice comes an arbitrary line where human empathy stops. Does the placement of that line make sense? Could some amount of money push chickens above that line?"

"Do you *want* to do that?"

"The reason to consider your question is if it would be less distracting to have made a decision."

This was the time for the CIO to die on the ridge, prove that Marvin had incomparable foresight. Shake here, and the CIO would (somehow) make it happen. Eleven billion dollars for complete naming rights. Hermann University—the University of Hermann?—a top-five school in an instant, the new fucking Stanford. They could even start a billion-dollar program for chickens.

But he was the chicken. He said to the back of the monitor, “So there’s nothing you spend money on?”

“Do you think I drive a Kia to signal frugality? I invest to reduce distractions.”

Do I have the right from Wirbin to cite Wirbin, the CIO thought as he heard his mouth saying, “Ben Wirbin told me that you don’t like distractions.”

Hermann turned on his monitor and began typing, looking between screens. The typing seemed to be getting louder. He eventually asked, “Does Ben Wirbin ever shut up? In the too many classes I took with him, he was more focused on being entertaining than finding the best answer.”

“I’ve found him unusually good at doing both.”

“Imagine that: you are impressed by a man who has abandoned his fiduciary responsibility by indulging your investment strategy of qualitative ‘heuristics’ and advice-seeking from Belorussian cab drivers. But, sure, Ben is not dumb. He is just lazy. In college, he led a crew that imagined themselves the campus’s true New Yorkers. Their referent system was Robert de Niro playing gangsters playing the Beastie Boys. I had zero interest in that act. I’m not surprised that he ended up in his position.”

“Most people think Ben is one of the most successful people they have ever met.”

“Was I the one begging him for 50 million dollars? Was I the one raging when I didn’t get it?

Could you draw any conclusion from that other than that upper-middle management at Goldman Sachs has left something missing in his life?”

Just leave. Leave Chicago, leave this life, leave being in the same line of work as self-satisfied Satans like Michael Hermann.

But first: win. Eleven billion dollars *couldn't* melt him with words. No one could melt anyone with words. The CIO himself could melt this conversation with the immolation of... of the judging by investment performance, every day. He said, with slow care, "One could also conclude that, being extraordinarily generous, Ben gets angry when other people don't act that way."

Hermann smiled the brain-tasting smile. "Do you believe that?"

The CIO was through. He was free. "Thanks. This has been very educational. I know much better now why people hate Wall Street."

"Is that where you're going with your 1.6-million-dollar salary?"

"It's not 11 billion dollars."

"Should I compare the transparency, honesty, and economic justification of how I made 11 billion dollars to how you 'earn' 1.6 million dollars per year?"

Stop talking.

"And tell me, what is wrong with having 11 billion dollars? Would the world be any different if I did not have 11 billion dollars?"

Stop talking.

"Would other people have more money? Who would have more money?"

Stop talking.

"What are the total financial assets of the world?"

The devil is intolerable because the devil is inarguable.

"You've already wasted twenty-eight minutes of my time. So humor me."

"A 100 trillion dollars?"

"You're off 100 percent. It's 200 trillion. Eleven billion dollars is .06 basis points of that number. Do you think that is material?"

The CIO needed to be his father, or at least Wirbin. His question instead came out exhausted: "Don't you think it's unusual to know off the top of your head what percentage of the *world's* wealth you personally own? Given that you represent one-seven-and-a-half-billionth of the world's population. This means that your share of the world's financial assets is equivalent to"—the CIO was desperate for a piece of paper to get the math ostentatiously right—"seven and a half... two hundred... equivalent to, like, 400 thousand people?"

Hermann smirked. "Did I say it was not 'unusual'? Is it 'usual' that Isaiah Berlin wrote the essays he did? Your argument seems only to be that being unusual, in this one case, is wrong."

"Well, is it *decent* that some immigrant hustles to death cleaning offices, working every bit as hard as you do to make in a year what you made in the half-hour I've been here? Is it right that all the people who work at much harder jobs than ours do so for wages that have been stagnant for forty years? That 30 million Americans still don't have health insurance, that an unconscionable number of families are desperate for minimally competent schools we fail to provide, that all that is nothing compared to the poverty, disease, and hunger suffered by a mind-blowing number of people in the world?"

Hermann showed no response.

The CIO started again, from a different spot. "If where you plan on heading now is cornering me with 'truth' about myself or my place in this world, trust me, I've been there. I *know* that I can't economically or morally justify my salary except by citing the same rigged-game facts that everyone cites: that the school's next best alternative *may* demand even more; that my salary is irrelevant if I can outperform by *three* basis points a year. But I am talking here about the hoarding of wealth. And I am pretty sure it's not crazy, or even 'uninteresting,' to imagine that some portion of the 11 billion dollars made by the mysterious methods of the Most Mysterious Man on Wall Street could come in handy to address some of the world's problems? Can you really think that 11 billion dollars has the right to tell the world to leave it alone because it doesn't want to be distracted? How is any of this just?"

"Again, did I claim something was just or unjust? I just stated facts. You, on the other hand, conflated wealth, wealth creation, and Wall Street. *Alpha* magazine does this, which is why I don't respond to them. Why do I have a certain amount of money? I have it because I invest in stocks that go up more often than not. The money I generate from providing financial services is an annoyance. So, what portion of my money concerns people like you? Or are you just bleating the old annoyance that some people are richer and some people are poorer? Your points *could* be logical if, one, 'Wall Street' controls the world's wealth or, two, Wall Street causes asset inequality. I look forward to hearing arguments about how either happens. Wall Street is a market of exchange and a collection of financial services around that exchange. Bezos's billions are, sure, in public shares. Did Wall Street *create* Bezos? Control him? Do you even know the statistics? Less than 15 percent of the world's billionaires are self-made through finance. Over twice that inherited their money. And the wealth of successful investors is not meaningful compared to the institutional pools of capital that own most of the world's financial assets.

"Now, to the second implication." Hermann began looking again at his monitors as he talked. "Have you spent any time thinking about a counterfactual? Financial markets exist everywhere. China has financial markets and one level of inequality. So does Sweden. So does the United States. Where is the correlation? If Wall Street disappeared tomorrow, would American children have better schools? Would Kenyans have more doctors? Would the reversion to the mean of Chinese wealth be reversed? Would a new manufacturing operation in Kansas become a better idea? Considering that there are five hundred times more people in China than Kansas, would this even be a good thing? Those are large questions. You pose small questions. So, again, how would a re-categorization of money now marked as belonging to Hermann Capital Management change anything?"

The CIO didn't speak. Marvin had tricked him. The world had tricked him.

"One has to make oneself get offended," Hermann added.

"But people *look*," the CIO said in what he hoped was not a whine. "It's clear to them that the over-rewarding, by an unimaginable multiple, of the minor human task of investing is revolting."

"Revolting?"

The CIO had accepted the inevitability of being crushed by logic and success and 11 billion dollars. But he would be at peace with dying here if he could draw one drop of blood with irreplaceable words. "Yes, it is revolting that some hedge fund kid can make 50 million dollars by calling a few trades right. It is revolting that so many kids, with all the useful and profound things they could be studying, major in economics at our school to get a job to make those trades. What conclusion can you draw from that other than that the world is a very fucked-up place."

"I understand that a hyperbolic and incorrect diagnosis that the world is worse than ever makes you feel sophisticated. I understand that this particular incorrect diagnosis is the central ideological belief of America's and Europe's progressive upper-middle class. But do you people think about facts before you talk? Do you know the facts? One, the world has less violence and poverty than it has ever had. Two, people are living longer and healthier lives than ever before. Three, there are more people living longer and healthier lives than ever before. Four, the world's ability to adapt to climate change has grown five hundred times faster than global warming. Five, by you people's measures of the highest virtues, the world has less bigotry, sexism, homophobia, child abuse, domestic abuse, rape, and animal cruelty than any time in human history. So the idea that Wall Street or even income inequality is the cause of the world's most severe problems sweeps under the rug the fact that the world has less severe problems than it has ever had. There is a growing number of rich people because an integrated, ever wealthier, ever better world offers greater rewards to people who provide products and services to a larger, growing market."

"I've read Steven Pinker, too. I don't attribute that to my wealth."

"I am not claiming that I am the cause of that, or even a part of the cause. I am just asking, would you prefer a world in which that human amelioration did not happen in order to ensure that my wealth creation did not happen?"

"It's not an either/or."

"Because this is all easy? To make a capitalist society, to invent new technologies, to build businesses that thrive, to create all that is necessary to increase global wellbeing? Should we just ask Congress to pass a bill to achieve this?"

"Am I asking Congress to do anything? I'm just questioning the hoarding of money for no end other than to impart a lesson to people so dumb as to not have become hedge fund managers. But I'm sure you're not worried about Congress, anyway."

Hermann had started typing, leaning towards his Bloomberg.

"You probably have all the political levers money can buy."

Hermann, grimacing, looked only at what he was typing. "Is this where we are going now? To yet another series of specious systemic diagnoses? Do you think taxes aren't higher because I am a part of a cabal that controls the United States? The Soros cabal? The Koch cabal? An upper-level cabal that controls both the Soros cabal and the Koch cabal? Well, I have never met a Koch. I have no interest in meeting a Koch. Taxes aren't higher because people observe how effective the government is at spending the 8 trillion dollars it already spends."

The CIO would one day return to gravity and language. "You have an answer for everything."

"I have the answer for how I spend my time and my money." He paused, waiting for the CIO. "Did I ask to come to your office to discuss how you spend your time and money?"

What was the purpose of not being angry anymore, in this world of 11 billion dollars deaf to need? What was the purpose of being better than his father? He was already far past anything his father could have accomplished. So he should be able to stuff Hermann's constant do-you-believes with a hard fist, grab his screen—*screen*—and crash it through the window, to bring in the shock of cold. The cold was the counterargument. The cold was the real world.

The CIO watched himself not standing up.

The CIO watched Hermann typing again.

And he felt failure wash over him. He had failed to learn the gears of Hermann's money machine, failed to learn anything about investing, failed to stand up for decency, failed to be violently angry, failed to get a consolation prize of 50 million dollars, failed to understand anything more than what he had already failed to uncover in ten thousand meetings with a thousand managers. Could he will himself now to be whatever Jane had become, a Mona Lisa, mysteriously content? Content without regard to accomplishment? Successful because contemptuous of success?

I really do hope you find what you are looking for.

"Do you want to know how I got here?" the CIO found himself asking.

Hermann was still typing.

"I... I don't know where I'm going with this."

Christ.

Hermann pushed the rimless glasses higher on his thin nose.

They neared his inconsistent eyebrows and called attention to the long plane rising to his hairline. He looked at the CIO and then at the screen. He began to read something. He then shifted his chair back to be less obscured.

And he turned off the monitor.

"I grew up in Jewish suburbia, Milwaukee version. We were comfortable, if not where my father thought he 'deserved' to be. I majored in American history at Williams and ended up in graduate school at NYU. My interest faded two months into it, so I never got to be the iconic PhD visited one night by visions of becoming Wall Street rich."

Hermann didn't invite the CIO to explain more about A.dV or Brian Park.

"I don't know if I dropped out because I was still smarting from not getting into Yale. Or maybe it was because of a conversation with a professor, on John Brown. She stared at me as if I had expressed approval of the lowest form of human output: the commercial biography. Which was kind of true. A friend of mine worked in equity research at CSFB. I was always better at math than I wanted to be. I had good grades. Back then, that was enough, especially as my boss and I understood each other's purpose. He got a non-idiot body to write first drafts of quarterly earnings notes and run primitive models. I got to save face when quitting graduate school.

"CSFB was thrilling, to my surprise. I had a *salary*. I bought suits. I could see how easy it would be to make way more than my father, even more than the people my father envied. That was pleasantly insane. But the bigger thrill was a realization that this could be my world of ideas—my intersection of theory and reality and contingency. Who was to say that these were *not* the most interesting ideas? The analyst I worked for destroyed telephones if he felt he was being fed anything less than pure truth. Did anyone in graduate school care that much about a text?

"Because life always has a next step, I went to the buy side, to Scudder. *Scudder*: it's like I'm reminiscing of my days on a whaling ship. And then, because I ended up on Wall Street without ever pursuing it, because none of this could be how things were supposed to progress in my special and destined life, I got an executive MBA at Columbia. That graduated me to feeling even more alien to myself, to real MBAs, to people who didn't need MBAs. But it got me a job at Alliance, where I eventually became a portfolio manager of a small sector fund. I established my professional personality there, a bit"—he paused—"professorial, a connoisseur of absurdity, prone to speeches like this. And then at an RJR Nabisco analyst day, an acquaintance at Nationwide Insurance mentioned that a sleepy but large family foundation in Columbus, Ohio, was hiring its first CIO. I can't say my wife and I burned to live in Ohio. But she wanted to leave New York before we started a family. And my professorial, absurdity-savoring act at Alliance was not translating into consistent outperformance. I was counting the hours before security guards brought in empty file boxes and ordered me to pack up my stuff. Many of those Days of Sisyphus, I wanted to bring in my own boxes. And so my elevation to CIO was, partly, another thing to do to not be doing something else.

"But I ended up liking the title more than I expected. I liked that the foundation needed professional management, given the nursing home of a board. I liked the money, too, especially how far it went in Columbus. And I did okay." He paused. "Better than okay. And then I was headhunted to the endowment. A very conventional story of a mid-successful American life. But after nine and a half years there, I barely think about what I've actually done. I just seem to ruminate on alternative paths not glanced at except in daydreams. I've never served in office, or the military, or even in a classroom except as an inconsequential guest. I've never brought the house down, as an actor or an athlete. I've never even fixed a car. I don't know how to fix a car.

"Really, what have I done? My first real professional victory was preserving value in '08–'09 with the most consequential market call of my life. And then I had a good run at the endowment, when I thought that I was proving that this work does not *have* to just be electronically categorizing wealth. My work meant, yes, fancy dorms and brittle, entitled academics but also scholarships and ideas given money to breathe. Ben Wirbin and my wife will tell you that my clothes never seem to fit right. But this job felt custom-made. It allowed me to do my work and feel the secondary contributions to an objectively not-worse world. It allowed me to be kindly ironic and coolly above it all. It allowed me to intellectualize things. Doesn't a college endowment *need* a quirky, professorial approach? Wouldn't the fulfillment of a true need be rewarded with success?"

Hermann didn't speak.

"And the salary? Making 1.6 million dollars a year *must* be evidence that the world thinks you're special. Was that my father's lifetime earnings? Not adjusted for inflation, maybe more. And there's this too: to me, *not* being the least bit hungry to make more than 1.6 million dollars was a sign that I was meant to be an LP, one step removed from the battlefield."

Was this getting through to Hermann? Beating Hermann, by showing him a reconciliation of—what?—finance and modesty, passion and comfort? But was this even getting through to himself? Everything that he had said was true, but none of it felt exactly enough. Should he tell him about Yeboah? Or this? Yes, well, then this: "There's a woman who works for me. Emily. Smart, overly serious, not completely sound of judgment yet but getting there, and, from the beginning, unintimidated. We once had a manager visit us, about a year after she started working for me. As we entered the room, I caught an IR woman looking at real estate listings on her phone, right swiping through pictures of fancy bathrooms. I was so bored that I kept wondering if I could find a way to make a joke about how my wife and I shared a single sink, like medieval peasants. But then I was jogged awake by how respectful and, simultaneously, uncharmed Emily was by this regional venture capital strategy.

"When she came into my office afterwards, we looked each other in the eyes and laughed. She has this way of pulling her upper lip over her gums after she laughs. But that time, she didn't. We laughed not because the fund was a totally stupid idea—Emily doesn't bring stupid ideas to the provinces—but because we were on the same page in our, our... souls or something. The risk just wasn't worth it. And the manager ended up doing horribly. Their largest position was in Rhode Island's biggest food delivery app that was, within a year, completely wiped out by national competitors. When I got an email about how the firm imploded, I forwarded it to Emily with a smiley face emoticon. She wrote back with the fist bump emoticon—a white one, interestingly. That afternoon, we both left the office at the same time even though she usually is the last to leave. Without thinking about it, we both stopped at the entrance to our building. We looked out at the campus, at all the students and learning, at what seemed at the moment totally carefree. And we brought those emoticons to life with shit-eating grins and a fist bump that filled me with, with, with..."

He stared at Hermann, trying to catch eye contact. Hermann was looking towards him, at least.

"When my numbers were really good, I was aware of two big choices I always had. First, because my money was 'found,' because it was never pursued, shouldn't this be the year in which I declare the money enough? Second, shouldn't this be the year in which I finally find the work that will allow me to be closer to the use of proceeds than the source of proceeds—the principal, not the enabler? But I never did anything about those two. And now, now when the numbers are not 'really' good or even good at all, I think about those two 'choices' all the time. And these choices seemed to be completely defined by this third thing, which is, can any of this"—the CIO circled his hand around the office, its billions—"be how the world really works?"

He stopped.

"Is there a reason you are telling me all of this?"

"Because I am talking to the ninety-seventh richest person on earth whose fortune was made through some level of genius and who—if this is true—sincerely thinks about giving it to chickens? Maybe reciting a life story that has, uh, lost its way is the only thing to do now. Because of all the times when I thought none of this could be how the world works, this—"

The CIO stopped, his tongue hanging over his lower teeth. Christ, he was thirsty. Christ, he would give anything to ask for a glass of water. And so, looking down, he slowly circled his rubbing hand over his forehead, hard then harder, and then down over his eyes and beard. He thought about the fist bump with Emily. He thought about his inability to make hard fists anymore. He thought that nothing would stop this hand from rubbing and rubbing forever, harder and harder. Hermann would go away.

The CIO stopped, though, when he heard Hermann turn on his Bloomberg. Hermann read something, then typed. The CIO assumed that Hermann was emailing his distraction reducer. Lye, the CIO's corpse, a bathtub, the end.

At least a bathtub might have water.

But Hermann took off his glasses and pinched the thin bridge of his nose as if he could get his fingers to touch. He put his glasses back on and shifted his chair back so that the CIO would be less blocked.

And then Hermann spoke. "I have always focused on how math was right, rather than where it circled upon itself." Hermann looked at the screen and then back at the CIO. "I am wasting my time with this, but okay. As a child, I was the cliché fascinated by share price movements printed in the *Journal.* I got a brokerage account when I was ten. I started reading *Barron's* in high school to listen to how professional investors thought. I ended up at your institution because Harvard wanted more well-rounded students. Once there, instead of finding people interested in investing, I found Ben Wirbin and his acolytes. They were interested in 'Wall Street,' Blue Sky Airlines, Darryl Hannah, and money. When I started working, it annoyed me that the Street's so-called competition was also around unproductive end goals and personal status. It annoyed me how people like Ben Wirbin stop when they find a short cut, an AUM trick, or a salary arbitrage. It annoyed me how people failed upwards. And, yes, it annoyed me that that a lazy mediocrity could get a bigger bonus than I did from two trades in the casino. And so I put a program in place to not be annoyed."

Hermann paused, stared at the CIO, and continued: "I choose to avoid pursuits in which, one, I have no aptitude and, two, the benefits do not justify the costs. I accept that it makes sense for most people to accept 'trade-offs.' Giving away a panda gets your name in the papers. Using adverbs can ease a conversation's fluidity. The data on the hedonic experience of having a spouse and children is mixed. But if a person cannot otherwise achieve personal satisfaction, it is perhaps worth wagering that you can beat the odds on that generic experience. I've assessed how this world works and my personality. And it is a simple formula: the costs of being distracted are subtracted from the benefits of deploying a talent undistracted. What is the opportunity cost of distraction to your office cleaner? What is it to me? Can you measure what it would mean if I implement my investment program over thirty more years?"

Thirty more years compounded at 10 percent would be, fuck: 200 billion dollars.

Hermann turned on his computer and began typing. The CIO couldn't tell if this was meant as an invitation to leave—if all the shifts back to the computer were invitations to leave. Much of the CIO wanted to leave, to be assaulted by the cold, to know again water and real air, to measure his own opportunity costs spending time away from all of the questions that haunted him.

And so why then did he care enough to find himself asking Hermann, "But what *is* your investment program?"

"Do you think I'm going to tell you?"

There was nothing more to lose. And so he said, "I do."

Hermann took off his glasses and pinched his nose again. The CIO realized that he had stumbled again—here comes an anti-Wirbin rant of—

But then Hermann said, "No one knows."

"How can that be?"

"It's a side effect of the conditions of the program rather than its purpose. Do you know what it takes to achieve superlative performance?"

The CIO didn't speak.

"Isn't your only job to be able to recognize the mechanics necessary to achieve superlative performance?"

The CIO didn't speak.

"The answer is: one, eliminate the agency problem; two, preserve offensive liquidity and an equity bias at the same time; and three, listen to the specifics of efficiency."

The CIO wasn't sure how to get more: to lean in, pretend indifference, bend to a knee in this chapel. Finally, he said, "I would really—I would appreciate it if you could explain more."

Hermann touched his glasses but didn't take them off. "I told you: the biggest problem with the investment management business is the investment management business. The agency problem—in which the self-interest of investment professionals acts against the collective interest of investment performance—is insidious. Take short-termism, compelled by innate desires to increase managed capital. Every journalist at *The New York Times* thinks they know enough about investing to denounce the effects of short-term performance focus. But agency problems don't just lead to higher risk trades. Asset aggregation also leads so-called investors to take on less risk than necessary for fear of public shame for allowing 'excess' volatility.

"Signaling is another agency problem. Why do hedge funds own the same positions? Because certain positions, in certain peer groups, signal intelligence. Scale is a major agency problem. Organizations arise to service pools of capital like CalSTRS or ADIA that demand high-volume asset management services. That business is profitable and easy. With enough management fees, you can guarantee market returns. If you manage capital in every asset class, you benefit from the option value of capitalizing on bubbles in sequential asset classes to construct a narrative about alpha. You can appeal to the civil servants or late-career investment bankers who work at these places by hiring your own late-career bankers to fly together on private planes and pretend that this is the way to invest. Does anyone who understands investing think investing is that easy?"

The CIO didn't speak.

"All organizations create incentives that distort the pursuit of their fundamental goals. Wall Street prides itself on being the most rational industry. It is, in fact, well below average, because of the entropy of talent as asset managers scale. Personal career ambitions are a cancer on performance. Deals are done and trades are made because of political power within an organization and jealousy of colleagues' shares of portfolio-wide decision-making. They are done for the 'morale' of younger people, who should function only in supporting roles. And who doesn't understand that the oxygen of the agency problem is asset managers inventing high-complexity investment strategies to justify high carry and other distorting fees?"

"So how do you solve this?"

"Do you think people *want* to solve this?" Hermann smiled his brain-eating smile. "Any idiot, if he is willing to forgo fee revenue, can do it. Optimize for market size, market liquidity, and efficient application of talent. U.S. mid- and large-cap equities are ideal for that. Then stop managing outside capital. Forgo whatever pleasure a small mind gets from seeing his logo on people's matching shirts. Forgo whatever social capital you glean for mating purposes. And then find high-quality support analysis that does not distort investment authority. I have found that the hardest to optimize. I had a hub-and-spoke program for six and half years: twenty-five-year-old analysts with no interaction with each other, no incentive compensation, term limits optimized to two years, tight NDAs, and high cash comp. I still found them distracting. No one believed me about the term limits. And what do people expect me to say about stupid analyses? The last four years, I've been using Indians."

"Indians?"

"Business and financial analysis by engineers, accountants, and two doctors in India. I have eighteen I pay through a service in London. I like the time zone difference. Someone here tracks their metrics, manages their data, and keeps them coded by number. I am not interested in anthropomorphizing data as Rahul or Rajiv. This system is still not perfect, but it is much better than the cancer of the agency problem. I am not convinced that AI is there yet, although it might be worth some of my time to study that.

"So, one: eliminate the agency problem. Two: maintain an equity bias. What does Dalio say? 'Diversifying well is the most important thing you need to do in order to invest well.' That is the most important thing if you are a diversification salesman. But the stupidest invention in finance is the long-short hedge fund, followed by the multi-strategy hedge fund. Yes, being a long-only investor is hard. But being a long-short is deciding that running a marathon makes your legs ache so you should run it on your hands. It is indisputable that the long-term outperformance of public shares is an investor's greatest advantage. Eliminating that for 'diversification,' for 'absolute return,' makes no sense. Except, again, for the agency problem. People like you don't want to scare other bureaucrats with volatility. Hedge funds managers need to fund alimony payments and charter schools in bear markets too.

"But why would I care if I was down 30 percent? Why would I care if I was down 90 percent? The only reason to not be 100 percent invested in the public equity market at all times is to allow oneself to be aggressive after corrections. I'm not talking about buying on the dips. That is for idiots. I am talking about the freedom to root for stupid valuations to correct. Keeping some cash, regardless of the short-term return drags, allows you to go long, with leverage, in three-standard-deviation events.

"I am not surprised that you did not eliminate the agency problem and do not maintain an offense-oriented equity bias. It sounds that you have taken the typical half—and thus ineffective—steps in those areas. That is unfortunate because those are the easiest parts of a successful investment program to put in place. They require good structure and rational asset allocation. The third one, respecting the market's efficiency, can be supported by good structure but not solved by it. There is a myth that the efficient market is just an economic issue. But who doesn't understand that market efficiency is more of a sociological issue? Once you solve that, though, you can develop an epistemology. The market is not efficient. There are thousands of idiotic valuations of liquid stocks every day. How could there not be, in a world whose two dominant characteristics are stupidity and laziness? What is Benjamin Graham's most famous line?"

Was that a real question? It had been twenty-five years. "I..."

"'In the short run, the market is a voting machine, but in the long run, it is a weighing machine.' The conventional wisdom is that the amount of capital in the market renders the weighing machine impossible. But most of that capital is in passive or de facto passive structures: automated voting machines. Most of the rest of the capital is in asset management structures optimized to distort good investing. The weighing machine business has been decimated. There are fewer people doing it than when I entered the business, with twenty times the liquidity. The business is getting easier."

The CIO reached up to his face with his hand but caught himself. He clenched and released an incomplete fist twice, behind his neck, before putting it down.

"The market is not 'efficient.' It is just *in*efficient in difficult-to-predict ways. This is where total commitment and rational thinking is necessary. Data from the Indians allows me to update the probabilities on my hypotheses. I am willing to spend a week—a month—full-time on an idea and do nothing about it. When the data is overwhelming that a stock is overvalued at a malicious level, I will short that stock 2 percent of the time. With the exception, of course, of 2007. Most times, however, I just avoid those shares. If, on the other hand, the shares are undervalued, I buy them. This is the least replicable part of the strategy. It's pattern recognition of having done it for forty years. It's possible only when you eliminate distractions. It requires probabilistic thinking superior to the moronic tricks of Bayesian hobbyists. Even then, I'm right, on average, 59 percent of the time. But I still benefit from the long-term equity bias by earning market performance when I don't outperform. And this still exceeds any diversified portfolio over almost all time periods. Only 18 percent of the time do I suffer material negative performance. I believe I can get that to under 13 percent."

The CIO waited for more.

Hermann said, "That is it. Reading Buffett and Munger would have gotten you an approximation of the most useful parts."

The CIO wanted to tell Hermann that this—that the truth is never *new*—was what he had recognized after Karen Kahn. He wanted to tell him that this was what his shapes had been born to systematize. He said instead, "I wonder what you'd think of the finance bros who come to the endowment's office and look around for signs that you've been there. I'm waiting for one of them to take a piece of Kleenex out of the garbage because he thinks it might have your DNA on it, so he can clone you as a sheep. It's not just that you are, uh, successful. I was trying to explain this to Meg Corso." He paused. "The president of the school. It's as if these guys' essential position in the world comes not from being Jewish or Southern or liberal or gay. Their central lens—seemingly the only lens for a lot of them—is being good at Excel, understanding the language of finance, and having modes of thought in which measurement is truth and the central value of superiority. I used to think that they couldn't imagine the reality of what goes on"—the CIO looked around the office, for Hermann—"here. But maybe they intuit it, somehow, as the ultimate exemplar of..."

Hermann looked at him, to finish. The CIO didn't understand why he couldn't finish. Hermann seemed to have an internal clock set to no more than nineteen seconds of wasted time. He turned on his monitor, began reading, and then started to type.

The CIO wondered why he hadn't finished. Was it because he was not talking about others? Because his own willed identity, too, was intelligence as everything?

Well, what identity had he inherited? What was his father's? What *was* the reason for his father's stock trading at the end? Was it more than an old man's need for a victory over his son?

Fuck me, the CIO thought, as he realized that he was seventy miles away from where he grew up, and it hadn't occurred to him to visit his parents' graves. He slumped in his chair, sitting on his hands, and felt his face decompose to slack-jawed passivity.

Hermann glanced at him, went back to his screen, but said from behind it as he continued to read, "Do you think there are secrets or shortcuts in life? There is little of what I do that people couldn't replicate if they were committed to returns."

"Except kind of stop being a human being."

"Is it in my interest for people to stop victimizing themselves with bad investment structures?"

"Did you hear what I said? I said that, according to the rules of your investment philosophy, people can do what you do if they agree to stop being a human being."

Hermann shut off the monitor, sourly. "And what is being a human being?"

"What?"

"What is being a human being? What rules are involved in being a human being?"

"Obligations to others, an urge for fullness. You think about this stuff."

"I think about this 'stuff'?"

"You just talked about where chickens fall on the spectrum of human empathy. Your mocking of your rivals' philanthropy is a judgment of their desire to believe in, or at the least perform, some obligation to others. Even if you've rejected it as an option, you've considered that path."

"What path is that?"

"Life. Family. Children. Society." He paused and swallowed. What kind of child was he? What obligations did he still perform? "Some sense of our place, metaphysically."

Hermann smiled. "Do you have a metaphysical system?"

"What?"

"Does God exist?"

The CIO didn't speak.

"So you don't, then, have a metaphysical system. Do you have a family?"

"Two children. A wife."

"Does that unique position allow you to understand how people should live?"

"You've made your point."

"Did I make my point? My point is that I should have never bothered wasting my time with you. Is there any person more pathetic than a sensitive Wall Street liberal? People like you argue that the world needs to be corrected. You believe every poor person is a victim. You spend an inordinate amount of time worrying about how to have more Black children educated alongside your own children as long as it doesn't affect the education of your children. You never deny a single personal appetite to fly more, own more, and consume more all the while mocking anyone who 'denies' climate change. Through all this, you attribute your padded spot in the meritocracy, your 1.6-million-dollar middle-manager salary, to a game that *is* fair. And so, to address the obvious dissonance that results from such points of view, you make monsters out of people. What is my crime? Isn't it being more successful by maintaining a rigor and focus you cannot?"

Hermann turned on the monitor and began reading. He pushed his glasses up as if he could make them display the screen's reflection. He clicked forward, ferociously absorbing facts more useful than the CIO's existence. "Do you know what the good part is?" he continued. "I don't need your validation or permission."

When Jane became giddily interested in his meeting with Hermann, the CIO at first wondered if she was hustling him with faked curiosity. But two nights ago, after Hannah went to bed, Jane began googling Hermann, for what little there was. She tried to recall the actor they had seen on Broadway who had Hermann's same thin nose. She speculated on whether the 11 billion dollars was real. Last night, she had helped the CIO find his gloves and teased him, with love, on where he had missed a spot shaving his head.

I really do hope, she had said, that you find what you are looking for.

And so now, the CIO asked, "Then how do you define decency?"

Hermann looked at him, confirming that the CIO had not melted under the prior exposure to the truth. He went back to reading the Bloomberg.

The money was enough. He did not need to be the enabler. The world was real.

The CIO said again, "I asked, how do you define decency?"

Without removing his eyes from the screen, Hermann answered, "Do you think I spend my time defining decency?"

"Well, do you believe in God?"

"Do you think I believe in God?"

"How about consequences?" The CIO leaned forward to see through the window of Hermann back into himself. To see if Hermann bled human blood. "Or is your plan really to die with somewhere between 11 and 200 billion dollars and declare it enough?"

"I will not declare anything. I will die. There will be consequences or there will not be consequences. But I have no interest in cutting off the proof of what happens when you do the work."

Hermann went, again, back to the work.

"You don't get to win," the CIO said.

"What are you talking about now?" Hermann was focused on his Bloomberg.

"You don't get to win."

Hermann started typing.

"You know this as well as I do. No one who has opinions on how his thoughts are more complete than Isaiah Berlin's could believe that pointing out the easy-to-point-out hypocrisies of the upper-middle class absolves you of anything. That 'I find it distracting' is some magic incantation that can close off the rest of human life. You asked what I believe. I really, really get it that you don't care. I really, really get it that you have concluded that *everything* I know is a subset of what you know. That may very well be true. But in that case, we both know the importance of not reducing life to a victory defined by your place on a list of billionaires."

Hermann forwarded a screen to continue reading. He started to type, stopped, then continued. Finally, he said, "You are in my office because I succeed at buying stocks. So what do you *want*? A pat lesson that I care about other people because it is good to care about other people?"

The CIO would get up. He would return to Jane. She would want to know everything that was said. He would return to Peter and complete the work of loving him as much as Hannah. He would return to Emily and his team because they still needed him, in their careers.

Hermann stopped typing and said, "At least Marvin Trotter just asked, 'Is it worth it?'"

Was this a warning? A favor? Indefinite gloating about the more he always knew? The CIO asked, stupidly, "Marvin was here?"

"Last year."

Had Marvin put this hour in motion a year ago, as a watchmaker God? But could a kind watchmaker God have put a world in motion to lead to this end? The CIO was too tired to not ask, "What did you discuss?"

"I just told you. He asked if it was worth it."

"Is what worth it?"

"Do you think I have any context for what Marvin Trotter repeats himself about?"

"So what did you say?"

"I did not say anything."

I can't do this much longer, the CIO thought. He nonetheless asked, "What would you have said if he was looking for an answer?"

"Trotter did not clarify the first 'it' from the second 'it.' Was he asking about the necessity of securities markets? A man like Trotter knows that data. On the benefit side of the ledger, you have the formation of risk capital, the distribution of ownership, the fuel of capitalist innovation, and the destruction of feudal power structures and stagnation. You also have people excelling at quantitative mental labor having more power than people who inherited status or captured mechanisms of state violence. On the cost side, you have people doing quantitative mental labor making more money than people wiping down office furniture. I understand that annoys some people. But does any sane person believe that it's better to not have financial markets?"

"What if Marvin was asking *you* the question."

Hermann rolled his chair away from the desk and took off his glasses. He pinched even higher on the bridge of his nose. "Do you think that he was asking me if it is worth it?"

"Why not? Because of the money?" The CIO could see the billionaire baguettes rising up to fuck the sky.

"Who doesn't know that the money is ridiculous? I am talking about work. Investing requires patience. It requires concentration.

It requires layers of contrarianism, total humility, total self-confidence, complete amnesia, and complete recall. It requires the ability to withstand maximum pain to seize maximum opportunity. It requires strength to forgo easy modes of thought, and life. There is nothing that can be faked or willed. The larceny of an Adam Neumann is inconceivable in true investing. And so do you think anyone who understands how hard it is, who understands, as Marvin Trotter understands, what differentiates a life, would ask me if it is worth it?" Hermann looked at his Bloomberg but didn't turn it on. "What is the first 'it' for most people in finance? It is a career, often a so-called successful career, that generates millions and sometimes billions in personal wealth. It is, however, most often a career in which the data proves that Trader, Banker, Analyst, or Investor X is unnecessary, replaceable, and/or counterproductive. Think about Ben Wirbin. Has he measured the performance of the IPOs he has encouraged? Has the M&A advice he's given created shareholder value? At least he says 'fucknuts' a lot, which has measurable entertainment value.

"For asset managers, though, what is the worst thing about the money on Wall Street? That it makes people stupid or that it encourages them to make stupid decisions? Your median Wall Street asset manager tells himself the story, from his good trades and deals alone, that he is an exceptional investor." Hermann was finally looking straight at him. "He spins his performance numbers to everyone, including himself. He claims that he is the essential employee to every institution in which he works. He is petty about colleagues' track records or utility. He has a core belief that the amount of money he has made is so unusual that it proves that he is special. So what motivation does he have to look at actual data if the result can already be measured by the 30 million dollars, or even 5 million dollars, he has captured?

"I have trained myself to let people live in that stupidity. It is distracting to point it out on a regular basis. For the data is clear that if someone can make twenty times more being an undifferentiated investor than excel at something else, he will always go for the money. Trotter should ask those people, 'Is it worth it?': the opportunity cost, the stress to perform at something they are not committed to, the constant presence of the market when they could otherwise be at whatever parental or marital activity they prefer."

Hermann stopped. A silence swamped the room. The end swamped the room.

The CIO said, tentatively at first, "I do ask them. The GPs. I ask them why they do it."

Nothing.

"I have never gotten the right response."

"Which would be?"

It was humiliating, but the CIO said it anyway. "To fly like this gives life meaning."

Hermann put his hands on his desk and pushed to the side for a fuller view of the CIO. "That's not what I expected from you. I would have expected something more unanswerable about being a human being. Nonetheless, it is stupid to expect that. Do you think of yourself as an investor?"

Sometimes the CIO felt like the victim. Sometimes, the perpetrator. But he answered, unequivocally, "Yes."

"Then don't you think it would be a good idea to be an investor and forgo the excess rent you extract through bureaucratic work?"

This was it, the CIO thought. Dying bad by doing well.

"Do you ever ask yourself why the customers of financial services don't revolt? What else can end the current level of profitability of those services? Increased regulation? Higher taxes? Elizabeth Warren? After two centuries of global economic growth, even 1 percent aggregate fees on the management and frictional costs of the world's financial assets equals 2 trillion dollars per year. Asset owners and corporations are willing to pay that. Do you ever ask yourself why is that? They can revolt. Look at investment banking revenue in research sales, equity trading, or fixed income: technology and consumer choice by intermediate asset managers have decimated those businesses. Does anyone miss the rent those people used to extract, other than steakhouse waiters and exotic dancers? No one is forcing your endowment to engage firms charging high fees to provide a supposed edge in niche asset management segments."

The CIO opened his mouth to speak. Or almost to speak. How heavy was this paradigm he had never broken out of. What could words do to smash it now?

He summoned all his strength to grip his hands. They still wouldn't close into fists.

"Take what would seem to be the most egregious example of Wall Street's uselessness: some person with a $300,000 portfolio paying a broker 1 percent to put him in active mutual funds that were selected for suboptimal and/or unsavory reasons. Is that guy as oblivious as passive management zealots think he is? At some point his TV has aired Warren Buffett and Diane Sawyer discussing the futility of active management. Did he yell at the TV that he will show Diane and Warren how smart he is with his Ameriprise Financial account?"

The CIO didn't speak.

"Why does he have a money manager? Could it be that he wants other psychic goods from outsourcing investment management than what Buffett wants or needs? He wants relief from the responsibility to do it himself. He wants peace of mind that someone 'smart' is working for him. He wants the feeling of control over his money. He wants a good doctor. Maybe he also wants excitement. Does Las Vegas exist to make gamblers rich? Whatever mix these psychic goods are worth, accepting 2 or 3 percent less annual appreciation may be the rational choice. For what is the real cost? Are there retired people out there playing less pickleball because they have suboptimal portfolio management? Or is it only people like you who confuse the investment management business with the investment performance business?"

The CIO was startled awake. "But an endowment is different," he said. "Institutions are different. Institutions matter." Hermann had to—had to—assent to this. "This is neither pickleball nor some Übermensch test of strength. Our endowment provides—must provide—a quarter-billion dollars to the school. That makes a difference in the world: to scholarship students, to their parents, to people who are trying to advance ideas other than that the accumulation of money is all that matters." The CIO's breath had accelerated. He tried to catch it, to not seem winded in weakness. Hermann doesn't get to win.

"Why would anyone believe that a college should be good at investing?" Hermann asked. "Why doesn't a college endowment try to generate 9 percent a year by starting a tangible, non-finance business with a 9 percent return on capital employed and a 5 percent free cash flow yield? How about an oil refinery? A commercial bank? An ice cream stand? Who would expect institutions staffed by more people sympathetic to hard left anti-capitalist views than any other mainstream institution in America to excel at capitalist economic functions? Why is there an exception for investing? I do not perceive you to be an idiot. But what are you, really?"

What verb tense did the devil want?

"Does Ben Wirbin really think one call to a headhunter can make an institution superior at something as difficult as this? How could anyone believe that a person like you could achieve irreplaceable performance? Your stated strategy is to execute an adverse selection process of finding managers compromised by the agency problem to seek your money. Can anyone imagine that this plan could work? Unless there is a category error. Why doesn't the college put the endowment in a passive strategy? Why don't they ask me to manage the entire thing?"

The devil is all you cannot do and have not done.

"One answer: because institutions are stupid. No one has enough standing to tell self-selecting alumni that they are sacrificing returns so that they can pretend they know how to invest. Or this answer: having 6 billion dollars is frightening to people. Why do the peddlers of mediocrity emphasize the 'risk characteristics' of their strategies, even though the best risk mitigant is duration plus the equity bias?"

The devil is undistracted.

"Having me manage everything would be scary to you people because it would expose you for having an original thought." Hermann looked at him and waited. "But more, it would seem too easy. Having 6 billion dollars at your disposal is facing the randomness of the world's distribution of assets as a result of talent, aggressiveness, inertia, and chance. Having 6 billion dollars exposes you to the burden of encountering the mysteries and volatilities of the market. The best way to make capital *seem* rational is to show that it 'earns' its returns, from effort. How is your endowment any different from the guy with the Ameriprise Financial account?"

Hermann stopped and looked at the powered-off screen in front of him. He waited for an answer from it, or the CIO. Then he said, ""If you know how to blow up your world, what is the need for you to be anything but who you are?" He reached for the screen but then brought his hand back to his desk. "I understand why a university would hire you. You appear academic. You can discuss philosophy at the shallow end. You are embarrassed by the money you make, which matches their embarrassment in paying you that money. But listen to the words: 'manage money.'

Your management of the money is more important to them than whether the endowment is up 6 percent, rather than 9 percent, due to fee drag and bad investment decisions."

The CIO could feel his temples getting sweaty, from the furnace of a heart beating loudly and wild. He needed to breathe, to explain again and again and again and again that Hermann didn't get to win. How could he *act* to make Hermann see, to get Hermann's hands off his throat? "No," he said. "You can't just pretend that returning 6 percent versus 9 percent doesn't matter." He looked hard at Hermann.

"Do you think that is the pretending we are talking about?"

The CIO scrubbed the back of his neck hard, feeling the sandpaper of his hands in the dry, sealed room. Being bigger than himself: that would win. "So what should we—they—do?"

Hermann took off his glasses, rubbed where they had rested on his nose, and put them back on. "Have I not been telling you what I told Marvin Trotter a year ago?"

The CIO didn't speak.

"I couldn't care less." He smiled his ate-your-brain smile. Maybe that was Hermann's only smile.

Then he turned on his Bloomberg, squinted at the near screen, and read something off the far monitor.

A hot gust was scorching through the CIO's parched throat. He managed to ask, "And what did Marvin say to that?"

"He told me that 'that was an answer.'"

The CIO looked at the closed door behind him.

Three minutes later, silently, he left.

Home
December 19

It was past midnight as the CIO opened the door from the garage as quietly as he could. He stopped, spent, halfway through the doorframe. His bones still felt O'Hare and the three-hour delay; his ears were still wormed by the Christmas music playing in the near empty airport when he arrived. It had taken all his energy to step over the extension cord of the rotary floor cleaner at the airport. He had wondered if the janitor was starting his workday or eager to finish it, when the last flight into town arrived.

The CIO managed to make it into the mudroom and peel off his shoes with the heels of the opposite feet. His bag slipped off his shoulder, almost catching his lapel.

He made it into the foyer. He turned on the lamp on the Chinese credenza and idled through the day's junk mail. Standing by the stairs, he listened upwards if anyone was awake.

Jane and Hannah wouldn't be.

Peter shouldn't be.

He heard nothing, not even Peter holding his breath as he powered something down.

The CIO walked into the new kitchen, the dining room wall broken through. It was all white, dominated by a subway tile backsplash, and yet—*and yet,* the interior designer had said—with "naturalizing" handles in unvarnished wood. He hadn't needed a room that looked like a hip London restaurant, or a morgue. But they had invested in the house, the town, comfort. He opened the

Sub-Zero, still impressed by the effort involved, and blinked at the soft Hollywood light illuminating fruit. Jane had left what appeared to be roast chicken in a Tupperware. He rooted past it, chicken welfare now forever associated. He opened another dish: sweet potatoes. Hannah had probably helped with the cooking. He could smell the cold of the Sub-Zero, which was less clean than the cold of Chicago, overpowering the whole bulb of garlic Jane must have used.

I really do hope that you find what you are looking for.

The CIO was starving or full or still under siege from the stupid decision—decisions—at O'Hare involving Good and Plentys, a hot dog, chocolate-dipped almonds, and gum. He had craved something to ground him to the human, to pleasure, but the Vienna Beef may have gone too far.

He thought he heard Peter. Or maybe it was the Sub-Zero humming its own digestive thoughts.

He put two unwashed grapes into his mouth. Midway through the third chew, he spit them into the sink and ran the faucet to push them down the disposal. He walked into the den and turned on the light. He sat on the couch, staring at the bookshelf. There were a lot of books. A lot of books of which nothing was retained. He had to go to the bathroom. But he couldn't stand up.

O'Hare. O'Hermann. He could wake up tomorrow and decide. But to wake up tomorrow and decide, he had to go bed.

It was late. Late capitalism.

He leaned forward to build momentum but stopped with his elbows on his knees. It was possible that Vienna Beef and whatever grape parts had made it down were going to end up on the rug.

He breathed in hard. He drummed on his bald head. When Hannah was younger, she would sit on his shoulders and sing, playing the bongos, playing the bongos.

At least he had performed that generic experience.

He was too tired to throw up. Was he too tired to throw the lamp against the bookshelf with a lion's roar to wake them all—Jane, the kids, the books that had led to nowhere? Wouldn't that rage better ground him to the human?

The CIO sat back up. He thought he heard a click. He hoped it wasn't Peter. He would have to have another discussion about moderation. He didn't know what to say to Jane. He didn't know if there was anything he had to say to Jane.

Hannah had left a *Hunger Games* book on the ottoman.

He listened closely to decide if a sound was Peter or his imagination.

How many times was Hannah going to read these books? Weren't these what every girl was reading? Weren't they getting Hannah off the track of an exceptional life?

Upstairs seemed silent. He would not need, right now, to talk about moderation.

But he was too tired to lift himself off the couch. Jane would understand if he slept on the couch. He could explain what had happened at O'Hare. Could he ever explain to her what had happened with Hermann? Should he wake her up as an act, again, of shared curiosity?

The CIO was too tired to wake her up because he was too tired to even lie down. He slid downwards on the couch, hoping that this would Swiss-army him, somehow, to a sleeping position with the cashmere blanket over him.

The action managed only to hurt his neck.

His neck would hurt more if he didn't change positions. He really should change positions.

Today—yesterday—didn't need to be important. He should just go upstairs to Jane and be in their bed. She would not wake up. Or she would understand and coo, Hi, honey, half-asleep, as she rubbed his chest. At least he had performed that generic experience.

He stood up.

He was back in the mudroom. He bent over with the will of a final surge to a peak, to get what he needed.

Today—yesterday—didn't need to be important.

He carried it with one hand, like a bowling ball.

He thought it was what he needed.

The house was paid for. The kitchen was paid for.

He walked back to the den. He didn't want to be doing this. He didn't know what he should be doing instead. He had responded with enough of a placeholder that they would be asleep, too.

He sat down again on the couch.

Also, to Emily? Is it important to also be to Emily?

He twisted the edges of the laptop he had brought from the mudroom. Should he destroy one again? Throw it against the bookshelf, at full violence, waking them all up?

Why did Jane and the kids get to sleep?

Who did he need permission from, to do anything?

Go to bed. Jane would understand and coo, Hi, honey, half-asleep, as she rubbed his chest. He shouldn't have tried to eat those grapes. He really had to throw up the hot dog and the candy, but the grapes would be last-in, first-out.

He opened the laptop. He looked at the picture of the four of them at the Maroon Bells Pass. Even Peter looked happy. This was also life, and privilege.

This didn't need to be important.

I really do hope that you find what you are looking for.

Isn't—isn't there always the need to be someone better than who you are?

Meg and Ben, he typed.

This is how the world works.

He paused, looked at the bookshelf, listened to hear if immoderate Peter was up. He wanted to be in bed with Jane. He couldn't be so tired that he couldn't be in bed with his wife.

He typed, I will continue to try to solve the problem of performance for as long as you let me.

And we'll leave the Michael Hermanns alone.

He read it again. He didn't know if it was right. He didn't want it to be wrong.

He signed it Aaron, and then he hit send.

Acknowledgments

I would first like to thank Abram Himelstein, GK Darby, and the entire team at the University of New Orleans Press for their encouragement and partnership and Gretchen Crary for her advocacy.

I would like to thank early readers and supporters for their feedback, patience, and advice: Ben Heller, Tom Bissell, Chris Parris-Lamb, Heather Schroeder, David Halpern, Thomas Lurquin, Cody Danks Burke, John McGuire, James Yockey, Josh Miller, Christian Busken, Mark Corigliano, Rick Greenberg, Carlin Flora, Andy Sernovitz, Andrew Miller, Diana Miller, and Jim Rutman. I would like particularly to thank Sam Douglas, Garth Risk Hallberg, and David McCormick for their editorial insights and enthusiasm.

I would also like to thank John Reynolds, Jonathan Farber, and all my colleagues at Lime Rock, past and present, for the space to write, to laugh, to be in the arena, and to listen. I'd also like to thank innumerable investors whom I've observed over the last quarter-century. Maybe this is what I saw.

Finally, I would like to thank my parents, in-laws, and other friends for their curiosity and gentleness during the long road to publication. I would like to thank Dora Sernovitz for sitting quietly beside me (sometimes) as I wrote this, and especially Molly Pulda for her constant and inspiring love, support, tolerance, extra domestic shifts, and constant commands for me to work harder and to push through frustrations. Every word remains ours.

About the Author

Gary Sernovitz has spent the last quarter-century working in and observing how money works, from Goldman Sachs to nearly twenty years at a private equity firm where he is now a managing director. He has also brought his keen writer's eye to America and business through two previous published novels, a non-fiction book, and numerous essays and reviews in *The New York Times*, *The New Yorker* online, *n+1*, *The Wall Street Journal*, and elsewhere. A native of Milwaukee and longtime resident of New York, Gary now lives in New Orleans with his wife and daughter.